SNIFFING
OUT MURDER

SNIFFING OUT MURDER

KALLIE E. BENJAMIN

BERKLEY PRIME CRIME

NEW YORK

BERKLEY PRIME CRIME
Published by Berkley
An imprint of Penguin Random House LLC
penguinrandomhouse.com

Library of Congress Cataloging-in-Publication Data

Names: Benjamin, Kallie E., 1964- author.
Title: Sniffing out murder / Kallie E. Benjamin.
Description: First edition. | New York: Berkley Prime Crime, 2023. |
Series: A Bailey the bloodhound mystery
Identifiers: LCCN 2023020271 (print) | LCCN 2023020272 (ebook) |
ISBN 9780593547359 (trade paperback) | ISBN 9780593547366 (ebook)
Subjects: LCGFT: Cozy mysteries. | Novels.
Classification: LCC PS3602.U767525 S65 2023 (print) |
LCC PS3602.U767525 (ebook) | DDC 813/.6—dc23/eng/20230803
LC record available at https://lccn.loc.gov/2023020271
LC ebook record available at https://lccn.loc.gov/2023020272

First Edition: December 2023

Printed in the United States of America
1st Printing

Book design by Elke Sigal

Dedicated to Mama Kallie, Elvira, and Benjamin Burns

Chapter 1

"Like any detective worthy of the title, Bailey knew that the only way to catch a criminal was to put his nose to the ground and sniff out the clues. With any luck, he'd pick up the scent quickly to help take a bite out of the crime wave hitting the city."

I walked through the park reciting the lines out loud, letting the words marinate in my mind. It sounded okay, but it didn't make my heart race with anticipation. Nancy Drew's place within the annals of children's crime fiction was secure. The first book in The Adventures of Bailey the Bloodhound, Pet Detective, series, *The Case of the Missing Maltese*, had flowed out of my head and onto the page like . . . well, like honey. This second book felt forced. I felt like I was scraping words out of my head with a dull spoon. I wouldn't mind if I were digging out good words, but this draft certainly didn't have the same zing as the first book.

Kids had loved the first book and were clamoring for more, but these eight-to-twelve-year-old middle-grade readers have high standards. They expect books to be well written, funny, and relevant, even if they can't articulate that's what they want. As a former elementary school teacher, or soon-to-be former teacher, I knew that kids could be exuberant with praise and brutal with criticism. My insecurities went into hyperdrive. *What if I didn't have any more books in me? What if I was a one-book wonder?* "Ugh!"

With a strong tug on the leash, Bailey lurched me out of the pool of self-doubt where I was wallowing around like a baby seal. Bailey wasn't keen on wallowing, unless it involved mud, freshly cut grass, or his favorite eau de parfum—deer poop. The best thing about a bloodhound was also sometimes the worst thing. They were Grade A scent hounds known for their tracking ability, especially when it came to tracking lost or missing humans. Usually bloodhounds, although large, substantial dogs, were docile creatures. However, whenever they were on the trail of a particular scent, they were unyielding and stubborn. Bailey, my three-year-old bloodhound, was no different. When he was working, he was all nose, but we weren't working. This was supposed to be a casual walk. However, I could tell from the slight prick of his heavy ears, the wiggling nose that barely left the ground, and the pull on his leash that he'd picked up a scent and was determined to follow it to the end. I just hoped that he wouldn't track anything that would get us both into trouble, again. Every time I see a flower bed, I'm reminded of Bailey covered in dirt and the look on my former neighbor Mrs. Goldstein's face as her award-winning peonies were utterly destroyed. Bailey's nose and my inquisitive nature could be a bad combination. However, I was determined to avoid trouble, especially around this town.

I gave his leash a gentle tug. "Come on, buddy. We're not tracking anything today. We both need to keep our noses clean and avoid falling down any rabbit holes."

Bailey pulled his nose from the ground and glanced back at me. His eyes said, *I have no idea what you mean. My nose is always clean.*

"Don't give me that look. You know what I mean."

He snorted and continued to sniff.

"I quit my job so I could write full-time and finish our next book, not so you could hound out trouble. No distractions. No mysteries. Nothing. We're going to lie low and focus on writing. Besides, nothing ever happens in Crosbyville, Bailey."

This time Bailey didn't bother lifting his nose off the ground. He grunted and continued sniffing. I rolled my eyes.

The sun was setting, and it was unseasonably cool, but I didn't worry about walking Bailey in the evening. Bloodhounds were gentle giants, but to those unfamiliar with the breed, they seemed intimidating. At close to one hundred pounds, Bailey looked like a threat. I knew he didn't have an aggressive bone in his body, but strangers didn't know that. Bloodhounds weren't known for their ability to protect, but there was still something about having so much muscle on the end of the leash that filled me with confidence.

"Priscilla Cummings. How's Crosbyville's budding author?" A familiar voice called out nearby, and I whipped around toward the source. Lucas Harrison flashed a blindingly white, toothy smile as though he were auditioning for a toothpaste commercial. Lucas was the owner of Harrison Real Estate Properties. He was tall with unnaturally tanned skin that reminded me of leather, and dark hair, dark eyes, and a large dark mustache, which was probably intended to distract from a prominent nose. Like Magnum, P.I., from the 1980s TV show with Tom Selleck, Lucas Harrison wore shorts and Hawaiian shirts whenever the northwestern Indiana weather permitted. I'd known him since our high school days.

"Good evening, Lucas." I wondered if he'd heard me talking out loud. How long had he been there?

"You talking to yourself?" He chuckled. Drat.

"No, I was talking to Bailey." I forced myself to smile in the hopes that talking to my dog didn't make me seem crazier than if I'd been talking to myself. Based on the confused look on his face, I knew two things. First, he hadn't read my book, because second, he had no idea who Bailey was. "Bailey, my dog." I pointed.

His smile was frozen on his face. After a moment, he shook it off. "Well, are you ready to sign your life away? We close tomorrow at eleven."

The idea of buying my first house was both thrilling

and terrifying at the same time. My heart raced while my stomach did flips. "Absolutely," I lied.

"Are you out walking alone tonight? That's not safe. Crosbyville isn't the quiet little hamlet that it once was, and you have to be careful. Maybe I should walk you home. It's never good for an attractive woman to be out by herself at night."

He grinned, but it looked like a grimace, and I forced myself not to frown and back away. "I'm not alone. I've got Bailey."

Again, he looked confused for a split second until it registered with him that Bailey was my dog. He gazed at Bailey, who had stopped sniffing the ground. They looked at each other like two prizefighters. Eventually, Lucas must have realized that he wouldn't stand a chance in a one-on-one battle and glanced away.

"If you're sure, then I'll be on my way. Don't forget to bring a certified check to the title company tomorrow." He gave Bailey a sideways glance and hurried on his way.

When he was out of sight, I released a sigh of relief. Given a choice between being alone at night fending off Lucas Harrison—whom we used to call *the Octopus* back in high school—or a serial killer, I'd probably rather take my chances with the serial killer. With a population of around thirty thousand, Crosbyville wasn't exactly a mecca for crime. Having spent most of my life here, I felt as safe walking the streets at night as I did in broad daylight. Although, my aunt Agatha often reminded me that this was the twenty-first century, and even though Crosbyville may not have produced an ax-wielding murderer yet, there was nothing preventing criminals from hopping in their cars and driving to town. Personally, I think a killer would find a better selection of victims in a bigger town, but rather than argue with my aunt, I made sure the Taser and pepper spray she'd given me for protection were in my pocket before I headed out.

Bailey and I continued our walk along the quaint streets and kept our eyes open for suspicious strangers. Crosbyville's Main Street could be described as a cross between a Hallmark Christmas movie town and Mayberry from *The Andy Griffith Show*. The street was lined with brick storefronts, and a manicured central square stood in front of a limestone-and-brick spired courthouse. The names on some of the businesses had changed over the years, but little else had.

Even though Crosbyville was only three hours from the state capital and twenty-five miles from River Bend, the third largest city in the state, it felt as though it belonged to a completely different era. Whether due to the old-fashioned ice cream parlor with its red-and-white-striped awning, the antique stores crammed full of furniture and vintage knickknacks, or the horses and buggies that could often be found hitched in front of the fabric and yarn shop, this old-fashioned town didn't seem to fit into the twenty-first century.

Indiana had quite a few Amish communities in Shipshewana, Middlebury, Nappanee, and Elkhart County. Crosbyville was the heart of Elkhart County, at least according to the brochures that the local chamber of commerce passed out to visitors like candy on Halloween. As a teen just learning to drive, I resented getting stuck behind the black buggies driven by the Amish, which hampered my lead-footed progress. As an adult, I appreciated the homemade baked goods, quilts, and handcrafted furniture they sold around town. I also appreciated the dedication of the Amish to their religious beliefs and lifestyle. It spoke to a simpler time, but was, in essence, harder without the modern conveniences that most of us took for granted. Today, the bearded men and the bonneted women dressed in black were symbolic of Crosbyville's enduring diversity.

April was technically spring according to the calendar, but in Indiana, calendars don't mean much where weather is concerned. Mother Nature had a wicked sense of humor and liked to keep this part of the country on its toes. It wasn't uncommon to feel as though we were experiencing all four seasons in one day with snow overnight, frost in the early mornings, sunshine by midafternoon, and nippy early evenings. It was early, so the cool temperatures meant that our daily constitutional was done at a much faster pace than normal. Still, Bailey kept his nose glued to the ground and followed every invisible feline, canine, human, and squirrel trail that he could while stopping to mark each tree along the route. I knew bloodhounds had been bred for tracking for centuries, but one of the most surprising revelations for me was that Bailey's amazing ability to track wasn't limited to people or animals. He had a gift for locating lost socks, keys, and shoes, which inspired my idea for The Adventures of Bailey the Bloodhound, Pet Detective, books. I couldn't believe what a difference he'd made in my life in such a small amount of time. It had been only three years since I adopted him, but a lot had happened in those three years.

Two years ago, Bailey's inquisitive puppy antics inspired me to write a children's book featuring him, and my first book was published a year later. Then, when my grandmother died six months ago, I took a job as a teacher in my hometown of Crosbyville to help my aunt Agatha. But it hadn't taken long before I accepted the reality that while I love children, teaching was another matter altogether. So, with the success of my first book and the promising trajectory of the series, I finally decided to quit my reliable full-time job with benefits and a steady paycheck to write children's books. Today was my last day.

I closed my eyes and tried not to hyperventilate. "What am I doing?"

Bailey glanced up from the trail he'd been following across the yard of an abandoned building and gazed at me with his soulful eyes.

There was something reassuring about those eyes, and I took a deep breath. "We got this, right?"

"Woof."

My cell phone vibrated, and I glanced at the picture that popped up on the screen and saw the smiling face of my literary agent, Cameron Prescott.

"Pris, are you sitting down?" Her voice rang with excitement as soon as I answered.

"I'm just walking Bailey. What's up?"

"You did it! You're a bestselling author. *The Adventures*

of Bailey the Bloodhound, Pet Detective, made *American Magazine's* bestseller list."

We hooted and cheered and celebrated for several minutes. When I was finally able to speak, I asked, "So, what does that mean?"

She laughed. "It means you've sold quite a few books in the last week."

"Like how many?"

"Who knows. Bestseller lists are tricky. It could be anywhere from a few thousand to tens of thousands. You're number one hundred thirty-eight out of one hundred fifty, but you made the list, so let's focus on that. Plus, from now on, we'll be able to put that *Bestselling Author* label on all your books! You're in your third print run, and we have multiple offers for subrights."

Cameron was perpetually cheerful, encouraging, and enthusiastic, at least when she talked to me. After twenty-plus years in the publishing industry, she was also tough as nails when it came to negotiating with publishers and sealing deals. Prescott Literary Agency had a reputation for representing award-winning children's book authors and signing with her had been a dream come true. She provided all the enthusiasm and support I lacked.

"Subrights?"

"Audiobooks, Spanish-, German-, and Polish-language editions. I told you, you'd be glad you didn't sell those when you signed your initial contract. The subrights should make enough to keep that hound of yours in kibble for a while now."

I glanced over at Bailey, who was marking a tree, and

took a deep breath. "That's a relief." *Maybe moving home to Crosbyville to write and quitting my job as a teacher hadn't been such a bad idea after all.*

"Peter's been pressuring me for a date for Bailey's next adventure."

"I should have plenty of time to write now, starting tomorrow. I have one parent-teacher meeting left tonight, and then I'm done. I should have a finished draft ready in a month."

She paused for a few moments. "Editors are sticklers for timelines. They're working on their catalog for next year. One month seems quick. Are you sure?"

"I'm sure. I should have plenty of time to write . . . now."

"Pris, one month is an aggressive deadline. Are you sure you want me to tell him you'll have the manuscript done by then?"

"Absolutely. An aggressive deadline will be just the push I need to get things moving. Besides, Crosbyville is a small town and nothing much happens around here. I should have no problem meeting that due date."

Chapter 2

I finished with my agent, glanced at my watch, and then hurried back to the school for my last official teaching responsibility—a parent-teacher conference. It was going to be unpleasant, and I'd put it off as long as possible. I had arranged a meeting with Joe and Whitney Kelley to discuss their daughter, Clarice. Joe and Whitney Kelley had adopted Clarice two years ago when her parents, distant cousins of Whitney's, both died suddenly. I was surprised that two people who were as self-absorbed as Joe and Whitney were willing to take on the responsibility. Personally, I wouldn't have allowed Joe and Whitney Kelley to care for my pet rock, but at eight, at least Clarice would be able to speak up for herself. I reminded myself that raising a child was a huge commitment. Maybe I was wrong about them. I could be replaying old tapes from high school. Perhaps they'd changed. I needed to keep an open mind.

"Mr. and Mrs. Kelley, I'm not suggesting that Clarice isn't a bright girl. She's very intelligent." *She certainly excels at avoiding work and causing trouble.*

"Prissy. What's with the 'Mr. and Mrs. Kelley'? That sounds so formal." Joseph Kelley chuckled. "You and I go waaay back." He grinned and winked.

I cringed. Too many unpleasant memories associated with that childhood nickname. *Sissy, Pissy, Prissy.* After ten years away and never hearing that silly name, I moved home six months ago, and it started up again immediately. I took a deep breath. "Mr. Kelley, I feel it's best to maintain a professional relationship with my students' parents or guardians."

Whitney Kelley snorted and continued texting on her cell phone without ever glancing up.

In high school, Joseph Kelley had been considered a hunk. Six feet tall with thick blond hair and blue eyes. He'd been the captain of the football team, and every girl at Crosbyville High School had been madly in love with him. I considered myself fortunate when he'd asked me—a short, plump, introverted nerd—to "go steady." *Fortunate*, until I realized he was dating me only so I would write his papers, do all of his homework, and allow him to cheat off my tests. Even then, it had taken nearly a year before I developed enough of a backbone to "break up" with him. Not until I realized he was also dating Whitney Baxter, head cheerleader and ultimate mean girl, at the same time. Using me was one thing, but I wasn't going to stand by and allow the two of them to mock me . . . especially not Whitney, who had already been bullying me since I was a little girl.

I tried again. "Mr. Kelley, Clarice hasn't applied herself this year."

"Well, I was never one for doing homework, either, if you remember." He chuckled and winked again.

On first glance, Joe Kelley looked as attractive as he had a decade earlier, but like an impressionist painting, Joe Kelley's true image required closer scrutiny. His tanned skin was dark and looked like leather stretched over his frame. His once-muscular body was now soft and flabby. In the years since high school, he'd acquired a beer belly that extended over the top of his pants, and his hair was masterfully teased and moussed to cover spots where it was most likely thinning out.

I could feel a retort rising in my throat, but I wasn't going to allow him to bait me into losing my temper, so I swallowed the smart response. "She hasn't completed any of her homework assignments all year, and—"

"You should have said something sooner." Joe flashed a toothy grin and gave me his "Clark Kent looking for a phone booth" gaze. I recognized that look, like he was about to save Lois Lane and the planet from calamity. He sat up straight and puffed out his chest. In a few seconds, certainly, he was going to remove his glasses and rip off his shirt to reveal his red-and-blue superhero attire. He leaned forward. "You just give me a list of the homework assignments that Clarice needs to turn in, and I'll make sure you have those by the end of the week." He winked.

I was getting really tired of that wink. "Mr. Kelley, it's too late for that."

He shook his head and gave me a look I'd labeled *You poor, pitiful thing.* "You *really* should have let me know about this sooner. I could have fixed things right up for you." He clicked his tongue several times.

I should have . . . He was making Clarice's laziness my fault. "I sent home messages asking you to get in touch. Plus, I scheduled two previous parent-teacher meetings, but neither of you were available." *Why was I defending myself?*

He slouched in his chair and stretched his legs out in front of him. "Well, now, I'm a busy man. I've been running a successful insurance business, and now that I'm the state senator for the county . . . I don't have the time for these types of things."

"These types of things"? You don't have time for your daughter's education? Deep breath. "I called and left voice messages and even sent email and text messages, but I never got a response from either of you." Texts were certainly something Whitney should appreciate. She hadn't stopped texting since she'd sat down that evening.

Whitney Kelley rolled her eyes without even looking up from her cell phone. She was a talented multitasker, capable of casting shade and texting without a second glance.

"You've got an excuse for everything, haven't you, Pris?" Whitney shook her head and texted. *Yep, she had mad multitasking skills.*

"Perhaps, if someone could—"

"Could what? Do your job for you?" Whitney dragged

her glance from her cell phone long enough to stare at me. "Our tax dollars go to pay your salary. You're paid to teach. That's your job."

Deep breaths. "I'm sure we all want to do what's best for Clarice."

"Clarice is a sensitive child," Joe added.

The sensitive Clarice was sitting behind her parents, making the most outrageous faces she could at me. I was confident that her face wouldn't get stuck like that, like my aunt Agatha used to tell me, but for a split second . . . No, I shook my head to clear my thoughts. "She's fallen behind the other students in practically every subject except art. At this point, I can't possibly see how I can pass her to the next grade, but if she were to attend summer school and repeat the—"

"Wait!" A red molten lava of rage started at Whitney's neck and quickly rose to encompass her face and the roots of her scalp. I'd struck pay dirt. Here was something that could shock her away from her cell phone. "Repeat the school year? No one affiliated with me is getting held back because of an incompetent teacher who's too busy wasting her time writing outlandish books about dog detectives rather than focusing her energy on teaching."

I didn't need a mirror to realize that my face was red, too. I could feel the blood rush to my head.

In one amazing accurate assessment of trouble, Joe Kelley recognized the danger in front of him. "Whoa, hold up there." He sat up in his chair. "Don't you think you're being a bit . . . hasty in expecting her to repeat the year? Surely, she could just do some extra credit to make up the assignments she's missed?"

"I've given her multiple opportunities for extra credit, but she hasn't completed those, either."

"How can you expect her to concentrate on her work when you've got that animal in the room?" Whitney pointed at Bailey, who was curled up in his dog bed.

Attacking me is one thing, but nobody attacks my dog. "Bailey's a registered therapy dog, and I *don't* bring him to class every day. Normally, he only comes when we're working on reading skills. I merely brought him tonight because of the late time for this parent-teacher meeting." Why was I defending myself again? I could feel the heat from my face moving down my neck. I took a deep breath and tried again. "I really think we should focus on what's best for Clarice. I think—"

Whitney Kelley shoved her cell phone in her purse. She stood up so quickly she knocked over her chair. "I don't give a flying fig what *you* think. I'm not going to let you embarrass me by flunking my child. I'm the chairwoman of the school board. Do you know what a scandal like this would mean to my career?" She scowled. "Of course you do. You've always been jealous of me, even in high school. This is all some sick revenge of the nerds."

"Whitney . . . I mean Mrs. Kelley, I have no idea what you're talking about. I assure you this has nothing to do with you . . . either of you, or your careers. I'm only concerned about Clarice. If we could just sit and talk this through, I'm sure we can come up with a plan that—"

"I have no intention of talking to you about anything. I'm not going to stand for this . . . this . . . political sabotage. If you think I'm going to sit idly by and allow you to destroy Kaley's future, you've got another think coming."

"Clarice," I corrected her.

"Whatever." She grabbed her coat and marched out of the room.

Joe Kelley sat for a few awkward moments, but then rose and followed his wife.

Clarice was the last to leave. She skipped to the door and then turned to stick out her tongue before slamming the door.

Well, that went about as badly as I imagined it would. I dropped my head onto my arms. After a few moments of wallowing in self-pity, I felt a warm, wet sensation as Bailey slid his muzzle under my arm and gave my face a lick.

I sat up and gazed into the big, brown droopy eyes of my friend and canine companion. I wrapped my arms around him and buried my head into his soft, warm body and instantly felt better. The Kelleys may not think very highly of my teaching abilities, but here was someone who loved me unconditionally. And that mattered. I reached in my pocket and pulled out a dog biscuit. I always kept dog biscuits in my pockets. You never know when you're going to need one. These were peanut butter and pumpkin flavored, which I'd made the night before.

Bailey chomped the biscuit down in two bites and then sat and looked at me expectantly.

I laughed. "You know me too well." I reached into my

pocket and pulled out two more small biscuits and tossed them in his dog bed.

He curled up in his bed and munched on his reward for cheering me up . . . at least a little. Clarice was a bright girl and a brilliant artist. She was just lazy, and apparently didn't have anyone helping to complete her schoolwork at home. Could they have been right? Was there more that I could have . . . should have . . . done? Could I have done anything differently? I racked my brain, but nothing came to mind. One thing was certain, I just wasn't cut out for teaching. Today was my last day as a teacher. I'd turned in my resignation and apart from volunteering at pet-assisted reading programs with Bailey, I was going to focus on my writing.

I glanced around the classroom. I love children, and I love teaching. I'm just not cut out to be a teacher, at least not full-time. The kids were great . . . well, most of them, anyway. I loved helping them discover new things and watching them grow and develop. There was no greater feeling in the world than that moment when you looked into a student's eyes and saw the lightbulb go on and you knew, *they got it.*

Unfortunately, those moments were too often overshadowed by harrowing parent-teacher meetings like tonight, curricula that focused on teaching to standardized tests rather than educating, countless budget cuts, and a salary that's barely above what I could make flipping burgers at a fast-food restaurant. Although, the pay was the least of my complaints. I knew I'd never get rich as a teacher, but I had hoped I'd be appreciated and respected at least. Sadly, Joe and Whitney Kelley weren't part of the minority. Well, maybe they were, but they certainly weren't part of the *silent* minority.

I packed up my few personal belongings and the mementos that I'd acquired that never failed to bring a smile to my face. I locked my room for the last time and loaded my belongings into the back of my SUV.

*I*t was after seven and the sun was going down, taking away a good deal of heat with it. Bailey and I headed for Main Street to the Blue Plate Special Café. I parked and got Bailey's therapy dog harness from my pocket and secured it. I snapped on his leash and then we headed inside.

Most stores and restaurants allowed only service animals inside, but since the pandemic, a lot of the old rules had changed. Restaurants were less crowded, and many places in town had become a lot more dog-friendly.

Under normal circumstances, I wouldn't have trusted Bailey around the temptation that a restaurant provided. At three feet tall from the shoulder to the ground, his head was level with most tables. He could easily slide a sandwich from the plate of an unwary diner. However, wearing his harness helped him remember that he was working, and that meant no pilfering food, no matter how tempting.

The other advantage of the Blue Plate Special Café was that we knew the owner, Agatha Bell, my aunt.

"I've been saving something special for you." Aunt Agatha

rushed from behind the counter as we walked inside, hurried to my side, and dropped down to give Bailey a big hug.

I was used to playing second fiddle to my dog and waited until Aunt Agatha finished greeting Bailey.

When she had her fill of dog kisses and drool, she stood and pulled a large bone from the pocket of her apron and gave it to Bailey.

Completely occupied with his treat, Bailey slid down into a sphinx position and got to work on his bone.

Aunt Agatha turned and pulled me into a large embrace. "Sit down. I'll just go wash my hands and I'll make you a nice BLT."

My aunt hurried to the ladies' room and then rushed into the kitchen to make good on her promise. She popped out in a few minutes with a steaming hot bowl of corn chowder. "This will tide you over until I can cook the bacon the way you like it." She placed the bowl and a spoon in front of me and then hurried back to the kitchen.

The Blue Plate Special Café was a small, old-fashioned diner. There was a long counter that covered one wall with a narrow aisle separating ten booths. The wood floor was painted with black and white squares, and the barstools that lined the counter were covered in the same plastic-coated checkered pattern with shiny aluminum legs. Each booth had a Formica-topped table featuring a small juke-box with songs from the '50s and '60s that could be played for a nickel.

Cooking had always been Aunt Agatha's way of showing her love—which she had plenty to share—so opening a café had been perfect for her. She was in her early fifties. She, like all of my Bell family relatives, was the same height—short. She was dark-skinned with short, curly salt-and-pepper hair, and light eyes.

Corn chowder was my favorite soup, and my aunt knew it. She also knew that I had a love-hate relationship with bacon. I loved it, but my skin hated it. In record time, she was back with a BLT piled high with bacon minus the *T*. God bless her, she also knew I hated tomatoes.

I took a bite of the warm sandwich and moaned. The thick-cut peppery bacon was cooked crisp, exactly the way I liked it, and it was delicious.

She smiled. "Do you need a moment alone with that sandwich?"

I chewed quickly. "You make the best BLT sandwiches ever."

She smiled and leaned forward and whispered, "The secret is the homemade bread I get from the Amish. Best bread ever. That, and the homemade mayo. Plenty of folks think the secret is the bacon. That matters, too, but the bread is critical."

Aunt Agatha could talk about food for hours. The café wasn't packed, although there were still a good number of diners. She had two waitresses who had been with her for years, so she was able to sit down and take a break without ignoring her customers.

"Prissy . . . Plump Prissy Cummings!"

I cringed, turned around, and forced a smile. "Joe Kelley."

Joe grabbed me by the shoulders and pulled me to my feet and then wrapped me in a big bear hug that he held too long. He acted as though we hadn't just met less than an hour ago with less-than-stellar results.

I pushed away and he chuckled and then raked his eyes over my body as though he were examining a prize heifer at the fair. "I hope you aren't holding a grudge about earlier. That was . . . business."

Business? Your daughter's educational future was business?

"I wanted to tell you, Prissy, that I noticed . . ."

"Noticed what?"

"How you've changed. You've dropped all the baby fat, gotten rid of those Coke-bottle glasses, and your skin's much cleared. It looks like you've grown a few inches taller." He leered. "Who knew Plump Prissy Cummings would turn into a knockout? You look delectable."

There was a large mirror that spanned the wall behind the bar, but I didn't need to look at myself to know that I was blushing. I could feel the rage welling up in my chest. I took a deep breath, swallowed the emotion, and forced myself not to cringe. *Deep breaths. Deep breaths.* "Joe, I don't think your wife—"

"Joseph, what on earth is taking so long to pick up a lousy chicken salad sandwich?" Whitney Baxter Kelley flew into the diner like a cold, icy wind.

If Joseph Kelley was an impressionist painting, Whitney Kelley was somewhere between the simple beauty of Vermeer's *Girl with a Pearl Earring* and Leonardo da Vinci's richly dressed courtesan, *Lady with an Ermine*. Whitney was tall and thin with thick blonde wavy hair, deep-blue eyes, and peaches-and-cream skin. As much as I hated to admit it, I had to acknowledge that Whitney Kelley was as gorgeous today as she had been in high school, although her face was slimmer and her lips were too thin with a downward arch. Not a hair was out of place, from her perfectly manicured nails to her Louboutin shoes and a dress that something in my core recognized as Givenchy without ever looking at the label. With a spectacular diamond-and-ruby necklace, large diamond earrings, and a diamond bracelet that must have set Joe back a small fortune, she looked like a Hollywood star fresh off the red carpet.

Whitney walked beside her husband and hooked a possessive arm to stake her claim as she looked down her nose and sized me up. Where Joe's glance had made me feel like a piece of meat, Whitney's left me feeling like a lump of clay that someone was trying to pass off as an expensive ceramic vase. "Priscilla."

"Whitney." I swallowed the lump in my throat and forced myself not to straighten my T-shirt or brush off my jeans.

Joe chuckled. "Now, ladies. If we're all going to live in this town, we might as well be cordial. After all, now that you're not Clarice's teacher, I'm sure we will all get along great."

UGH!

"Of course, we called Dr. Freemont as soon as we left, and he told us that you turned in your resignation and that Clarice would not be held back." Whitney smirked.

I seethed.

"I'm sure that Clarice will flourish with another teacher who is one hundred percent dedicated to their students, rather than one whose attention is split between other *hobbies*." Whitney's words dripped with sugary spite.

Hobbies? Deep breaths. Deep breaths. I was no longer a teacher. This wasn't my problem, but it still burned my butt. I'd dedicated so much time and effort to all my students, including Clarice Kelley, only to have my principal ignore my recommendation to have Clarice repeat the year rather than moving her along and give in to parental pressure instead.

"I wish her luck," I said through my teeth.

Aunt Agatha narrowed her gaze and glared. "Pris was a great teacher. All her students loved her, but she doesn't need to teach. She's a highly successful author." She huffed.

Whitney Kelley glanced down at Bailey and frowned. "Hardly sanitary to have a dog in a restaurant." She turned to Joseph. "On second thought, I think I'll skip the sandwich."

Aunt Agatha shrugged. "Have it your way." She walked away mumbling, *"Some animals have better manners than humans."*

Whitney held up her ring finger and flashed a massive diamond that looked to be at least three carats. It certainly dwarfed her not-unimpressive wedding ring, which was stacked below the larger diamond. "Joe and I have been 'highly successful,' too, you see. He's a state senator and I just got elected to the local school board. I think it's vitally important to give back to the community, and I intend to help cut out all the fluff from the school's budget and make sure that Crosbyville is competitive in the national academic standings—"

"What fluff?" I asked.

Whitney halted in what was undoubtedly her election spiel and glanced at me. "Did you say something?"

"I asked what fluff you were talking about cutting? I was a teacher for the past five years in River Bend and then here in Crosbyville, and I can't imagine that any schools around here have anything remotely resembling *fluff* in their budgets. The population of Crosbyville hasn't increased a lot, and with inflation, the rising cost of infrastructure, advancing technology, and the dwindling tax base, I was just wondering what 'fluff' Crosbyville had."

"Art, music . . . special programs, like that dog reading program." She waved her hand as though swiping at a fly. "I heard your artistic friend, Maria—"

"Marcie."

"Whatever." Whitney rolled her eyes. "She coerced Amelia Cooper Lawson to fund that trivial program. If Amelia had talked to me before she wrote that check, I could have told her that she was tossing away her money. If students are struggling to read, then it's up to their parents to find and pay for private tutors. Public schools can't afford to foot the bill for programs like that when our students need to focus on math and science to be competitive in the global job market."

I felt my chest constrict and my fists clenched by my sides. Five years of anger from paying for supplies from my own pockets and watching school boards cut humanities programs like art and music when they were deemed *nonessential* welled up inside, and I nearly exploded. Math and science were important, but I was frustrated by people who treated the arts like redheaded stepchildren.

"You can't do that. The arts and special programs are important."

"I can. And I will." Whitney smirked and I knew that's exactly what she would do. She'd always gotten her way and now that she was on the school board, she'd manipulate the other members of the board until she got exactly what she wanted, just as she'd just done to keep her daughter from repeating a grade.

"You won't get away with it. Someone will stop you."

She leaned closer so only I could hear her. "Who's going to stop me?"

"I will. One way or another. I'll stop you if it's the last thing I do." I could feel my blood pounding in my ears, and I knew my neck and face were flushed, but I didn't care.

I thought Whitney was going to laugh in my face, but at that moment, the door opened and the new chief of police, Gilbert Morgan, walked into the café along with his daughter, Hannah.

Gilbert Morgan was tall, muscular with dark hair and

eyes, square-jawed with a five-o'clock shadow and a rock-solid chest. Our new chief of police had rugged good looks.

Whitney glanced at the chief and then seized her opportunity. Bailey was sitting by my side with his back to her, and she stepped on his tail.

That's when all hell broke loose.

Chapter 3

*B*ailey yelped as he turned and lunged at her.

I grabbed his collar, pulled him back, and got him calm.

Whitney screamed and cowered behind Joe, who stood by with a blank expression on his face.

"Chief Morgan, I want this dog removed immediately. He's a loose cannon. I can't believe she brings him around innocent children. He's a danger to the public. At a minimum, he needs to be muzzled whenever he's out. The reality is, he needs to be put down," she yelled.

"Put down? Are you kidding? He didn't do anything. You vicious shrew. I almost wish he were dangerous. You deserved it." I was so furious I could barely see straight.

Chief Morgan came up behind me. "What's going on here?"

"That vicious mutt nearly ripped my throat out. That's what happened. Then Priscilla here threatened me. I want her arrested." Whitney turned around and asked everyone in the diner. "You're all witnesses. You saw and heard everything."

Chief Morgan turned to me. "Can you tell me what happened?"

"She deliberately stepped on my dog's tail. He wasn't going to rip her throat out. He was surprised and it was just a reflex action. He'd never hurt anyone. He's a registered therapy dog and gentle as can be." I could feel the tears welling up behind my eyes, but I forced them back. I would NOT cry in front of Whitney Kelley.

"Gentle? He's a menace to society and I expect you to do your job and arrest her," Whitney shrieked.

Aunt Agatha came from behind the counter. "Now, hold up, Chief. This is my diner and I have a right to say who stays and who leaves, and as far as I'm concerned, Bailey stays." She put both hands on her hips and glared at Whitney.

"Well, I never . . ." Whitney huffed.

"It's about time someone told you that you're not the center of the universe, Mrs. Kelley. The sun, moon, and nary one of the planets revolve around you. Now, if you don't like how I run things in my diner, then you can just get to stepping." Aunt Agatha pointed at the door.

Whitney looked as though she could bite the head off nails.

She narrowed her gaze, and I could see a cutting remark

ready to come, but the look on Aunt Agatha's face would have stopped a bear dead in his tracks. Whitney opened her mouth, but before she could speak, my best friend, Marcie, swept into the café.

"Pris! I'm so glad you're here." She walked past Joe and Whitney and hugged me. She whispered in my ear, "I don't know what's happening, but she's just trying to get you riled up. Don't let her."

Marcie dropped to one knee. "Bailey, you are just the bestest doggy and I wuv you. Yes, I do." She cuddled and scratched him in all his favorite spots as the drool dripped from his jowls.

When she stopped, he shook himself, flinging drool on Whitney's perfect dress.

"Ugh. It's completely unhygienic to have a dog in a restaurant. If you don't do something about it, I'll call the health department." She spun around and marched out. "And I'm sending you my dry-cleaning bill."

Joe Kelley stood awkwardly for a few moments before finally turning and following his wife. As the door closed, I heard him muttering about his chicken salad sandwich.

Marcie smiled and held up her hand to Bailey for a high five, one of the few tricks he knew. Then she turned to me. "Remind me to give him a big treat for that later."

I shook my head. "You did that on purpose. You deliberately worked Bailey up into a lather, knowing he'd . . ."

Marcie gave me her most innocent, doe-in-the-headlights look. "Who, moi? I have no idea what you're talking about."

After Whitney and Joe left, the tension in the diner

dropped. Several of the patrons applauded. Everyone else returned to their meals and the noise level returned to normal.

Chief Morgan tipped his hat and returned to his daughter.

Aunt Agatha took a deep breath and then went to take care of the chief's order, still muttering, though now about where Whitney could shove her dry-cleaning bill.

I was still shaking, and Marcie gave me a hug to steady my nerves and then pushed me back down into my seat and slid into the seat across from me.

"It's okay. Whitney Baxter was always a mean girl. Now Whitney Kelley is a mean woman. How is it you've been back for nearly a year and haven't run into her?"

"Good luck?" I shrugged. "According to Clarice, Whitney's been out of town quite a bit the last few months. She's been helping Chelsea move back."

"I forgot about that. The only person more dedicated to Whitney Kelley has to be her younger sister, Chelsea." Marcie shuddered.

"Whitney's awful. She deliberately stepped on Bailey's tail. Can you believe that? She deliberately hurt my dog. I was so furious I could have strangled her."

Aunt Agatha brought Marcie a large chocolate shake, which she knew was her favorite. "You want a chicken salad sandwich?"

"Absolutely, Miss Agatha. You know I love your chicken salad." She glanced at my dishes. "Is that corn chowder?"

Aunt Agatha smiled. "One chicken salad sandwich and a cup of corn chowder coming up."

Marcella Rutherford and I had been best friends since

we were five years old, when my parents both died suddenly and I was brought to Crosbyville to stay with my grandmother and my aunt Agatha.

My mom joined the Peace Corps right after college. She had been a teacher, which is probably why I became one. My dad was a doctor. I'm proud of their commitment to service. From everything I've heard about my mom, she was always giving. That generous spirit and desire to help led both of my parents to Africa, where they met, fell in love, and had me. Their commitment also led to their death, when disease broke out in the tiny village where they worked. My parents made the decision to stay and help the villagers but sent me to a convent until arrangements could be made to send me home. Neither of them survived the outbreak. Isolated at a convent, I stayed with the Sisters of the Holy Cross until a missionary was cleared to bring me to stay with my family in Crosbyville.

I looked around the restaurant and caught several of the diners staring at me. I gazed at myself in the mirror behind the counter and confirmed that the heat I'd felt rush up my neck had settled in my face. I stole a glance at the chief and our eyes locked. He smiled, and I drew my glance away and prayed the ground would open and swallow me alive.

Marcie gave my arm a squeeze. "She's a horrible person who likes making others feel bad, but a wise woman once said, '*No one can make you feel inferior without your consent.*' Don't give her your consent."

"Eleanor Roosevelt." I took a deep breath and wished I could shake off the poisonous cloud that Whitney Kelley had left just as Bailey had done. Joe hadn't been wrong—I'd lost fifty pounds since high school, exchanged my thick glasses for contacts, and reinvented myself. Yet, two minutes with Whitney Kelley, and I was a fifteen-year-old, chubby, four-eyed teen again, with a mouth full of metal and zero self-esteem, who was looking for a hole to crawl in to hide.

"Forget about that witch. If we're lucky, maybe a house will fall on her, but if it does, I'm calling dibs on those shoes. Did you see them?" Marcie joked.

I laughed. Marcie was always able to find the bright side of any situation. Her glass was always half-full, and she was a perpetual optimist. "Those were some pretty amazing shoes. Maybe we could arm-wrestle for them."

"Deal." She chuckled. "Now, let's eat. We need all our strength for your big move tomorrow."

At twenty-eight, Marcie and I were the same age. Unfortunately, that's where the physical similarities ended. Marcie was almost six feet tall and able to maintain a perfect model-thin figure regardless of how much she ate. While I was barely five three with more curves than a snowman, regardless of how *little* I ate. Marcie had a smooth, dark complexion, which she inherited from her Nigerian mother, and straight, dark hair and dark eyes, which were gifts of her Taiwanese father. She was stunning but didn't realize it. My skin wasn't smooth like Marcie's. My face was prone to acne unless I watched my diet like a hawk and limited dairy, fried foods, chocolate, and Diet Coke, which I seldom did. My eyes were light gray like my dad's and my hair was dark and curly like my mom's, but my wavy locks had a mind of their own with a tendency to frizz at the slightest sign of humidity. Our interracial lineage was probably one of the things that drew Marcie and me together as children. A shared interest in mysteries, dogs, and old movies cemented our long-term friendship for nearly a quarter of a century. Marcie was an art and music teacher in Crosbyville, so after I'd recounted the entire argument to her, she shared in my furor over Whitney's goal to eliminate special programs and the arts from the Crosbyville schools.

When I graduated from high school, I couldn't wait to move as far away from rural, midwestern America as possible. I wanted to move to a big city with skyscrapers, nightclubs, museums, concerts, and a diverse population filled with people who looked more like me. At least, that was my original plan. When the time arrived, I chickened out. The two popular state colleges in Indiana were both bigger than Crosbyville, and I felt lost in the crowd. So when I was accepted at a prestigious private university less than an hour from home, I accepted. The University of Our Mother by the Lake was a Catholic university in nearby River Bend. Our Mother was a great school, and River Bend was the third-largest city in the state, so even though I was a lot closer to home than I planned, I was still in a larger city. Turns out being closer to home was a good thing. My grandmother and my aunt respected my privacy and didn't visit too often . . . well, not after my freshman year anyway. Plus, I appreciated being able to come home on weekends whenever I was feeling homesick for family and a home-cooked meal. When I graduated, I got a job teaching in River Bend before moving back to Crosbyville six months ago. Now, if I was honest with myself, I had to admit it felt good to be home.

"How excited are you about buying your first home tomorrow?"

The smile that broke out over my face answered that question without my saying one word. "I love living with Aunt Agatha, but there's nothing like having your own place."

"I wish you could have moved in with me. I would have loved having you and Bailey around more."

I barely noticed the whine at the end of that phrase. "If it were just me, I would have moved in a heartbeat, but . . ."

"I know. I know. My apartment's too small."

"Not to mention the fact that your landlord hates dogs. There's no way we could hide a one hundred–pound bloodhound without her noticing."

"I know, but I really want a dog and I love Bailey so much."

"Well, you'll get to see him as much as you like. I'm only going to be a few blocks away."

We chatted a bit longer, but then went our separate ways. Marcie helped to calm my nerves, but I was still shaky from the altercation with Whitney. The short drive home to the colonial house where I lived with my aunt Agatha wasn't long enough to bring peace, either. I tried to push the incident at the diner out of my mind, but it kept popping up like a jack-in-the-box. Just when I thought I'd moved on, "Pop Goes the Weasel"—I was back in the midst of my argument with Whitney. Each time, I came up with a hundred stinging retorts that I wished I'd said. It was too late now.

Sleep was elusive, and my tossing and turning must have distracted Bailey, because he eventually stood on his hind legs with his front paws on the bed and gazed into my eyes. When I looked back, he leaned closer and licked my nose.

Nothing like getting a sloppy kiss from a dog to wash away all your troubles.

I wiped my face with the pillow and couldn't help smiling. "Thanks, buddy. You're right. Everything will be all right."

Bailey barked, wagged his tail, and looked at me expectantly.

Eventually, I caved, sliding over to make room, and he jumped up on the bed. I had been working to keep him off the bed, but my goofball always knew how to get exactly what he wanted.

He stretched out next to me and I snuggled up and held him close. Within minutes he was snoring. It took me a little longer, but feeling the heat from his body, watching his chest heave up and down with each breath, and listening to his snoring made me sleepy, and before long, I was drifting off into dreamland. My last waking thought was *Maybe, the next book in The Adventures of Bailey the Bloodhound, Pet Detective, should feature Bailey's defeat over Cruella de Vil, a villain who bore a striking resemblance to Whitney Kelley.*

Chapter 4

The next morning, I was eager to get up and get the day started. I glanced at Bailey. "We have a lot to do today, buddy. So, this morning's walk is going to be superfast. No marking every tree. No tracking critters, and no putzing around."

He yawned and did a full-body stretch.

Somehow, I knew he wasn't paying attention. Nevertheless, onward, and outward.

It was going to be a long day and I wouldn't be giving Bailey much of my attention, so I wanted to make this morning's walk special—quick, but special.

I loaded Bailey into my SUV and drove downtown. Crosbyville Elementary School was next to his favorite park. The park technically belonged to the city, but its proximity to the school meant the students had access and used it almost exclusively. A walking path at the back edge was popular among joggers and power walkers. There was a formal area with a fountain, bench, and some brightly colored begonia borders. The fountain was in the middle of a hedge maze that we used to call *make-out maze* when I was in high school. Bailey headed straight for the maze with a dogged determination that meant he was on a trail, and nothing short of a miracle—or a hot dog—would be able to distract him from his mission.

I glanced at my watch. I could spare another fifteen minutes before we needed to head home so I could move forward with the 153 things on my to-do list. Besides, I hated pulling him away from something he loved to do, especially since he'd been such a good boy during our pet-assisted reading sessions at the library earlier in the week. He'd tolerated rough-and-tumble petting, ear flapping, jowl jiggling, and being used as everything from a pony to a pillow by a group of second graders from Crosbyville Elementary. He'd endured all these indignities with barely a whimper. The life of a pet-assisted reading therapy dog was taxing, but he'd done good work. Students who struggled with reading curled up with whatever book I handed them and read aloud as long as Bailey would listen. Even Clarice Kelley had participated, and that was saying a lot. If only her parents were more involved, she might stand a fighting chance at growing up to be different from her self-absorbed parents.

Thinking about the Kelleys only put a frown on my face and tightened the knot in my stomach. I didn't want to think about any of the Kelleys right now, especially Whitney Kelley. Instead, I smiled at Bailey's biggest breakthrough—Hannah.

Hannah Morgan was the only child of Crosbyville's dishy new chief of police. They'd moved here from Chicago a year ago after her mom died. She was shy and withdrawn and was having a hard time adapting to life in small-town Crosbyville. According to Marcie, she'd barely spoken ten words for over a month when she first arrived, but this week she read aloud to Bailey for nearly thirty minutes.

"If there was ever a reason to continue the pet-assisted therapy reading program, Hannah Morgan was it. Surely, even Witless Whitney Kelley could see that." I looked at Bailey for confirmation, but he was engrossed in his scent trail.

"You're right. I don't need to think about Whitney Kelley." I took several slow deep breaths. "I need to think about our next book." I allowed Bailey to lead me while I focused on the story that formed in my subconscious mind.

Bailey, the relentless detective, put his nose to work. Head down and with a new determination, he sniffed his way across miles of fields until his tongue hung from his mouth, exhausted. His focus never wavered. Through the dense forest filled with creatures big and small, he plowed forward, not veering to the left nor the right. Nothing could distract him from the trail left by the jewel thieves.

"Jewel thieves? I wonder where that came from." I rolled the idea around in my brain. "Actually, I kind of like the idea of Bailey catching a jewel thief. What do you think?" I looked at Bailey and he was indeed focused, but not on a trail of jewel thieves. Instead, he was engrossed in a newly planted bed of begonias along the trail.

I pulled back on his leash. "Whoa, boy. Where are you going?"

Bailey's response was to continue his path through the greenery, even if it meant dragging me along.

I adjusted my grip on the leash and was just about to plant my feet and give him a tug when he lurched forward and bolted around a bench. Zigging and zagging, he made a beeline into the flower bed.

"Bailey, stop!"

I'd like to think his abrupt stop was due to the hundreds of dollars and millions of hours I'd invested in obedience school, but I wasn't quite that naive. No, Bailey stopped because he'd reached his destination, the begonia bed.

He stopped and quickly began digging fast and with a fury. He flung dirt, mulch, and whatever the municipal gardeners used to fertilize the plants.

"Bailey, stop. No digging up the flowers. Do you want to get us banned from the park?" Visions of Mrs. Goldstein's flower bed flitted across my brain.

He ignored me and continued digging with a vigor and determination that meant he had come to the end of his trek and had no intention of stopping until he'd unearthed his prize. Bloodhounds were stubborn, and Bailey was all bloodhound.

When the dirt and debris stopped flying, I leaned forward to assess the damage. With any luck, I could stick the flowers back into the ground, brush off any evidence that would link us to the destruction, and sneak out of the park. I picked up a mangled begonia that was lying nearby and reached down to return it to its hole when I saw a glimpse of a shiny black patent leather pump with a flash of red. It was a shoe—an expensive shoe. There was only one person in Crosbyville whom I'd seen wearing shoes that cost more than most teachers made in a month. I looked closer and got a clear view of what Bailey had uncovered. It was a body lying facedown and half-covered in dirt.

Chapter 5

I felt light-headed, and for a few moments I closed my eyes and took several deep breaths. When the park stopped spinning, I opened my eyes a smidge and peeked out. Yep. Still there. My knees felt wobbly. I closed my eyes again and took several more deep breaths. Maybe this was all some really bad dream . . . a nightmare. Maybe, just maybe, when I opened my eyes, it would all disappear. I squeezed my eyes tighter, shook my head like an Etch A Sketch, and then slowly opened them. No luck! She was still there . . . still dead. No matter how much I wanted to believe that this was a bad dream, it wasn't. It was real.

I was standing in the park, staring down at the body of Whitney Kelley.

One part of my brain wanted me to run back to my car screaming like a banshee, but my feet were concrete blocks, and I couldn't move. As I grasped the situation, fear stabbed my heart. My gaze darted from one side to the other. I slowly reached my hands into my pockets and grasped my Taser and flipped the cap off the pepper spray. I edged closer to Bailey and whispered, finding comfort in the sound of words. "What if the person who killed Whitney Kelley is still here . . . watching and waiting, prepared to jump out from behind the hedge maze and—"

"Woof."

I glanced at Bailey and stood still and listened to the sound of birds singing, planes flying overhead, and the distant clip-clop of a horse from an Amish buggy trotting through the streets in the early morning. We were alone. That knowledge should have brought comfort, but still I tightened my grip on my Taser.

Bailey sat and looked back at me with his head tilted to the side. He wasn't the least bit worried. Bloodhounds may not be the ideal breed for protection, but they wouldn't stand idly by while a chipmunk walked by, let alone a person. There was no way he'd be this calm if there was a killer waiting to take us out. "You're right. There's nobody here." I released my hold on the Taser. Without the fear of needing to fend off a killer, I was free to have a mental meltdown. I walked in a tight circle. "WhatamIgoingtodo? WhatamIgoingtodo? WhatamIgoingtodo?"

Bailey gave way to a very loud yawn.

I stopped walking in circles. "You're right. We can't panic. There's no need to panic. Panicking won't solve anything. We have to be calm, right?"

"Woof."

"Right. I'm an adult. I can't panic." I took a deep breath and steadied my nerves. "I've always said I wanted to try search and rescue with you. This is what we'd do, right? We'd search for lost people and . . . sometimes, we'd find bodies." I took another deep breath. "What would Bailey the Bloodhound do? He'd . . . look for clues and call the police, right?"

Bailey tilted his head.

"I can do this. We can do this." I forced myself to open my eyes and look at the scene. "It's Whitney Kelley, and she's dead. You don't need to be a psychic or a medical doctor to know that."

Bailey barked.

I fixed my gaze on the body. I was grateful the scene wasn't gross, and even though my stomach felt like I'd just been on an ocean liner in the middle of a hurricane, I wasn't about to lose my breakfast. Mentally, I knew Whitney was dead, but she just looked like she'd fallen asleep in a flower bed. She was facedown, so I didn't have to see her face, only the back of her head. I'd spent much of my early years sitting behind Whitney Kelley, formerly Baxter, in school. Cummings always followed Baxter. So almost a decade after high school graduation, I still could have identified the back of Whitney's head from a police lineup if put to the test. I'd stared at that cowlick coated in Nice'n Easy 9G Light Golden Blonde for way too many years to be mistaken. Plus, she was wearing the same expensive Givenchy outfit she'd worn yesterday when we'd had a public shouting match in front of everyone in my aunt's diner, including the local chief of police. That incident had nearly gotten me arrested. "Ohmygod."

I didn't want to look, but like a rubbernecker at a traffic accident, once I looked, I couldn't stop myself. I surveyed her lifeless body, but . . . something was missing. "What's missing?" I had no idea. I was tempted to move closer, but I'd read enough mysteries to know better. "Nope. Not going to do it. We need to call the police."

I pulled out my cell phone and turned toward Bailey, my curious bloodhound, who sat nearby smiling at me with one of Whitney's red-soled, expensive Louboutin pumps in his mouth. "Drop it."

Bailey could be stubborn, but he must have recognized that now was not the time to push my buttons. He dropped the shoe and gave me a sad-yet-adoring look from his large, soulful eyes.

In my heart, I knew it wasn't his fault. He was merely doing what bloodhounds had been bred to do for centuries.

"We'd better get this over." I dialed the emergency number. "This is Priscilla Cummings and I need to report that my dog, Bailey, just found a dead body . . . It's Whitney Kelley. I'm positive it's Whitney Kelley. Yes, I'm sure she's dead . . . No, I haven't touched anything."

The officer asked a lot of questions, ordered me not to touch anything, and then promised that someone would be here shortly.

I hung up and flopped down on a nearby bench to wait.

Bailey meandered over and put his big head in my lap.

I stroked his droopy ears and scratched the spot behind his left ear that made his leg jiggle and his eyes roll back in his head. "I know it's not your fault, buddy, but Whitney Kelley is dead. Someone is bound to think that maybe we . . . okay, I, had something to do with this. Even if they don't, which they shouldn't because I didn't, it could be . . . difficult." I sighed and gave myself a mental kick in the rear for focusing on myself and how Whitney Kelley's death might inconvenience me. She was dead. A human being whom I knew had lost her life. I shivered. I wrapped my arms around Bailey and allowed his warmth to seep into my soul.

"I'm sorry, buddy. You did good. You found her. Good boy," I mumbled in his ear. Still, in the core of my being, I couldn't help wishing that just this once, he didn't have such a keen sense of smell and a knack for finding things.

Chapter 6

The gravel footpath inside the maze wasn't wide. Two people could comfortably walk side by side. Or, one person and a large bloodhound, but not much more than that. When I was young, the walls of the maze were tall, at least six feet. However, with time comes wisdom—or a fear of lawsuits. After a toddler wandered away from their parents and the irate parents sued the city and won, the inner walls were cut back to three feet tall. There was a large hedge that surrounded the outside of the maze, enclosing it in a wall of green. However, once inside, the pattern was clearly visible to anyone standing. Benches were placed throughout the maze, providing opportunities for rest.

Rest was the last thing on my mind. Nervous energy prevented me from sitting on the bench for more than a few seconds. My mind raced with questions. *How did Whitney*

Kelley end up in the maze? Was the killer still here? Hiding? Watching me? I hopped up again and looked over the top of the hedges, turning in a circle to survey my surroundings. Nothing. It was early and the only living creatures apart from Bailey and me were either flying overhead or scurrying under the hedges. I sat back down on the bench. The thought of being alone should have put my mind at ease. However, one glance at Whitney's remains and I was back on my feet.

My stomach growled. I'd skipped a big breakfast in favor of a granola bar in order to get to the park. Bad mistake. I'd worked hard not only to lose weight, but to change my eating habits. I stopped eating when I was bored or nervous and concentrated on only eating when I was hungry . . . like now. Of course, the thought of eating sent a wave of nausea that made me want to puke. I closed my eyes and took more deep breaths. When the queasiness left, I rummaged in my pockets looking for an antacid. I found a stick of peppermint gum and stuck that in my mouth. Peppermint was good for digestion, or so my grandmother used to tell me. I sucked the gum and hoped there was enough of the peppermint flavoring to do the trick.

I glanced at my phone to check the time. Less than one minute had passed since the last time I'd checked. *Where were the police?*

Bailey tilted his head, stood, and barked.

I froze and strained to follow his gaze. It wasn't until I saw his tail wag that I realized the woof wasn't a *There's a deadly killer coming so be ready* bark. It took a few additional seconds before I heard the sirens and realized it was a *Help is coming now* bark.

"Breathe," I said out loud. My shoulders dropped a quarter of an inch, and I allowed myself to follow the words with the action.

The first person I saw walking through the hedge wall was Chief Morgan and I felt my breathing quicken for an entirely different reason. *Breathe. Breathe. Breathe.*

Chief Morgan's eyes darted around as he marched toward me. "You found the body?"

"Yes," I said. All of the saliva had evaporated from my mouth and my voice squeaked. I cleared my throat. "Yes," I said slightly louder and a few octaves lower on the squeak-o-meter.

He squatted down and examined the scene. "Did you touch anything?"

"No. Of course not."

He turned and glanced up at me.

"Everyone knows not to touch anything at a crime scene."

He rolled his eyes toward Bailey. "What about him?"

"Bailey is a highly trained therapy and search-and-rescue dog," I spat the words out. Unfortunately, my chewing gum came out and landed with a splat two inches from my foot. Before I could bend down to pick it up, I felt a tug on Bailey's leash. I turned in time to see him hike his leg and pee on the leg of the bench.

Chief Morgan sighed. "Miss Cummings, would you and your 'highly trained therapy and search-and-rescue dog' please exit the maze and wait in the parking lot. I'll be over to take your statement shortly."

Grateful for the opportunity to exit before either Bailey or I did anything else humiliating, I practically ran toward the parking lot and away from the chief.

Bailey and I walked around the parking lot as an army of police and EMTs traipsed from the parking lot to the maze. I counted ten police cars barring access to the park. Their flashing lights served as a beacon attracting people who stood on the perimeter and gawked.

I kept my head down and avoided eye contact with anyone who might recognize me. I hoped no one would notice me—but clearly, Bailey was impossible to miss. My phone vibrated as text messages from my aunt Agatha and Marcie came in at once.

I started a reply and glanced up in time to see Chief Morgan headed in my direction. I cut my text short and sent both the same message.

Bailey and I both fine. Will explain later.

I resisted the urge to pat my hair in place and mentally kicked myself for not using the time while I waited in the parking lot to touch up my face. I didn't have makeup with me, but I had a lipstick. Oh well, too late.

"Miss Cummings, can you tell me what you and your *highly trained therapy and search-and-rescue dog* were doing in the park and how you happened to find the body of the woman I saw you arguing with less than twenty-four hours ago?"

Not how I wanted the conversation to start. "It's a public park. I was walking my dog and he caught a scent and followed it. That's what bloodhounds do."

The chief wore sunglasses that shielded his eyes, so I couldn't tell what he was thinking. "Tell me what happened."

"There's not much to tell." I replayed the morning's events in my mind and realized there was absolutely nothing that would be helpful.

"Is this part of your regular routine? Do you come every morning?"

"We've come here several times since I moved back to Crosbyville six months ago. I don't usually come this early, but I have a busy day today and . . . Oh my God." I pulled out my phone and looked at the time. "I'm buying a house. I close today in two hours. I still have to go to the bank and get a cashier's check. I have to go." I turned to leave, but Chief Morgan grabbed my arm.

"Wait. We're not done. You need to provide a statement and sign—"

"Can't it wait? I promise that as soon as the closing is over, I'll swing by the police station and give a statement, but I have a ton of errands to do first. It's not like I strangled—" I clamped my mouth shut, but I felt sure he knew what I was going to say. We'd both noticed the scarf tied around Whitney Kelley's neck, but that didn't mean I was the one who'd tied the knot.

He paused for a few seconds, but his radio squawked. "Fine. I expect you at the station later today."

I saluted. "Aye, aye."

His lips twitched, but he didn't let them smile or scowl. Instead, he turned and walked away as he answered the radio.

I didn't wait for him to change his mind. I hurried to my car and drove to the bank.

Crosbyville Savings and Loan had been in the same spot for over one hundred years. The name had changed many times in the past century. The current trend away from Wall Street and bigger franchise banks with no roots in the community in favor of hometown businesses had led to a change back to the original name that was still chiseled into the building's masonry.

I hadn't intended to bring Bailey inside with me, but I didn't want to waste time taking him home, so I pulled out his therapy dog harness and took him inside the bank with me.

Technically, only service dogs were allowed inside the building, but I hoped I wouldn't be inside long enough to get kicked out.

Inside, I glanced around. Thankfully, it was still early and there were only a couple of people in line. I waited my turn and then hurried to the first available window. Thankfully, it was someone I recognized.

"Eli, I need your help. I'm closing on my house in"—I glanced at my phone—"less than two hours and I need a cashier's check."

"No problem." Eli Yoder smiled. "Congratulations."

"Thank you."

Eli Yoder was in his late twenties. He was a Mennonite, a Protestant sect that is similar in many ways to the Amish in their beliefs. Both Amish and Mennonites believe in a simpler way of life, although they differ in how that simpler life is practiced. Unlike the Amish, Mennonites use motorized vehicles, electricity, and some, like Eli, are clean-shaven. He was tall, thin, and slim with dark hair and dark eyes. He wore glasses and was handsome in a Clark Kent sort of way. "How's Marcie?" He blushed.

Raised Amish, Eli lived on a farm in the country. When he turned sixteen, he participated in the Amish practice of rumspringa, which allowed Amish youth the freedom to experience the world before choosing to be baptized into the Amish faith. He had an older sister who had turned away from the Amish faith, moved away, and was shunned by the community.

"Marcie's great. She's coming to the house later to help me move. You should swing by."

Eli blushed and dropped his head. He fell head over heels for Marcie years ago. However, his life as a Mennonite, although less restrictive than the Amish, posed a problem. Both groups still frowned on marriage outside of the faith. And Marcie, although a Christian, was much too liberal for Amish or Mennonite practices.

Eli finished processing my cashier's check and handed it to me with a big smile.

I gazed at the small piece of paper. This small paper represented years of savings and the advance I'd received on my book. My heart raced and, for a brief moment, I felt like I was going to puke.

"Pris, are you okay?" Eli asked.

I swallowed hard and nodded. "Fine. It's just so much money."

He nodded. "True, but you're not losing the money, you're simply investing it in a different asset."

I nodded. He was right. I focused on the positive. Buying a house was the biggest purchase I would ever make. But it was an investment. I wasn't just giving my money away. I was buying something in return.

In the car, I gave Bailey a hug. "Eli's right. We're buying land and a home with a yard for a bloodhound to run and play." I scratched his ear.

Bailey gave a short bark and smiled. Well, it looked like a smile. My vet said dogs can't smile and claimed he just had gas. Still, it looked like a smile to me.

I arrived at the title company in time for my appointment. I signed a mountain of papers, handed over my hard-earned money, and walked out with my head spinning, a packet of papers, and the keys to my new house.

My new home had once been a carriage house belonging to one of the town founders and Crosbyville's first mayor, Josiah Cooper. The extra-large brick carriage house later became the town's first post office. It had a lot of history and charm and, up until today, had belonged to one of our most prominent citizens, Amelia Cooper Lawson.

Originally home to the Miami, Peoria, and Potawatomi

peoples, Crosbyville was later resettled by Puritans after the Indian Removal Act of 1830 had the Indigenous people "relocated" west of the Mississippi River. The history books made it sound like a peaceful and fair transaction that the native peoples entered willingly rather than the forced exile it really was. They painted the Europeans who followed as though they were Noah's family disembarking from the ark, sent to repopulate the Earth after the great flood. Amelia Cooper Lawson's family took pride in its label as the "founders" of the town, which was named after one of Josiah Cooper's children, Crosby. Josiah Cooper built a large farmhouse near the church in the early nineteenth century. As the town and the family prospered, they built a second, massive house atop a hill overlooking the town. The original Cooper farmhouse burned to the ground a decade later, but the large brick carriage house remained. The stone carriage house was used as the post office for nearly fifty years, but when a newer, modern building was built, the old carriage house was left to the proprietors.

Marcie met me at the house with flowers and food.

"You really lucked out. I didn't think Amelia Cooper Lawson would ever sell this old place." Marcie sat on the floor with her legs crossed. She was wearing cutoff jeans and a paint-splattered T-shirt and still managed to look like a model for a Sherwin-Williams paint commercial.

I glanced down at my outfit. I'd spilled ketchup on my T-shirt and ripped my jeans dragging in an antique metal bed I'd bought from a secondhand shop downtown. The humidity made my hair look as though I'd stuck a wet finger in a light socket. I looked like a hot mess. Nope, I wasn't bitter.

I bit into my burger and used the back of my hand to wipe away the mustard that dribbled down my chin. "Frankly, I was surprised, too. Lucas Harrison had been trying to get her to sell the building for years, but she wouldn't even consider it until now. At least, that's his story." I looked around the small room that was now my living room. The room had dark wood paneling and wide wood-plank floors that were at least one hundred years old. "Anyway, it needs a lot of work, but it has great bones."

"It's going to be perfect, and you know I'll help."

"I'm counting on it." I laughed. "You're the artistic one, I'm just going to provide the checkbook and the labor."

"It's going to be so much fun. I've been scouring the Internet for ideas and looking at paint swatches, wallpaper, and fabric for drapes." Marcie's face lit up. I worked to keep my expression neutral, but I should have known I couldn't fool my best friend.

"I know you *hate* wallpaper, Pris, but it's making a comeback. Besides, some of the walls upstairs are so bad, I really think wallpapering them will be best."

"I do hate wallpaper. Anyone who's ever had to remove old wallpaper hates it, and I still have nightmares from removing it from my room at Aunt Agatha's. I have no idea why I ever thought it was a great idea to have a room covered in Pepto Bismol pink flowers. Paint is so much easier, but I know you're right."

The first thing Marcie and I did was paint. The original building housed the Cooper family's carriages. The structure had to be large enough for the driver to drive both the carriage and the horses into the building and turn around. The original structure had large doors, high ceilings, and a loft space upstairs for the carriage driver to live in. Over time, when the building had been turned into a post office, walls were added. However, despite the high ceilings, the building had windows only at the front. The walls cut off the light to the back rooms and made the rest of the building feel dark. I wanted something bright to lighten the space and suggested white, but Marcie had convinced me to go with a bright, creamy yellow on the walls and golden-yellow trim. The color reminded me of sunshine, lemons, and flowers. It was a bold choice, but it worked, and I was glad I listened.

"This color makes me happy," I said.

"I knew you'd like it. White walls are so boring." Marcie smiled. "Besides, if you get tired of the yellow, we can always repaint it."

While we ate, I told Marcie about finding Whitney Kelley's body in the park. The joy or curse of living in a small town was that news traveled fast. We may not have liked Whitney, but neither of us felt up to discussing it while we were eating.

We finished eating and spent hours painting the first floor, which would now be my living room, kitchen, dining room/office, and a small bathroom. When we finished the first floor, we moved upstairs. I painted while Marcie wallpapered.

It would be a long, cold day in Hades before I would be in the mood to paint again.

"Are you sure Whitney was murdered? Couldn't she have tripped and hit her head or something?" Marcie asked.

I shook my head. "Not unless she tripped, hit her head, fell neck-first into a scarf, and then rolled around until the scarf became wrapped too tightly around her neck and stayed there until she died."

"Ugh."

"No one could be that clumsy."

"So, who do you think did it?" Marcie asked.

"No idea. I mean, she was a horrible human being. Still, who would want her dead?"

"You mean other than you, me, and every arts teacher in the Crosbyville school system?" Marcie said.

"I didn't want her dead . . . just . . . directing all of her energy in a different direction."

Marcie turned to stare and raised an eyebrow. "She stepped on Bailey's tail."

"Okay, I wanted to take one of those Louboutins and shove it up her—"

"Pris! You'll never guess who I found hanging around outside." Aunt Agatha surprised us both when she poked her head around the corner; we hadn't heard her come inside the house.

I turned to look at her and lost my balance on the ladder where I was cutting in the upper trim. I flailed my arms to find my balance and smacked the full paint tray on the rung beside me. In what felt like slow motion, a wave of yellow paint hit my face. Blinded by the paint, I stumbled backward and lost my footing on the ladder.

I braced myself for a crash that never came. Instead of hitting the ground, I was caught in midair. My chest hit what felt like a solid wall, but the thud onto the wood floors never happened. I blinked paint out of my eyes as I turned to see what stopped my fall and found myself gazing into the dark, smoky eyes of Chief Morgan.

Chapter 7

*T*his *can't be happening.*

I blinked several more times to clear my paint-splashed vision, only to have a large glob of yellow paint fall from my forehead onto my face. I lifted my T-shirt and wiped the paint from my eyes. I squinted but when I opened my eyes, the image was still the same. Staring back at me was in fact the chief of police. "Chief Morgan . . . I'm sorry . . . Oh my God . . . I'm sorry. I've got paint everywhere . . . I'm—"

"Be still," Chief Morgan ordered.

I obeyed the authority in his voice, despite the awkward situation. Despite the weight I'd lost since childhood, I wasn't a lightweight. But Chief Morgan's arms were strong. His knees weren't buckling. I squinted through my paint-splattered eyelashes and didn't notice any visible signs of strain. Nevertheless, I regretted the extra cookies I'd eaten earlier.

Chief Morgan shifted my weight in his arms, leaned forward, and placed my feet on the ground.

Upright on my own two feet, I turned to look at the chief of police. His uniform was speckled with yellow paint. He had paint on his cheek, but he had managed to avoid the yellow tidal wave that had drenched me.

"Pris, you're dripping paint everywhere." Aunt Agatha gaped at my mess.

I closed my eyes to avoid the eye roll that I felt coming. "Thanks, Captain Obvious," I mumbled.

"What was that?" Aunt Agatha asked.

"Nothing." I knew better than to repeat my lippy comment to my aunt.

"I didn't think you were talking smart to me, young lady," Aunt Agatha muttered.

For a few seconds I was grateful to be covered in yellow paint. At least Chief Morgan wouldn't be able to see the flush that I felt rising up my neck. With any luck, the yellow paint mixed with the red flush of embarrassment made me look like a giant orange. Sad that I considered that to be an improvement.

Marcie handed me a damp towel that I used to remove as much paint from my face as possible. I mustered as much dignity as I could. "Can I help you?"

"I need your statement."

"What time is it?" I asked.

"Five thirty," Chief Morgan said.

"Oh, I'm so sorry. I had no idea it was so late." I glanced down at my paint-covered T-shirt and jeans. "If I can just get cleaned up, I can—"

"I brought tea, scones, and some of my chicken salad sandwiches. Why don't you come downstairs and let me fix you a little snack, Chief, while Pris gets cleaned up." Aunt Agatha wasn't involved in law enforcement, but when it came to food and maneuvering people, she was an expert.

I removed my shoes and socks, scurried to the bathroom, and hopped into the shower. I started with the intention of a quick rinse, but as the warm water pelted my skin, I felt compelled to do a thorough job. I shampooed my hair, scrubbed the paint from my body and fingernails, and tried not to think about the spectacle I'd made of myself. I couldn't stay in the shower forever, no matter how much I wanted to. When the water at the bottom of the tub ran clear and I felt clean, I got out.

I wiped the film from the mirror and confirmed that I was no longer covered in yellow paint. I quickly dried off, wrapped myself in a towel, and peeked out the bathroom door. Seeing the path clear, I scampered across the hall to the room that would be my primary bedroom. On the bed, Marcie had laid out clean undergarments and a sundress, as well as some shoes.

I held up the dress. This was a bright fuchsia A-line sundress that was more of a "Let's go out for drinks and tapas" dress than a "Thanks for stopping by to take my official police statement" dress. I looked around for something else but couldn't remember which one of the thirty boxes I'd thrown my jeans into. "Phooey." I pulled the sundress over my head. I slipped my feet into the sandals Marcie had placed nearby, rushed to the bathroom to corral my hair into a ponytail, and hurried downstairs, ready to get this over with.

The narrow stairs formed an L and ended at a small foyer. To the right was the kitchen. To the left, the living room. Snatches of conversation told me that Chief Morgan, Aunt Agatha, and Marcie were in the kitchen. I turned to join them but stopped when I heard a soft voice from the living room.

"'Bailey the Bloodhound lifted his head and sniffed the air.'"

I didn't need to see the cover to know those were my words. That was my book, *The Adventures of Bailey the Bloodhound, Pet Detective.*

I tiptoed closer to the door and peeked my head around the corner.

On the floor, Bailey lay curled up near the wall. Also on the floor was Hannah Morgan, Chief Morgan's eight-year-old daughter. Using Bailey as a backrest, her long dark hair splayed across his back. Even without his therapy dog scarf and special harness, he lay perfectly still and listened while she read.

"There you—" a voice thundered from behind me.

"Shhh!" I turned and found myself face-to-face, or rather face-to-chest, with Chief Morgan.

He had changed out of his uniform and was wearing a

crisp, clean white T-shirt with the Fraternal Order of Police logo over his chest and a pair of jeans. He must have had extra clothes in his car. There were no signs of yellow paint, so he must have washed off the few splatters he'd had earlier. His brow rose, his gaze narrowed, and a tiny vein on the side of his head pulsed. He reminded me of a kettle ready to whistle, missing only steam coming from his ears.

With my finger, I tapped my lips in the universal symbol for quiet and pointed around the corner.

To my surprise, he obeyed and turned his head to look.

"'Bailey followed his nose down a long, winding country road. He pranced. He trotted. He jogged, and then he walked. Mile after mile, stopping only to sniff the air and the ground. His too . . . nun . . . gaaa.'" She sounded out the word. "Oh, 'tongue hung out of his mouth and his ears drooped. Bailey did not stop. He would not stop until he found the missing girl.'"

Chief Morgan and I stood—very close together—silently and listened as Hannah slowly worked through the book. His breath warm near my ear, I could smell his aftershave, and the combination of pine and citrus filled my head. My pulse raced.

"'The end.'"

I turned to face Chief Morgan and for a moment, the veil was lowered. The eyes that stared back at me were not the cold, impersonal gaze of a cop. I saw the soft, warm look of a father.

"She's reading," he whispered. "She's actually reading." His eyes wide with astonishment and pride.

I nodded.

"Cookies and milk." Aunt Agatha's voice rang out from the kitchen.

That broke the spell and Hannah, followed closely by Bailey, hurried around the corner and nearly collided into us.

"Dad, is it okay if I have a cookie?"

So engrossed in eavesdropping, we didn't hear Aunt Agatha approach from the kitchen until she spoke. "Of course it's okay with him." She gave Chief Morgan a stare that dared him to oppose her.

He may be the law, but when it came to food, Aunt Agatha was the boss.

"Just one. You haven't had dinner."

"Yay!" Hannah skipped the short distance but stopped right before entering the kitchen. She turned and glanced back at me. "Bailey, too?"

I nodded. "Bailey, too!"

"Woo-hoo!" Hannah ruffled Bailey's ears. "Come on, Bailey. We get cookies."

Cookies was one word that Bailey knew well. He woofed his approval and followed Hannah and Aunt Agatha into the kitchen.

My gaze followed Bailey. "He is such a good boy. He deserves a treat."

Chief Morgan motioned for me to follow him into the living room. He paced from the fireplace to the back wall, rubbing the back of his neck. "That was amazing." He rubbed his neck and paced. "Ever since Sarah . . . her mom, died, she's been . . ." He struggled to find the right word, but gave up. "Her teachers in Chicago wanted her to go into a remedial class for kids with special needs. They told me she couldn't read."

I took a deep breath and searched my mind for the right words. "I'm not a doctor, but I'm sure there are people who, for whatever reason, are unable to read. During my time as a schoolteacher, I've seen children with learning disabilities, traumatic injuries, and developmental difficulties. Generally, with help, they can be taught to read at some level. Most teachers are overworked, underpaid, and don't have the time or the resources to spend the extra time needed to help individual students who are struggling. That's why programs like the pet-assisted reading program are so beneficial."

"That's the program that Whitney Kelley wanted to stop?"

I nodded. I'd studied the benefits of pet-assisted therapy for years and could spout off about the benefits of Reading Education Assistance Dogs (R.E.A.D.) in my sleep. "Pet-assisted reading isn't new. It first started in 1999 in Salt Lake City, but is now practiced in most states as well as Germany, Italy, the Netherlands, Norway, and Sweden." I launched into the studies that showed the empirical evidence of the effectiveness of canine-assisted read-aloud intervention. After several minutes, I glanced up and noted a smile on Chief Morgan's face.

"I'm sorry. I can talk about the benefits of pet-assisted reading for hours. It's a subject that I'm very passionate about."

"I can tell." He grinned, but quickly got serious. "Never apologize for your passion."

Something in his eyes brought a wave of heat up my neck. "Well, I should have handled myself differently yesterday." *Was it only yesterday that I'd had that argument with Whitney?* "I should have . . . I don't know, just walked away. Whitney always knows—knew—how to push my buttons."

"You went to school together?"

"Yes. From elementary school through high school, we attended the same school, and she never liked me." I shrugged. *Whitney didn't like anyone, though she especially didn't like me, but I certainly wasn't going to say that.*

"Tell me about that."

Idle curiosity? Or did he really believe that I held some deep-rooted grudge against Whitney Kelley from childhood? Regardless, it was bound to come out. I folded my arms across my chest. "Do you want to hear this now? Or do I need to get a lawyer and meet you at the police station?"

"I'm just asking, but if you'd feel more comfortable with an attorney present, that's your choice."

I took a deep breath and tried to let down my defenses, knowing that sharing whatever information I had would be the fastest way to find Whitney's killer. I unfolded my arms and glanced around. "I don't have much furniture yet. Would you like to go in the kitchen? We can sit."

He cocked his head to the side and listened. Laughter

came from the kitchen as Aunt Agatha, Marcie, and Hannah joked. "Perhaps we could . . ." He pointed outside and let the sentence trail off. I nodded and we went out the front door and walked around to the side of the house.

An arched gate connected to a stone wall that enclosed the courtyard. Chief Morgan lifted an old wrought iron latch and held the gate open.

I sidled through. Inside the courtyard, overgrown privet hedges created green walls on either side of the yard. A gravel path led from the back of the house to the back wall, which held a fountain. On either side of the path, ground cover crept from the beds onto the path.

There was a rusty bistro table and two small rickety chairs that I planned to have hauled to the dump, and a wooden bench that looked capable of supporting both of our weight.

I walked to the bench and sat down.

Chief Morgan gazed around the courtyard. "Someone was an avid gardener."

I followed his gaze and squinted. "All I see are weeds."

He walked around. "It's overgrown now, but those are lilac bushes, roses, forsythia, azaleas, and rhododendrons." He pointed. "The ground cover, pachysandra and ivy, has taken over, but I'm guessing when that's cleaned out, you'll find all kinds of flowers."

I glanced around. "Really? Do you think they'll come back? I mean, I assumed I'd have to have everything pulled out and start over from scratch."

He walked over to one of the dense bushes. He took a

small knife out of his pocket and sawed at one of the branches deep inside the brambles. When he was done, he came back holding a yellow rose. He held the rose out to me. "You've got a ton of weeds, but someone invested a lot of time and money into this garden."

I took the rose and sniffed the sweet aroma. "Are you a gardener?"

He smiled. "When I have time, which is never. I love working with my hands. My wife used . . ." His smile faded. "Anyway, we should get to work." He sat down. "Now, tell me what happened today."

I repeated the story I'd told him earlier in the day. It was just as short.

"Did you see Whitney Kelley after she left the diner last night?"

"No."

"You didn't arrange to meet her in the park?"

"No. Why would I?"

"Were you friends?"

"No."

He looked up from his notepad, raised an eyebrow, and waited.

The silence became too much. "We weren't friends. Whitney Kelley was never a nice person. She was . . . cocky, arrogant, entitled, and spoiled. She thought she was better than everyone else since elementary school. She had to have the lead in the school play, or she didn't want to be in the play at all. She had to be the head cheerleader or nothing. Which was fine when it only involved her. But she begrudged everyone else a sliver of the limelight, too. If she wasn't the homecoming queen, then she made sure no one was." I fumed.

"How? This seems specific."

I felt my cheeks flush as I thought back. "I used to be a lot heavier than I am now. My senior year of high school, I was determined to lose weight, and I did. My classmates were so proud of me, they nominated me for homecoming queen. The only problem was, Whitney Kelley was also nominated. She spread rumors and . . . well, let's just say she made some accusations that weren't true."

"How do you know it was Whitney?"

"She told me."

That got his attention. "She told you that she spread lies about you?"

I nodded. "She eventually wanted me to know it was her."

"Did you report her?"

I shrugged. "What good would it do? She would just say it was sour grapes or something like that."

He squinted at me for a few moments. "Did you hate Whitney Kelley?"

"No."

"No? Why not? It sounds like she was an awful person who liked to torture you and other people."

"She was, but that was more than ten years ago. I moved on. I moved away and went to college, then got a job. I wrote a book—a very successful book." I lifted my head and stuck out my chin.

"Why'd you move back?"

"To write. To be closer to Aunt Agatha. I certainly didn't move back to kill Whitney Kelley."

"Can you think of anyone else who would want Whitney Kelley dead?"

"How about anyone who'd spent more than fifteen minutes with her? Or anyone who had the misfortune of being on the receiving side of her acidic tongue and hateful attitude?" I folded my arms across my chest. As soon as the words were out of my mouth, I regretted them. If I could roll back time, I wouldn't have spoken ill of the dead, even Whitney Kelley. Especially in front of a police officer, but it was too late. The words were out there.

I opened my mouth to apologize but was interrupted when I heard Bailey barking. There was a commotion, and the chief and I both stood and turned to face the back of the house.

Bailey ran out, chased by Hannah. He had a toy in his mouth and his leash was trailing behind him. From the joyful look in his eyes, I knew he was enjoying a game of keep-away.

When he was close enough, I reached down and grabbed his leash.

Hannah lunged for the toy to remove it, but Bailey wasn't done yet. There was still about eight feet of leash left and he was stubborn. He wouldn't give up without a fight.

Bailey ran, but I kept hold of the leash. His movement was limited, and he ran around me and Chief Morgan, encasing us in the leash.

"Bailey, STOP," I yelled.

I'd like to believe it was the authority in my voice that made him halt, but I suspect it was due to the fact that he had finally run out of leash. With nowhere to go, he skidded to a stop and sat.

"Drop it," I ordered.

He thought about it for a few moments, but then opened his mouth and let the toy drop.

Before I could untangle Chief Morgan and myself from the leash, the back door slammed and out marched Whitney's younger sister, followed by Joe Kelley, Marcie, and Aunt Agatha.

Chelsea Baxter-Davis was thin, blonde, and petite. She wasn't as pretty as her older sister, Whitney, but she used her familial assets to her advantage. From childhood, Chelsea worshipped her older sister.

Chelsea marched straight up to Chief Morgan, stopped, and folded her arms across her chest and glared. "Well, isn't this cozy? I want to know why this woman hasn't been locked up yet." She stretched out her arm and pointed her finger inches from my face. "Priscilla Cummings is a murderer. She killed my sister, and I want her arrested, now!"

Chapter 8

*C*helsea Baxter-Davis fumed.

Chief Morgan worked to get untangled from the leash and stepped forward and positioned himself in between me and Chelsea Baxter. "Mrs. Davis, as I told you earlier, this is an active police investigation. We are working—"

She snorted. "From what I can see you aren't working fast enough."

"Mrs. Davis, I would advise you to go home and leave this to the police," Chief Morgan said.

"It's *Ms. Baxter*, not Davis," Chelsea said.

"Ms. Baxter."

In school, Chelsea Baxter had always been smarter than Whitney, but she lacked her sister's acting ability. Whitney pretended that she liked you while she plotted your demise, while Chelsea's emotions were always clearly displayed on her face. Today, her face clearly showed what she thought of me, which was less than scum on the bottom of her shoes. "Chief Morgan, you need to do your job and arrest this . . . this . . . murderer. She killed my sister."

"Chelsea, I know you're upset, but I did *not* kill your sister. I did not murder Whitney. She was already dead when we found her body. Now, let's go inside and talk—" I extended an arm, but she brushed it off.

"Don't touch me. Don't you dare touch me." She glared.

"Ms. Baxter, you need to go home and let me do my job. I—"

"Your job?" Chelsea shrieked. "If you'd done your job, Whitney would be alive today. Whitney told you that she was dangerous. She *told you* Priscilla threatened her." She turned to Joe Kelley. "You were there. Didn't she tell the chief to arrest her?"

Joe Kelley tugged at the collar of his shirt. He looked at me. He looked at the ground. He looked everywhere but at his sister-in-law.

"Well?" Chelsea stamped her foot.

"Umm, well . . . yeah, but I don't think that—"

"That's your problem, Joe. You don't think." Chelsea rolled her eyes. She turned her back to her brother-in-law and faced the police chief. "If you aren't going to do your job, then I'll need to take matters into my own hands."

Chief Morgan narrowed his gaze. "What exactly does that mean?"

"It means that if you're too incompetent to do the job that the taxpayers pay you to do, then maybe we need to find someone to replace you." She folded her arms across her chest and then gave a saccharine-sweet smile. "Did you know that the state senate oversees the police budget?"

Chief Morgan's eyes flashed and the vein on the side of his head pulsed. Through gritted teeth he said, "Until I'm removed, I'm still the chief of police, and I suggest you turn around and leave."

His voice was steel, and Chelsea visibly shuddered. For a few seconds she glanced around like a frightened rabbit. After a few moments, she huffed, turned, and marched away.

Joe Kelley forced a pitiful apologetic glance toward the sheriff, nodded, and then followed Chelsea.

"Good riddance to bad rubbage," Aunt Agatha muttered.

Hannah's eyes filled with tears and her bottom lip fluttered. "I'm sorry. This is all my fault. If I hadn't been playing with Bailey, then he never would have run out and wrapped you in his leash and . . ."

In an instant, Chief Morgan shed his role as law enforcer and became Dad. He knelt on one knee, pulled his daughter into an embrace, and held her close. "None of this is your fault. You didn't do anything wrong," he whispered.

"But . . . I—"

"Shhh. No buts. It's all right. I promise." He stood up and turned to me. "We should go."

"Of course. I'll come by the police station first thing tomorrow and give my official statement."

Chief Morgan nodded and then led his daughter around the side of the house and away.

I stood and watched them leave and tried to make sense

out of the jumble of emotions that were flittering through my body. I was so absorbed, I forgot that Marcie and Aunt Agatha were still there until they spoke.

"You know, I wish I'd never joked about a house landing on Whitney like in *The Wizard of* Oz. Now we've got real life imitating art," Marcie said.

"What do you mean?" I asked.

"Just like in the movie, Dorothy's house may have landed on the Wicked Witch of the East, but it was her evil sister, the Wicked Witch of the West, that proved to be the real problem," Marcie said.

"Well, I'm not going to the wizard and I'm not melting anyone." I closed my eyes and clicked my heels three times. "There's no place like home. There's no place like home. There's no place like home." I opened my eyes and sighed. "It didn't work."

Aunt Agatha smiled and wrapped her arm around me. "Sure it did! You're home. You're surrounded by friends and family who love you. But you can't wait for some stranger behind a curtain to tell you what to do. If you want to have peace, you're going to need to screw on your courage, put your brain to good work, and set your heart on figuring out who killed Whitney Kelley, or that witch just might destroy you."

Chapter 9

*A*unt Agatha's words stayed with me long after she and Marcie were gone. Not the *Wizard of Oz* references. The part about figuring out whodunit. In fact, I lay awake most of the night thinking about it. I knew I hadn't killed Whitney Kelley. I didn't believe Chief Morgan thought I killed her, either. He would have arrested me by now if he thought I was a killer. Wouldn't he? I punched my pillow, rolled onto my back, and studied the ceiling. *No. If he thought I was a dangerous killer, there was no way he would have brought his daughter to my house and let her eat cookies. He didn't think I killed Whitney.* For some reason, that realization put a smile on my face.

I rolled onto my side and looked at Bailey. He wasn't lying awake, worried about arrest. He was sound asleep on his side. His jowls lay on my pillow. Bailey snored and I smiled again, but the smile didn't last long.

It didn't matter if Chief Morgan believed I was innocent or not. Chelsea Baxter was determined to have me arrested. I was accustomed to the Baxter sisters' tactics, and while I didn't like them, I knew that I could weather the onslaught of lies, negativity, and ill will. I'd dealt with them most of my life. I had years of experience.

I released a heavy sigh and rolled back onto my back. I may have experience ignoring the Baxter/Kelley family, but Chief Morgan and Hannah didn't. *Hannah was new to the school and didn't have a lot of friends yet. She was quiet and insecure. Clarice Kelley was well on her way to surpassing Whitney's skill at "annoying the new kid." Hannah was still grieving her mom's death. The last thing she needed was to have Clarice stirring up trouble. Besides, Chief Morgan didn't need Chelsea Baxter trying to ruin his career. He was still new to Crosbyville, too.*

Bailey gave a yip and shuddered.

I turned to look, but his eyes were closed. His paws were stretched out in front, and he was still asleep. He yawned and snored.

Chelsea Baxter and Joe Kelley could make trouble for Chief Morgan and Hannah. Neither of them deserved that. No one deserved that. Maybe Aunt Agatha was right. Maybe I could help. I sat up and turned on the light.

Bailey opened his eyes and looked at me. He stood up and turned around in a circle a couple of times. Then he turned his back to me and curled up in a ball. He was snoring again as soon as his head hit the pillow.

Chief Morgan didn't know Crosbyville. He didn't know Whitney Kelley or her evil sister, Chelsea. He probably thought he was able to handle them because he was a policeman. He was smart and supercute and . . . strong. He'd caught me and held me as though I weren't still packing an extra fifteen pounds of post-Covid weight. He was muscular and . . . rugged, but he didn't know what it was like in a small town where gossip can spread like poison ivy. He was from Chicago. Things were different in big cities. I bit my lower lip and wished I hadn't given up overeating as my emotional crutch, because I could really go for some potato chips.

I took a deep breath, turned out the lights, and lay back on my pillow. There was only one solution. Aunt Agatha was right. I was going to have to find Whitney Kelley's killer.

Chapter 10

I woke up with a hairy paw in my mouth. I panicked when I opened my eyes, because I couldn't see. Then I realized my temporary blindness was caused by Bailey's ear, which was covering my eyes. I brushed the ear out of the way and glanced at the one hundred pounds of dog that was hogging two-thirds of the bed and 100 percent of the pillows. I rolled him over onto his side and slid out of bed.

Bailey lifted his head and glanced at me for a few seconds and then lay back down and went back to sleep.

I stuck my tongue out at him, went to the bathroom, and hopped in the shower.

It took longer than normal for me to get dressed. There was a small voice in the back of my head that was sure I was struggling to find an outfit to impress Chief Morgan.

However, I refused to listen to it. I chalked my wardrobe struggle up to the move. Not all my clothes were unpacked and easily accessible for comparison, and for some reason everything I tried on made me look fat. I sighed. "Black is supposed to be slimming, right?" I pulled out my go-to outfit and considered it a win that the wrinkles were minimal. No iron needed. I looked at myself from all sides in the full-length mirror Marcie had hung before leaving yesterday.

I glanced at Bailey. He was lying on the bed staring at me like the Great Sphinx.

"What?"

He yawned big.

"Black is serious. I think this outfit says, 'I'm telling the truth when I say I didn't murder Whitney Kelley.'"

Bailey dropped his head on his paws and closed his eyes.

I glanced down at the black leggings, black shirt, and black shoes. "Darn. It is boring, isn't it?" I pulled the shirt over my head. "I hate it when you're right."

My cell phone rang while I was removing my pants, and I hopped to the bed, reaching for the phone that was charging on my nightstand. Unfortunately, I misjudged the distance and tripped over the pant leg that I'd managed to wrap around my foot. My upper body hit the bed, but I slid to the floor as I answered the call with a huff.

"Hello."

"Why do you sound muffled and out of breath? Please tell me I interrupted a romantic interlude? And, if I did, why are you answering the phone?" Marcie said hopefully.

"Sorry to disappoint you, but I'm just getting dressed." I kicked my legs until I got out of the pants and stood up. "Bailey didn't like my outfit, so I'm changing."

"What are you wearing?"

"I had on a—"

"Please tell me you weren't wearing all black?"

I paused and glared at the phone. "No, of course not. Why would I wear all black? Besides, what's wrong with my black pants? Black is supposed to be slimming."

"There's nothing wrong with black, if you're going to a funeral, but if you're going to talk to a hot policeman, you should wear your blue-and-white dress and show off your legs."

"I'm going to give a witness statement, not go out on a date."

"And you won't get a date in black. Trust me. The blue-and-white dress is beautiful. Oh, and don't forget the red pumps."

I walked to my closet. "I don't know. That's my 'I'm an author, buy my book' dress. I need something that says, 'I'm not a murderer, please don't arrest me.' I think I need to stick to something serious." I picked up the black pants from the floor.

Marcie paused. "Okay, maybe wear your black leggings. He can still see how shapely your legs are in those. Oh, and wear that black-and-white-striped top, but you're going to need a pop of color." She paused. "Oh, what about if you add a scarf? You should add the yellow scarf your aunt gave you for Christmas and those yellow flats."

I looked in the closet and pulled out the black-and-white-striped shirt. It was made out of some type of fabric that didn't need ironing, so that was a plus, but I wasn't sure about the scarf. "I don't know . . . Are you sure?"

"Absolutely. And put your hair up in a high ponytail. That way, he can see your slim neck."

"Good grief. Let's stay focused on the important thing. Not getting arrested."

"So, we're back to the blue-and-white dress with pumps?" Marcie chuckled.

I cupped the phone in my neck and stepped back into the black leggings. "Fine. I'll wear the black and white, but I sure hope these stripes are kept as a fashion statement and not a permanent lifestyle change."

I promised to meet Marcie at the diner after I finished giving my statement, so long as I was free to wander the streets of Crosbyville, and we hung up.

As much as I hated to admit it, she was right. The black leggings with the striped top and yellow pumps gave me a "Parisian artist/Mary Tyler Moore from *The Dick Van Dyke Show*" vibe. I didn't look like I was trying too hard to impress, but I also didn't look like a murderer. At least, I didn't think I did. I turned to Bailey. "What do you think?"

He sat up and barked.

"I'm glad you agree." I grabbed my phone and gave one last turn in the mirror. "Let's go."

Bailey jumped down and we went downstairs.

I opened the door and Bailey went outside to take care of business. He put his nose to the ground and followed a trail that led from one bush to the other.

I stuck a K-Cup in the Keurig and made a cup of coffee. When it was done, I decided to join Bailey outside. I sat on the bench where Chief Morgan and I had sat yesterday. I sipped my coffee and glanced around at the overgrown yard. Everything still looked like weeds to me, but knowing that there were roses, azaleas, and lilacs under there brought a smile to my face. I wondered how much it would cost to pay someone to bring the garden back to what it had once been. Regardless, it was probably more than I could afford.

Bailey stood on his hind legs with his paws on the trunk of a tree and barked at a squirrel. Instead of cowering in fear, the impudent squirrel tossed a nut down that bounced off Bailey's head. He stumbled backward with a yelp of shock, shook his head, and then continued to howl at the squirrel from a distance.

"Bailey, you're hilarious. No wonder the kids love you." I laughed and then paused. "Wait. You are hilarious. And children really love you—or at least your stories. You made one of the national bestseller lists! We are successful. I'm not an impoverished teacher anymore. I'm an author of a bestselling children's book." I glanced around at the yard. "It's a small yard. I can afford to have someone clean this up—right, Bailey? I may not be able to afford an expensive landscaping company, but I could pay someone in town to do the heavy work, and I can get some books from the library and teach myself to do some of the work myself."

Bailey barked his approval.

"I can make some flyers and put them up on the community board at the library to get someone to do the yard cleanup." I glanced around at the yard and then got up. "Okay, well, first things first. Let's go give our statement to the police and then we'll head over to the library. Who knows, maybe while we're there we can find some information that'll help figure out who killed Whitney Kelley."

Chapter 11

*A*ccording to a plaque in front of the building, the Crosbyville Police Station was established in 1868. The first chief of police was hired in 1914. Today, the department had sixty-four sworn, full-time officers, two special police officers, eight sworn reserve officers, ten civilians, and two part-time ordinance-compliance officers. It was a lot bigger than I imagined. I turned to Bailey as we stood by the entrance. "Who knew?"

"Who knew what?"

I jumped at the unexpected response—Bailey's usually the quiet listening type—and turned in time to see Chief Morgan standing a few feet behind me.

"Holy moly. You scared me." I patted my chest and took a deep breath to slow down my racing heartbeat. "I didn't see you behind me."

His lips twitched. "Who did you think was talking?" He glanced at Bailey and raised a brow.

I followed his gaze. "Of course not. I just wasn't expecting . . . I mean it startled me to hear . . . Never mind."

His face was kind as he waited for me to stop rambling.

"Pastry?" I shoved the box of muffins, pastries, and assorted goodies at his chest, grateful that I'd stopped at the diner before coming.

He focused on the box in his hands, and I faltered.

"I was raised never to arrive empty-handed, so . . . Oh, I didn't think there might be a rule against pastries? I mean, it's not a bribe or anything. I didn't think . . ." I reached for the pastries, but he pulled the box out of my reach.

"No rules about giving pastries, but once you give a policeman a box of goodies, we do have rules about taking them back. I might have to call in a 129 and have you arrested."

I was fairly certain he was joking, but I was a suspect in a murder investigation, and he had a great poker face. "What's a 129?"

"It's a request for backup. There's no way you're getting these pastries from me." He cracked a rare smile.

His face lit up when he smiled, and I found myself staring like a lunatic. Was he flirting with me? I was so far out of practice with flirting, I had no idea. Maybe he was just a naturally nice, funny guy. Thankfully, Bailey chose that moment to make himself known and stood on his hind legs, reached up, and licked the side of Chief Morgan's face.

I pulled on his leash. "Bailey, no. Down."

His tail wagged and he ignored me. In fact, they both ignored me. Chief Morgan wrapped his free arm around Bailey. He patted his back and leaned down and baby-talked to him. "You're a good boy, Bailey."

I cleared my throat. "Ah, excuse me."

He gave Bailey a final pat. "Okay, off."

Whether due to the authority in his voice or the hopes of getting a treat from the pastry box the chief was holding, Bailey obeyed. He returned all four legs to the ground and wagged his tail expectantly.

"Now, let's get that statement." He turned and walked toward the door and Bailey followed, dragging me on the end of his leash.

Chief Morgan held the door open, and Bailey and I entered the Crosbyville Police Station for the first time. I glanced around, wondering if there was anything here that I could use for my books. I stopped and turned around to ask.

I stopped so abruptly that Chief Morgan bumped into me. When I turned around, we were mere inches away from each other.

"You might want to signal next time."

"I'm sorry. I was just wondering if it would be okay if I took some pictures."

He narrowed his gaze. "What kind of pictures?"

"Of the police station. You know, for inspiration for my books. I write children's books. Well, you know, The Adventures of Bailey the Bloodhound, Pet Detective." I pulled out my cell phone and held it up.

He pointed to a sign on the door of the building—cameras and any type of recording device were strictly prohibited.

"Humph."

He must have read more attitude into that huff. "What's that supposed to mean?"

"What?"

He glared. "I recognize that huff."

"It just seems sketchy, that's all. I mean, if you don't have anything to hide, then why prevent people from taking photos or recording things?" I shrugged.

He started to speak, but a man walked into the station. He was covered in tattoos and had long hair that he had pulled back into a ponytail. He looked like a member of a biker gang, someone who would be dangerous in a dark alley.

Bailey stood and stared at the man, but after a few moments, he wagged his tail and sat.

The biker smiled at Bailey, winked at me, and nodded to Chief Morgan. Then he must have felt the tension because he rubbed his upper arms as though he were cold. "Brr . . . it's a bit chilly in here." He chuckled and then, noticing the pastries, extended a hand for the box. "Why don't you let me take those off your hands for you."

Chief Morgan hesitated, but eventually handed over the pastry box and watched while the biker entered the department offices.

He glared at me for a few seconds as though it were my fault the biker took his pastries. He folded his arms across his chest. "Did it ever occur to you that maybe the reason we don't allow recording devices isn't to hide something, but maybe we're doing it for protection?"

"What do you mean?" I tilted my head to the side.

"For example, that man who just took my pastries used to be an undercover detective in Chicago. If pictures of him had gotten out, the organizations that he'd spent years infiltrating would have slit his throat in an instant."

I looked at the door the biker had just passed through. "I had no idea. He looks like a dangerous criminal."

"That's the point." He stepped forward and opened the door to his department, the same door that biker-slash-detective had disappeared through. Then he clasped my arm and guided me inside.

We walked past a series of desks and cubicles. Eventually, we went to a small office at the back of the station. There was a name plate on the side of the door that read, GILBERT MORGAN, CHIEF OF POLICE.

Gilbert. His first name is Gilbert.

He guided me inside the office. The office was functional but sparse with a desk, two padded chairs, and a file cabinet. On the desk, the biker had left the pastry box. The chief glanced at the box as he walked around the desk to sit in his chair. He extended a hand for me to sit in one of the guest chairs.

Once I was seated, he picked up the box and held it upside down. It was empty except for a few crumbs that fell out onto his desk.

He shook his head and shoved the box into his wastebasket. He mumbled something that sounded like *locust*, but I wasn't sure.

Bailey stood up on his hind legs and started to lick the crumbs from the desk.

"Bailey, down," I said.

He ignored my protest.

"It's okay, boy. You're just cleaning up, right?" Chief Morgan said.

Bailey snorted and finished his cleaning job. When he was done licking the desk, he turned to Chief Morgan, wagged his tail, and barked. Morgan gave his ear a scratch.

If I hadn't already had a major-league crush on him, seeing him interact with my dog would have done it.

A knock on the door startled me back to attention.

"Come in," Chief Morgan said.

The door opened and the biker who'd taken the pastries entered. He had a cinnamon roll on a napkin.

Chief Morgan leaned back in his chair.

The biker grinned and placed his offering on the desk. "We know how much you like cinnamon rolls, so we saved you one."

"One? Gee, thanks," Chief Morgan said sarcastically.

The biker saluted, then turned around and winked at me. Then he marched out of the office.

Bailey drooled and his tail wagged faster. He leaned forward, but Chief Morgan was faster. He slid the cinnamon roll out of reach.

"Sorry, boy. That's mine."

Bailey placed his head on the chief's lap and gazed up at him with adoration.

Chief Morgan gazed into those sad eyes and folded like a stack of cards. "Well, maybe a small piece." He looked up at me and his eyes asked for permission.

After a brief pause, I caved. "You're as bad as Aunt Agatha. Here . . ." I reached in my pocket and pulled out one of the dog biscuits I'd brought. I tossed it across the desk.

He reached up and caught the treat like a baseball player. He gave it to Bailey, who took his treat, moved over to a corner, and lay down. He clasped the treat between his paws and began gnawing away.

The chief then turned his attention to his cinnamon roll. He took a big bite and moaned. In two more bites, he had eaten the entire cinnamon roll and was licking his fingers. "Hmm, that was delicious."

I smiled. "My aunt will be glad to know you enjoyed it."

"Coffee?" he mumbled around a mouthful of cinnamon roll. I shook my head and declined his offer. "Be right back."

He picked up his coffee mug, stood, and stepped around Bailey, who barely moved, and left. He was back within minutes with a steaming cup of coffee. He took a large sip. Returned to his seat.

He opened a desk drawer and pulled out a tape recorder and put it on the desk. He pressed two buttons, glanced at his watch, and then recited the date and time. "Chief of Police Gilbert Morgan taking the recorded statement of Priscilla Renee Cummings."

I wondered how he learned my middle name, but then

my mind wondered what other information he had. I'm sure he could just look up my driver's license, which made me grateful I hadn't updated my official weight in a while.

"Miss Cummings?"

"Oh, sorry. Yes."

"Tell me what happened that morning from the time you arrived."

I took a deep breath.

Bailey must have sensed that I was nervous, because he abandoned his biscuit and came over and put his head in my lap.

I gazed into his eyes and then recited everything that I remembered from yesterday.

Chief Morgan asked a few standard questions—Was there anyone else around the park that morning? Had I seen anything suspicious after our argument the night before?—which I answered, and then he turned off the recorder. "I think that's it for now. I'll have someone type this up and then we'll call you to read it over and sign."

"Is that it?"

"That's it. Unless, you have something else you want to tell me."

"Like what?"

"Like who you think killed Whitney Kelley."

I thought for a few moments and then shrugged. "I have no idea. But I thought the police always looked at the spouse as the prime suspect."

His lips twitched. "Let me guess, *CSI* or *Law & Order?*"

"*Murder, She Wrote.*"

He rolled his eyes. "Contrary to what you may have seen on television, we don't automatically assume the spouse is guilty, though they're often a suspect. We investigate everyone."

I glanced around his office. "Yeah, but do you make any of those crime boards?"

He stood. "No, we don't create crime boards with pushpins and index cards. At least, not here."

"Oh."

"Now, if you think of anything else, please feel free to give me a call." He handed me a card with his name and the telephone number for the police station.

He waited for me to stand, but I didn't budge. If I was going to help him figure out who murdered Whitney Kelley, I was going to need some more information.

"Was there something else?" he asked.

"I was just wondering if you noticed Whitney Kelley's shoes."

"Her shoes?" He sat down. "What about them?"

"They were Louboutins," I said.

He raised a brow and waited.

"Surely, you've heard of them?"

He shook his head. "Should I have?"

"Well, most people have. Christian Louboutin is a famous fashion designer."

"Okaaay. So, what's special about that? I imagine lots of women have designer shoes."

I shook my head. "Not Louboutins. Certainly not in Crosbyville they don't. Those shoes cost a small fortune.

The cheapest pair of Louboutins cost around seven hundred dollars, but I'd estimate that those heels she was wearing probably cost three times that much."

His eyes widened. "You're joking."

I shook my head.

"For a pair of shoes?"

"Yeah, and her purse was a Louis Vuitton. That was probably fifteen hundred. Then there's her jewelry, and while I'm not an expert, I'm sure those stones were real."

He opened a drawer and pulled out a folder. Inside the folder, there were pictures. He shuffled through the pictures until he found what he was looking for. Then he placed the picture on the desk.

The picture was from the crime scene. It was a photo of Whitney Kelley's body lying in the park. My stomach roiled. I closed my eyes and swallowed hard to keep my breakfast from coming up.

Chief Morgan came around the desk and eased my swimming head down between my legs. "Take deep, slow breaths."

I followed his instructions until I felt sure I wouldn't hurl all over his desk.

"You okay?"

I nodded, sitting back up.

"I'm sorry. I shouldn't have—"

I waved away his apology and forced myself to stare at the picture. I barely noticed the shake in my hands and the quiver in my voice. "See the red bottoms on the shoes? That's how you know they are Louboutins. And the distinctive *L* and *V* on the purse are the logo for Louis Vuitton. When Whitney was at the diner, she was wearing large diamond earrings, a diamond-and-ruby necklace, and a huge diamond ring along with her smaller wedding ring, but she's not wearing them in this picture. Just her wedding ring."

He glanced at the picture. "Okay, so what? Whitney Kelley had expensive taste and wore expensive clothes, shoes, and jewelry. Are you implying that Whitney Kelley's murder was a robbery gone wrong?"

I thought for a few moments and then shook my head. "Maybe. But why not take all the jewelry? Why take the necklace, earrings, and diamond ring, but leave her wedding ring? I mean, it wasn't as big as the other diamonds she'd been wearing, but it's a decent size and probably still cost Joe a tidy little sum of money."

He glanced at the picture. "Maybe the killer couldn't get it off. Or maybe he didn't have time." He shrugged. "Can you describe exactly what the rest of the jewelry looked like?"

"It was big and gaudy." *Like Whitney,* I thought but didn't say out loud. Instead, I took a notepad and a pen from a container on his desk and drew two strands of diamonds braided together with a row of large ruby ovals through the middle. I studied the drawing and frowned. I was no Picasso, but I think he got the idea. "The earrings were similar but there were only three stones that dangled from each one."

He glanced at my finished drawing. "I'll ask her husband for an inventory of her jewelry. If it's not at her house, then we'll check the pawn shops."

"You might ask Chelsea, too. Joe might not remember

exactly what jewelry Whitney had, but Chelsea would know."

"Thank you. I will." He stood up, indicating that our conversation was over.

"If there's anything else I can do . . ." I stood up.

"I'll call you." He walked around the desk to the door, squatted, and gave Bailey an ear scratch. Then he stood and opened the door.

I hesitated for a second and then grabbed Bailey's leash and hurried out of his office. I wasn't paying careful attention and took a wrong turn. I wandered around the sea of tall cubicles and down a hallway that I didn't recognize. I stopped and glanced around in an attempt to get my bearings. I looked for the exit signs and realized that just like on airplanes, *your closest exit may be behind you.* I turned quickly and collided with the biker. "I'm so sorry!"

"You look lost?" He smiled.

"I followed Chief Morgan when I entered, and I must not have been paying attention to the route," I stammered.

"Now, who is this handsome guy?" He extended a hand toward Bailey.

Bailey sniffed his hand. He must have been okay, because Bailey wagged his tail and then got up on his hind legs and gave the undercover cop a face wash.

"Hey, I already bathed once this morning." He laughed.

"Bailey, off." I tugged on his leash until he got down. "I'm so sorry. Again."

It took all his energy, but Bailey sat like a jack-in-the-box ready to spring up at any minute.

"He's usually so well behaved, but for some reason—"

He waved away my apologies. "He knows dog lovers when he sees them." He scratched Bailey's ear in the place that made his leg twitch and his drool pour like a fountain. "I think I found your spot. Is that the spot? Is that it?" He worked Bailey into a lather until he couldn't take it anymore and he let out a howl.

"Bailey!" I glanced around.

The biker laughed. "Oh, don't blame him. It was all my fault. Wasn't it, boy?"

Bailey barked his agreement.

The biker stood up and smiled. "Now I know his name is Bailey, but what's your name?"

I extended a hand. "Priscilla Cummings."

"What a beautiful name for a beautiful lady." He grinned. "I'm Pitbull."

"Hello, Mr. Pitbull."

He laughed. "No Mr. Just Pitbull."

"I'm sorry. I—" Apologizing was getting to be a habit. "Nice to meet you, Pitbull."

Pitbull was a big man, more than six feet tall. He looked tough as nails on first glance and very scary. But up close, I was able to get a good look at him. I saw that his dark eyes had a softness around the corners. He had an easy smile, and most important, Bailey liked him.

"Now, what brings a beautiful lady like you down to a place like this?"

I had known this man for less than five minutes and he'd called me beautiful twice. He didn't look like someone who threw out compliments at the drop of a hat. I felt the heat come up my neck, and I had to lick my lips because my mouth was suddenly dry. I didn't have to question if he was flirting with me or not. He was definitely flirting with me. "I found a dead body. Well, technically, Bailey found the body. I had to give my statement to Chief Morgan."

"I heard about that." He tilted his head to the side. "You off her?"

I should have been offended by the question, but I wasn't. "No."

"Good. Give me your phone." He extended his hand.

Without thinking, I reached in my purse, entered my passcode, and handed him my cell phone. He swiped the screen and then pushed several buttons and then handed it back. "Follow me." He turned and led us back down the hall we'd just taken.

Bailey followed him like the Pied Piper, and I followed Bailey. More like I was dragged after them, but it had the same result.

Pitbull took us down a corridor and turned, and suddenly I was at the front of the police station.

"Thank you."

He nodded. "If you or Bailey need help, you call me." He gave Bailey one last scratch and then stood up and winked at me. "I put my number in your phone. And I got yours." He turned and walked away.

Chapter 12

I walked to the car and opened the door for Bailey to climb in the back. Once he was settled, I got in and put on my seat belt. When I glanced in the rearview mirror, I noticed a stupid smile on my face.

It had been quite a while since I'd flirted with anyone. Crosbyville was never ideal for singles to meet up, and I'd convinced myself back in River Bend that I was getting too old to hang out in bars or clubs. Well, maybe I wasn't technically too old, but when you have to get up early to be ready for school the next day, you feel old. Besides, in small, midwestern towns, elementary school teachers were expected to behave like nuns. Heaven forbid that Little Johnny's mother or the school board should find out that a teacher was drinking. But I wasn't a teacher anymore. That thought made my smile even larger than it was before. I looked in the mirror. "Pull yourself together. It's not like he asked you out on a date."

True, but he had given me his telephone number.

Pitbull wasn't attractive in the same way as Gilbert Morgan, chief of police. Pitbull was a tough guy. There was something dangerous about him, and that danger held its own attractions.

Someone leaned on their horn across the way, and the sound pulled me out of my dazzled state. I pulled away from the curb and drove the short distance to the public library.

Ever since I'd gotten Bailey registered with Therapy Dogs International, we'd visited hospitals, nursing homes, libraries, or schools at least once per week. When I was a teacher, visiting a school was easy. I just brought Bailey with me to work. The kids loved it, and even those who didn't have challenges reading loved pet-assisted reading time. Even though I was no longer a teacher, I still planned to continue our work in the school system. Today was Thursday and one of the professional development days for teachers to learn new skills, so the kids were out of school, and we were scheduled to read at the public library.

Bailey hopped out of the car and waited patiently while I put on his special harness and bandanna that indicated he was a working therapy dog.

"Okay, boy. You know the routine. I need you on your best behavior." I gazed into his eyes. He woofed and I kissed his nose. "I know, you're always a good boy, aren't you?"

We walked inside and checked in with the librarian at

the main desk before making our way to the children's reading room on the lower level.

The main branch of the Crosbyville Public Library wasn't huge, but a robbery and an electrical fire a few years ago at the Lawson Jewelers building located next door resulted in most of the original building being demolished. The jewelry store was brick and the fire damage there was minimal, but a spark had made its way over, and the old Victorian house that had housed the library for the past fifty years went up like a box of matches.

Amelia Cooper Lawson was devastated when she learned of the damage to the original library. Always generous, she had donated many of the new books, along with a substantial financial contribution that funded the reconstruction. The new library was light and airy with cozy chairs, plenty of windows, a media room, and a café. The town was so grateful, the city council was entertaining a proposal to rename the library the Amelia Cooper Lawson Public Library.

Stepping off the elevator, I heard the children before I saw them. Today was going to be a full house. I glanced down at Bailey and smiled when I saw his tail up wagging with excitement and the drool pouring from his jowls. He was excited. I stopped and pulled a wet wipe from my bag to remove the loosest of the drool, although I knew it would be replaced in a matter of minutes. I clasped his head and gazed into his eyes. "Okay, boy. It's time to go to work. Now, you know the drill. If you're a good boy, there will be some special liver treats with your name on them when we get home."

His tail swished faster at the mention of liver. Scientists may debate how much a dog can actually understand, but I had no doubt that Bailey knew the L-word when he heard it.

Stepping off the elevator, we walked down a hallway to a set of double doors that led into a large, open playroom. I took a deep breath and secured my grip on Bailey's leash and then opened the door.

The room erupted into cheerful screams as children danced up and down and clapped. The noise was almost deafening, but Bailey was trotting with extra pep in his step toward the throng of screaming kids with what I can only describe as a smile on his face. He always was a bit of a ham.

We had a routine we followed when visiting excitable children at schools or libraries, which differed from our routine when visiting children who were sick or the local nursing home. Bloodhounds were not known for their energy, but we generally trotted around the perimeter of the crowd before we settled down for reading or petting. Bailey got a good chance to take in the millions of new scents, plus it helped tire him out a bit. My training instructor had drilled into me the motto *A tired bloodhound is a good bloodhound.*

Bailey and I took our places at the front of the crowd, and I signaled for the children to settle down. After a brief introduction, I took a couple of minutes to share a bit about bloodhounds and their amazing ability for tracking scents. "Bloodhounds' noses are millions of times better than humans' and they can even follow a scent that is more than one hundred and thirty miles away. That's farther than Crosbyville to Chicago."

I waited for the "oohs" and "aahs" to settle down before continuing. I'd worked out a plan with the head librarian to showcase Bailey's skills.

"Because of the bloodhounds' amazing ability to track a scent, they are great at finding lost objects and missing people. In fact, I believe one of the children is missing." I glanced around as though looking for someone.

On cue, Mrs. Charlotte Littlefield, the head children's librarian, stepped forward. She was a short woman with a round face, brown eyes, and brown hair streaked with gray, which she wore pulled back in a bun. "Oh my, I'm so glad you're here. One of the children is missing, but luckily, I have this sweater. Do you think Bailey could help me find her?"

Charlotte handed me the sweater, and I put it under Bailey's nose and let him take a good whiff.

Once I was certain he had the scent, I stood up and gave him a command. "Bailey, find."

He put his nose to the ground and got to work.

Charlotte Littlefield usually identified one of the children who arrived early to be our "missing child." With parental consent, she then had the child leave a scent trail that zigged and zagged all over the room. Once a trail was laid, she secured an item of clothing and had the child hide. Having just arrived, neither Bailey nor I knew who the child was or where they were hiding. It was completely up to Bailey to find them.

Today's volunteer had left a good trail, which included

loops and circles around the entire room, behind shelves, and computers. Eventually, the trail led to a storage room behind the checkout desk. At the door, Bailey scratched with his paw and then sat, his signal to me that he had found his target.

I opened the door and out came Hannah Morgan, Chief Morgan's daughter.

Hannah flung her arms around Bailey's neck and gave him a great big hug. "I knew you'd find me, Detective Bailey. You're the best tracker ever."

Bailey gave her a sloppy lick.

I returned Hannah's sweater, and we went back to the crowd of children, who were all clamoring to be the next target for Bailey to find. However, this wasn't our first rodeo, and I was prepared with a distraction.

"Who would like to see Bailey do some tricks?" I asked.

"Yay!"

"Tricks!"

"Me! Me!"

Many of the tricks that Bailey knew were just extensions of the basic obedience training that all dogs need in order to be good family dogs. Once a dog is first consistent with "sit," "stay," and "down," then adding on to those commands is easy. Well, easier. Bloodhounds are large with a stubborn streak. Unlike breeds like poodles and border collies, bloodhounds are not easily trainable. However, string cheese, hot dogs, and dried liver had the power to coerce even the most stubborn breed to comply. Bloodhounds were no different.

Bailey's repertoire of tricks wasn't spectacular. He shook hands. High-fived. And rolled over like a circus dog when he could smell dried liver or cheese.

The children applauded and we finished with Bailey taking a bow. He really was a ham who loved the attention.

When the demonstration was over, I allowed time for the children to pet Bailey, and then we said our good-byes.

There were a few tears as children didn't want Bailey to leave, but we promised to come back again if the children all promised to be good.

Promises were made, and Bailey and I made our exit to the staff break room, away from the noise and Bailey's adoring fans.

I filled a container with water and put it down for Bailey to get a drink.

Mrs. Littlefield came in and gave Bailey a pat. "You and Bailey are always such a big hit with the children."

"I wish I could take the credit, but it's all Bailey." I glanced down at my buddy, who had finished his water and was lying down at my feet.

"I think he's remarkable, and I'm so glad that shrew Whitney Kelley didn't get her way and that you'll be able to continue your pet-assisted reading program in the schools."

I'd never heard the mousy librarian say an unkind word about anyone, so I was taken aback by the passion behind her words. "You heard that she was going to end the pet-assisted therapy program?"

She nodded. "Oh yes. The school board often meets

here at the library. That's where I heard her bullying the other board members into agreeing to cut the program. And I tell you, it was shocking."

"Well, I suppose it's hardly surprising. I know that as a teacher, I'm biased because I see the benefits of special programs firsthand. But, as valuable as I feel programs like pet-assisted therapy are, I have to say, Whitney Kelley isn't the first person to attempt to eliminate art, music, and special reading programs to tighten up a school's budget."

She was shaking her head before the words were out of my mouth.

"But that's not the shocking part."

"What do you mean?"

Charlotte Littlefield glanced around the empty room and then leaned closer. "Well . . . Amelia Cooper Lawson offered to personally fund those programs."

I frowned. "Wow. I know Amelia Cooper Lawson's family was wealthy, but I had no idea she was that rich. That would have cost millions."

She nodded. "Exactly. The other board members were all in favor, but Whitney Kelley refused to give up. She said that if Amelia Cooper Lawson had so much money to toss away, then those funds should go to improve the math and science departments."

Before I could figure out what to say, Charlotte Littlefield dropped another bombshell.

"And she didn't stop there."

"What else did she say?"

"She said that unless the other board members supported her plans, she'd open up all of their closets and pull out every skeleton they had."

I didn't think anything Whitney Kelley did could surprise me, but this did. It took a few moments for me to realize that my mouth was open. In fact, I blinked and shook my head. Clearly, I couldn't have heard that properly. "You're not serious."

Charlotte nodded vigorously. "Oh, but I am."

"Whitney Kelley actually threatened the other board members?"

She nodded.

"But someone must have stood up to her. Surely they told her to go jump in the river."

Again, before the words were out of my mouth, Charlotte Littlefield was shaking her head. "Not one of them stood up to her. In fact, they all rolled over and played dead, just like one of Bailey's tricks. I don't think one of those board members is sorry that Whitney Kelley was murdered. I'm just wondering which one of them did it."

Chapter 13

Charlotte Littlefield may have looked mousy, but there was obviously passion behind those mousy brown eyes. However, when it came to action, her passion seeped out like air from a balloon. Try as I might to convince her to share the conversation she'd overheard with the police, she refused.

"I don't want to get involved. However, if you were to suggest that the police question the other school board members, then . . . surely, that will be just as good as if I told them?" she said. "Besides, I would prefer not to be implicated in anything like a murder."

No matter how hard I tried, *and I tried*, Charlotte Littlefield would not budge. I tried from every angle I could think and left the library feeling like Sam-I-am, the character in the Dr. Seuss book *Green Eggs and Ham*. When it came to the police, she would not go see them at the jail. She would not call them on her cell. She would not talk to the police from her house. She would not talk to the police with her spouse. I was exhausted from trying and had a new respect for the persistent Sam in the book.

By the time I arrived at the diner, I was moody. Last night, everything seemed so straightforward. I was going to use my knowledge of Crosbyville and Whitney Kelley to figure out who murdered her. I was confident that I was going to save Chief Morgan's job. But today, reality set in. If I couldn't convince a sweet, civic-minded librarian to make an anonymous call to the police, how was I going to track down a killer?

I must have worn my frustration on my face because Aunt Agatha took one look at me, turned, and came back with a slice of apple pie, which she placed in front of me.

"Guaranteed to fix whatever ails you."

I opened my mouth to protest, but the look on her face and the hand on her hip told me that I needed to follow orders.

I took a bite and could feel the spicy mixture seeping into my bloodstream. It felt like a warm hug. My shoulders dropped a quarter of an inch. My muscles relaxed, and the corners of my lips slid upward.

Aunt Agatha nodded her approval and filled my mug with coffee. "Now, I don't know what had you in such a knot, but you eat that pie and calm down."

I followed instructions and by the time Marcie arrived, I was in a much better frame of mind.

After greeting Bailey, who was sprawled under the table, she slid into the booth. "You're eating apple pie? I didn't see apple pie in the display when I came in."

Aunt Agatha smiled. "That's my emergency pie. I keep it on hand for folks that need an attitude adjustment."

Marcie glanced in my direction and raised an eyebrow. "Should I even ask?"

I licked my fork. "Probably not."

Even though Marcie didn't need an attitude adjustment, Aunt Agatha still brought her a slice of apple pie, which she ate with her eyes closed while moaning in between bites.

When she scraped up the last bit of apple-cinnamon delight, she leaned back in the booth, closed her eyes, and put her head against the seat.

"If you're done, I'll fill you in," I said.

She opened her eyes and gave me a look that I would have taken for drunkenness if I didn't know she'd consumed only pie and not alcohol.

I told her about my decision to help Chief Morgan. I outlined my activities from the morning, skirting around my conversation with Pitbull and rushing ahead to my encounter with Charlotte Littlefield. Something in the way Marcie looked screamed, *I know you're hiding something*, but she merely sat and watched me. When I finished, she waited.

"What?" I asked when her silence grew too much.

"Nothing. I'm just waiting for you to spill the part you thought you could omit from the police station. Did he ask you out on a date?"

"Who?" I picked at my napkin and avoided eye contact.

"Who? Chief of Police Gilbert Morgan."

"How'd you know his first name was Gilbert?" I asked only partly to stall for time.

"It was in the newspaper when he came to town. Now, spill it."

I took a deep breath and was about to mention the undercover policeman I'd met in the most boring, nonchalant manner I could when my phone vibrated. One glance down and I could feel the heat rush up my neck. I forced the corners of my lip down and typed a quick response. When I glanced across at Marcie, I knew all attempts at subterfuge would be useless.

"Well?"

I told her about meeting Pitbull and how he had just asked me out on a date.

"Pitbull? Sounds like a tough guy and nothing like the type you typically pick." She leaned closer.

"I know. If you saw a guy like him in a parking lot at night, you'd clutch your purse tighter, start walking faster, and make sure your pepper spray was ready."

"And yet . . ."

"And yet, he also seems like a big cuddly teddy bear. Plus, Bailey liked him."

"Well, if Bailey liked him, that seals it." She chuckled.

We chatted a bit longer about Pitbull before getting down to serious business.

"Are you going to work on Charlotte Littlefield again?" Marcie asked.

"No way. I know when I've met my match, but I was

thinking . . . if you can't bring Muhammad to the mountain, then maybe I can bring the mountain to Muhammad."

"Okay, you've lost me."

"If Charlotte Littlefield won't go to the police to tell them what Whitney Kelley said at the school board meeting, maybe I could get the police to go to the school board meeting. One of those board members is bound to crack under pressure and spill the beans. Don't you think?"

Marcie didn't seem as confident as I felt, but then she hadn't had as much time as I had to mull things over.

"Whenever Hercule Poirot brings all of the suspects together and confronts them with the evidence, the guilty party usually confesses."

"Hmm . . . I don't think that will work in the United States or the twenty-first century, but it's worth a shot." Marcie shrugged.

"You two want real food to go with your pie?" Aunt Agatha brought two hamburgers and placed one in front of each of us and took a seat.

"I'm not going to be able to fit in any of my clothes," Marcie said around a mouthful of hamburger.

We ate our hamburgers quickly while Aunt Agatha watched and sipped a Tab soda. For the life of me, I couldn't figure out how she managed to swallow that god-awful-tasting beverage, but she grew addicted to the sludge as a teen and had been drinking it for more than thirty years. When Coca-Cola announced they were discontinuing them in 2020, she stockpiled cartons in the diner's storage room. She said she was weaning herself off the synthetically sweet beverage and allowed herself only one per day. By the end of the year, she expected to be completely free and would probably need a detox program to get it out of her bloodstream.

The bells over the diner door tinkled, barely audible over the customers' noontime conversational buzz. However, Aunt Agatha was conditioned to hear that bell. She glanced at the door every time someone entered.

Sitting across from her with my back to the door, I didn't need to see the door to know that whoever just entered was a person of interest. I could tell from the one raised brow that something was afoot. That one brow screamed loud and clear. The mirror opposite the door meant I didn't have to draw attention to myself by turning to look, as Joe Kelley entered the diner with a platinum blonde with big hair.

"Hmm . . . that's just plain tacky." Aunt Agatha sipped her beverage.

The quiet that descended on the previously humming diner indicated that Aunt Agatha wasn't the only one who found the situation tacky.

"Who is that woman with Joe Kelley?" I asked.

Aunt Agatha sipped her drink and glanced down her nose at me in a look Marcie and I referred to as her *You poor, deluded fool* look. "Well, I'm not one to gossip."

That was always the opening for a great gossip session and we both leaned closer, careful not to miss a word.

Aunt Agatha wiggled in her seat and took her sweet time responding. "Well, that platinum blonde is Betty Wilson.

She runs The Big Tease, that beauty shop on the corner of Main and Hamilton."

"Oh no. Not the Pink Palace?" Marcie asked.

The Pink Palace was the name we'd adopted for the hair-and-nail salon that opened about a year ago. Based on what I'd seen through the front windows, the salon was a shrine to all things pink. The floor, walls, and chairs were various shades of pink from the light-blush curtains to the fuchsia uniforms worn by the stylist. There were even bubble gum–colored salon chairs with matching hooded dryers lining one wall. While most shops, especially shops catering to hair and nails, were modern establishments that could fit any urban city, The Big Tease capitalized on a retro vibe from the 1950s. The staff, and especially the stylists, embraced big hair. As bizarre as it sounds, there was a demand for big hair in town. Women with thin hair went to get their hair teased to appear thicker. Beehives, bouffants, French twists, and roller sets were surprisingly popular, especially for weddings. However, the proprietor, Betty Wilson, wore her 1950s poodle curls with pride year-round.

Aunt Agatha nodded. "Rumor has it that she's been doing more than *teasing* that snake oil salesman Joe Kelley's hair for the past six months."

Marcie gasped and I gawked.

"Better close your mouth or you'll catch flies," Aunt Agatha said with a smile.

"Seriously?" I casually turned around to remind myself what Betty Wilson looked like.

She was probably about five feet two and wore four-inch heels. Her platinum blonde mane added another six to eight inches to her height. She was thin and made up with false eyelashes that looked as though it took amazing eyelid strength to blink.

Aunt Agatha glanced over her shoulder and leaned forward. "Word on the street is that Joe Kelley was handling a lot more than insurance for Betty." She gave us a meaningful look.

"How?" I asked.

Aunt Agatha gave me a look that seemed to question my understanding of the birds and the bees. I felt myself flush. "No, I mean, how do they *know*? What made them . . . whoever *them* is . . . think that? Just because a man and a woman are having lunch together doesn't mean there's anything . . . romantic going on. Maybe they're just friends. Or maybe she's got questions about her policy and he's explaining it."

"Nobody has questions about insurance after midnight." She pursed her lips. "And, if she did, then why would he need to *explain* those questions at the Dew Drop Inn?"

That stumped me.

"Eww. The Dew Drop is such a sleazy dive." Marcie shuddered.

"True, but it's on the outskirts of town. There's not a lot of traffic. They take cash. Charge by the hour. And don't ask questions." Aunt Agatha ticked off each of her points on her fingers.

"How do you know all of that?" I tilted my head and worked hard to keep my lips under control.

"Pshaw. Everybody knows that. Besides, I haven't always been old." She chuckled and then took a sip of her Tab. Then she got serious. "Macy Thompson was driving home from our Thursday-night poker game and just after she passed the Dew Drop, she got a flat tire. It was February, so it was cold. She was low on gas and didn't want to risk running out of gas by sitting in the car and running the heater while she waited, so she walked to the Dew Drop to wait for her nephew to come and pick her up." She rolled her eyes. "That's why I always told you to make sure you don't let your gas tank get lower than a half tank in the winter, and make sure your tires are properly inflated. You never can tell what the weather will be and—"

"Aunt Agatha, focus. We're talking about Joe and Betty, not automotive maintenance," I reminded her.

"Yeah, well, when she went into the lobby, she caught a glimpse of Joe Kelley and Betty Wilson going down the hall to one of the rooms and they weren't talking about insurance." Aunt Agatha winked.

"Eww . . . just eww." Marcie shivered.

"Has anyone told the police?" I asked.

"Beats me. I'm not one to pass along gossip," she said with a straight face that amazed me. "Besides, adultery may be a sin, but it's not a crime."

"Actually, it used to be, but not anymore," I said.

"Do you think it makes Joe a suspect?" Marcie asked.

"In books, the police always consider the spouse a suspect. Either Joe or Betty could have wanted Whitney dead." I shrugged.

"Maybe they were in it together," Marcie said. "That makes more sense than for them to be looking at you as a suspect, especially if they don't have an alibi."

"I wonder how we can find out if they have an alibi?" I asked.

A lightbulb went off in Marcie's head and she sat up and smiled. "I have it."

"What?" I had a bad feeling about that lightbulb.

"You could go to The Big Tease and ask around. You know what hair salons are like. Whitney Kelley's death is bound to be the topic of the day. It'll be a piece of cake to find out where Betty was two nights ago." Marcie smiled like a cat who had just brought home a dead rodent as a gift and expected praise.

I was shaking my head before she finished talking. "I don't think that's such a good idea."

"Why not?" Marcie tried to hide the hurt in her voice, but I could see the disappointment in her eyes.

"I don't know how to ask questions without drawing attention to myself. Besides, why would anyone answer me? I'm not a detective," I whined.

"That's exactly why they will answer you. No one wants to talk to the police. No one wants to get involved," Marcie said.

"She's got a point there," Aunt Agatha said.

"Of course I do. Plus, you're not going to be asking questions. You're just . . . making conversation with your stylist," Marcie said.

"And that's another problem. *The Big Tease?* Are you

kidding? Why would I go to a place like that? Why me? Why not you? Or Aunt Agatha?" I glanced from one to the other of them.

Marcie gave another Cheshire cat smile. "Because you're the one with a hot date tonight."

Chapter 14

"Hot date? What hot date? Don't tell me that police chief finally asked you out?" Aunt Agatha smiled.

"No. He didn't. I'm going out with someone else." I glared at Marcie.

Before Aunt Agatha could pump me for more details, she was called away by Luellen, one of her waitresses, to help with a problem in the kitchen.

"Remind me to buy Luellen a gift." I sighed.

"Sorry, I guess I got carried away. I didn't mean to spill the beans about you and Pitbull." Marcie reached out and squeezed my hand.

"It's a small town. She's bound to find out sooner or later, but I would have preferred later." I sighed.

"It's still a good idea." Marcie tilted her head and looked me over. "Your hair is a bit . . . unruly."

I reached my hand to my hair. My hair had been wet when I'd pulled it back into a ponytail this morning. Now that it had dried, it was no longer lying flat. I dropped my head onto my arms. "It's hopeless. My hair has a mind of its own, and going to a salon called The Big Tease is not going to make it sleek and manageable. I'm going to look like one of those actresses from the '70s shows that Aunt Agatha used to watch."

"You do not look like Phyllis Diller."

"Okay, Don King, then," I mumbled, not bothering to lift my head.

"Look, maybe you should stop trying to make your hair be something it isn't."

I propped my chin on my palm. "Are you suggesting I shave my head?"

"Of course not. I'm saying you should go to a professional who can help you find your hair's natural curl pattern and see what happens . . . What do you have to lose?"

She was right. I'd been fighting with my natural hair for years, since I'd finally stopped applying straightening chemicals, which were damaging and caused my hair to break and fall out in clumps.

I glanced at myself in the mirror and admitted that I needed help.

"Then I'd better do this before my courage fails." I got up. Took Bailey's leash and marched out of the diner.

*T*he salon was only a few blocks from the diner, but I sat in the car for five extra minutes giving myself a pep talk.

"It's just hair, right? I mean, the only difference between a good haircut and a bad haircut is two weeks, right?" I glanced at Bailey in the rearview mirror.

He yawned.

"I could always buy a wig if all else fails." I got out of the car and opened the back to let Bailey out. There was a sign in the salon window that indicated the facility was dog-friendly and through the large picture window, I saw a woman sitting under one of the Pink Palace's hooded dryers with a chihuahua on her lap.

A bell tinkled as we entered, and the hum of conversation stopped as all heads turned to see who had invaded their lair.

I walked to the receptionist and said a silent prayer that despite the sign that stated WALK-INS WELCOME, they wouldn't be able to see me today.

The receptionist was thin with a big smile. The right side of her head was buzz-cut and dyed magenta while the left was dyed in a rainbow and gelled to stand up in spikes. Her eyeshadow matched her hair. "Welcome to The Big Tease. Would you like a treat?"

"Excuse me?"

She came around the counter and squatted down and planted a big kiss on Bailey's head. She reached in her pocket and pulled out a dog biscuit and held it up. "Treat?"

"Oh, sure."

She gave Bailey the treat and then petted his ears while he chomped down on his biscuit. "You're a beauty. Now, what do you think we should do for your owner?" She glanced up and flashed another smile at me.

Bailey liked her, even before she gave him the treat. So, I took a deep breath and decided to do the same. "I don't know. I don't really want anything drastic, but I have a date tonight and I—"

"Oh, you want to impress. Gotcha." She stood up.

"No. I mean, I just don't want to look like a mad scientist or like I just stuck my finger in a light socket."

She glanced at my hair. "Mind if I take it down?"

I shook my head.

She removed my ponytail holder and ran her fingers through my mane. Well, she tried to, anyway. She got about halfway before her fingers stuck in the tangled mess that my hair had become. "What time is your date?"

I started to answer before I saw the sparkle in her eyes that meant she was only teasing. She extended a hand. "Tabitha, but you can call me Tabby."

"Priscilla, but everyone calls me Pris, and that's Bailey."

She jiggled his jowls. "Bailey. You're just the most handsomest boy, aren't you?"

He barked his agreement and then gave her a sloppy kiss.

Tabby guided me to her station near the back of the salon. Once Bailey was lying down and I was seated, she put a pink cape around my neck and spun me around so I was facing the mirror. "Your hair is dry, so we'll do a deep-moisturizing masque to hydrate and detangle. Then, I want to trim your split ends. Contrary to those ads on television, the only thing that will help them is to cut them off. Then, once we have a good foundation, I'm going to apply a product that'll define your curls and make them pop. If we had time, I'd love to add some highlights to frame your face. Maybe another day." She looked at my reflection in the mirror. "The question is, Do you trust me?"

I gazed at the reflection of the buzz-cut, spiked, rainbow-colored stylist and realized that everything she'd done to herself suited her. It wasn't my style, but it looked amazing on her. The asymmetrical cut showcased her high cheekbones and hazel-colored eyes. She was talented and I made the decision to trust her. "Go for it."

Her smile broadened and she actually jumped up and kicked her heels. "I promise. You will look stunning when I finish, and *you* will love it. She rushed to the back of the salon and grabbed bottles, gloves, and an armful of containers. She mixed, poured, and chatted the entire time she worked.

Marcie was right. I learned a lot sitting in that salon. At first, Tabby talked about herself. As she shampooed my hair, I learned that Tabby was born and raised in Brooklyn. Both her mom and dad were accountants. Even as a small child, she hadn't fit into their upper-class, country-club mold. When she came out to them in high school, they sent her off to a private boarding school in Europe.

"I'm so sorry," I said.

"For what? I thought I'd died and gone to heaven."

I sat up from the shampoo bowl and looked at her in confusion.

"A lesbian at an all-girls school? Seriously? They should have thought that through."

I chuckled and put my head back into the bowl.

"As long as there was no PDA in front of the staff, it was all good. Things are *very* different in Europe than in the US."

"So, how'd you end up back in this country?"

"My partner got a job at a CPA firm here in Indiana. Can you believe that? I spent my life trying to get away from accountants. Just my luck, I fall in love with one. Go figure."

Tabby explained that she'd always had a flair for hair and makeup and went to cosmetology school. She'd been at a few other salons before landing at The Big Tease.

"I like it here. The other stylists are friendly, and Betty's a hoot."

"Really? I don't know much about her," I said.

We were back at her station, and she had pulled out a pair of scissors and was cutting what felt like more than my split ends, but I closed my eyes and sat still.

"If you just look at her on the outside, you'd think she was uptight and rigid, one of those ultraconservative types who act like their poop don't stink, but you get a few drinks in her and she loosens up."

I opened my eyes. "Really? How so?"

She glanced around and leaned closer to my ear. "Well, first off, she's sleeping with that insurance salesman."

"Oh my—really?"

"Now, between you and me, I think that's just not okay. I mean, if my dad cheated on my mom or heaven forbid,

Carla cheated on me, well I'd take these scissors and stab them right in the heart." She took the scissors and demonstrated just how she'd do it.

Whitney had been strangled, not stabbed, but it was a shocking demonstration. "Oh my."

Tabby continued, "I don't think it's right to cheat, but hey, they're all adults. And, besides, I guess they must have had one of those open marriages or something. After all, since Whitney was having an affair, I guess it's only fair that her husband did, too. What's good for the goose is good for the gander, right?"

Chapter 15

What?" I turned around and gaped at her. "Whitney Kelley was having an affair?"

She'd yanked the scissors away before they could catch my head. "Hey, watch it. You keep turning your head while I'm cutting your hair, don't blame me if you end up with a buzz cut."

I froze.

"You should see your face. Oh my goodness." Tabby laughed.

I looked at myself in the mirror.

"You're fine. I promise, but you do need to sit still while I'm working." She twirled the scissors on her fingers like a gunslinger in the Wild West.

I nodded and sat back in the chair.

She returned to cutting. "Now, where were we?"

"You were about to tell me how you knew Whitney Kelley was having an affair?"

"Betty told me."

"Oh, but how does she know? I mean, maybe she was just making it up to justify her own affair with Whitney's husband?"

"Maybe you're right." Tabby shrugged.

The door of the salon swung open, and Betty Wilson waltzed in, arrogant and cocky, like she owned the place. Which, technically, she did. Betty's triumphant entrance sparked a response like Norm walking into the bar on an episode of *Cheers*.

"Betty!" voices called to her.

"Good afternoon, my lovelies!" Betty waved and smiled broadly at the stylists and customers.

"Maybe we should ask her," Tabby said.

"Wait. I didn't—"

"Hey, Betty. We were just talking about you." Tabby turned and invited the salon owner to join us.

I sank down in my chair and wished I could slide my head under the cape like a turtle retreating inside its shell.

Betty Wilson smiled and marched over. "Oh yeah? Whatcha talking about?" She laughed. "Whatever it is, I didn't do it. At least, that's my story and I'm sticking to it." She stood beside Tabby and gazed at me. "Do I know you?"

"No." I croaked and cleared my throat, which was suddenly as dry as the Sahara desert. "No. We've not been introduced."

Tabby took the reins and completed the introductions. "Betty Wilson, proprietor of The Big Tease, this is my new customer, Priscilla . . ."

"Cummings."

"Nice to meet you." Betty turned her head to the side. "You look familiar."

I prayed her memory lapse would continue, at least until my hair was done and I could skulk out of the salon.

Bailey had been asleep in a corner next to Tabby's station, but he'd awakened at Betty's entrance and was now stretching as though he were exhausted before he sat.

Betty may not have remembered me, but Bailey was unforgettable. She snapped her fingers. "You were at the Blue Plate diner." She looked from Bailey to me and back. Her face went from recognition to surprise to bewilderment and finished with suspicion. "You're related to the owner of the diner." She frowned.

"She's my aunt."

"You're the one that found the body." She folded her arms across her chest.

I nodded. "Technically, Bailey found the body, but . . . yeah."

"The one they're saying killed Whitney Kelley."

All conversation in the salon had stopped and all eyes were turned to us. You could have heard a pin drop. After what felt like an eternity, Betty Wilson threw back her head and laughed. "Whitney Kelley was a thorn in my side. If you did her in, then I'm in your debt. Your services are on the house."

Everyone laughed and then returned to their conversations.

"I didn't kill Whitney Kelley." I sat up straighter in the chair. "I didn't kill anyone."

Betty shrugged. "Honey, I don't really care whether you did or not. You found her body and that's good enough for me." She walked over to a station that was larger and more bedazzled than the others and put her purse in a drawer. She took a pink smock from a hook nearby and put it on. She took a dog biscuit from a tin on her counter and handed it to Bailey, who snapped it up and lay back down, munching away.

Betty returned to stand next to Tabby. The two of them conferred about my hair. After a few moments, Betty decreed, "I'd recommend cutting out more and creating a layered bob. It'll give her more volume." Betty held out her hand and Tabby passed over the scissors.

For a few minutes, Betty snipped away in silence while I studied my reflection and watched as larger sections of my hair were cut away. The fear was evident in my eyes, but I tried to suppress it.

"Now, why were you two talking about me?" Like Edward Scissorhands, she quickly whacked away with her scissors.

"Oh, I was just telling her that Joe wasn't the only one fishing in another pond," Tabby said.

Betty chuckled. "You got that right. Whitney always walked around like she was so perfect. She had the perfect hair. The perfect house. The perfect marriage. HA! What a big phony!"

"Umm. I agree that Whitney liked to . . . show off, but how do you know that she was . . . um, I mean . . . having an affair?" I stammered.

"Oh, I have my ways. Joe and I had been seeing each other for months, but I have no intention of always being the *other* woman." She huffed. "I told Joe he needed to make a choice. Of course, he chose me. He wanted to call it quits—get divorced—but Whitney wouldn't have it. She wasn't about to be humiliated by having him marry anyone else, especially a common little piece of goods like me." Betty smirked and snipped. "But Joe and I are in love. I wasn't just going to stand around and wait forever for him to get free. I heard a rumor a few months ago that Whitney wasn't as pure as the driven snow, so I decided to find out for myself."

"What did you do?" I asked.

"I hired someone to get the dirt on Little Miss Whitney 'I'm Better than Everyone Else in Town' Kelley. She was cautious, and it took him a while. But my private investigator finally found out that she was sneaking off to River Bend and checking into a hotel to see her lover."

She had my full attention now. "Who was it?"

Betty snipped a bit more and then turned me around, so I was facing her directly instead of her reflection in the mirror. Her facial expression hadn't changed. I wasn't sure she even heard me. After a few moments, she spun me back around and spoke to my reflection. "Why? Why should I tell you? I haven't even had a chance to tell Joe about it, and she isn't an issue anymore. She's dead now and Joe's free. When things die down a bit, we'll go to Vegas and get married. No point dragging her name through the mud with more details. No matter how much I want to."

"I don't want to drag anyone's name through the mud. All I want to do is to clear my own. I didn't kill Whitney Kelley, but . . ."

"But what?" Betty asked.

"Someone did."

She tilted her head to the side. "So, you came here to blame me?"

"No. I came here because I have a date tonight and my hair looked like birds were about to make a nest."

Tabby nodded. "She's right. It was dry, brittle, and her ends were damaged."

"My best friend suggested I come here and . . . well, Tabby's been wonderful." I ran my fingers through my hair. "I can actually get my fingers through my hair."

Betty grinned. "Tabby's great. You're going to love your hair when she's done." She handed the scissors back to Tabby.

She turned to return to her station. "Look. I didn't kill Whitney Kelley, either, although I would like to have done it."

Now that she was no longer holding scissors, I felt emboldened. "Do the police know about you and Joe?"

Betty shrugged. "Beats me. No one from the police has questioned me, if that's what you're asking. But I figure it's just a matter of time. This is a small town. Sooner or later, someone's bound to tell them about us." She took a deep breath. "In fact, I wish they would, so we could just get everything out in the open." She turned to me. "You're friendly with that police chief. At least, that's what Joe tells me his sister-in-law thinks."

"That's not true. We're just friends . . . actually, not even friends. I'm a teacher. I taught his daughter. We're friendly . . . not friends . . ." I stammered.

Betty and Tabby exchanged glances and then burst out laughing.

"Well, if you want to be the one to drop the bomb, be my guest. You tell your friend-who's-not-a-friend that Joe Kelley and I are in love. You can also tell him that neither of us killed Whitney Kelley."

"He'll probably want to know if you have an alibi," I said as nonchalantly as I could.

"We do, in fact. We were together." I must have looked skeptical because she continued. "Ask the night manager at the Dew Drop Inn. Every Sunday, Tuesday, and Thursday night for the past six months. He'll tell you." She winked at me and patted her hair.

The door to the salon opened.

"Opal, come on over. I'm ready for you," Betty said.

Betty Wilson guided her customer to her station and the two women were lost in conversation before I realized Betty hadn't shared the name of Whitney Kelley's elusive lover.

"Betty's a magician with a pair of scissors." Tabby spun the chair around, so I was able to see the results of Betty's layering from all sides. Even wet, I could see the precision cut I'd received. I turned my head from side to side and admired the bounce and shape. It was great. My eyes looked larger and the color richer, and the biggest surprise was that I now had visible cheekbones. Awed, I stared at my reflection and glanced at Betty, who was absorbed with her customer.

Betty must have sensed my gaze because she turned and winked at me before turning back to her customer. In that wink, I knew that Betty Wilson was no lightweight. She might look simple but she was as sharp as a pair of barber shears. She hadn't revealed Whitney's lover, and something told me this wasn't an oversight. Betty Wilson was shrewd. She'd maneuvered the conversation with finesse and with as much skill as she'd used when wielding a pair of hair shears. Was she not only a magician when it came to hair, but did she have other secret abilities? Hypnosis? Illusion? Murder?

Chapter 16

*W*hile I sorted through my feelings about Betty, Tabby went to the back room and came back with a spray bottle and a Tupperware container that looked like it held salad dressing. She filled the spray bottle with water and gave my hair a thorough spray until it was dripping wet. My wet hair looked like a lion's mane. I was surprised when she dipped her hand in the thick liquid and then started to apply it to my hair. She parted my hair and ran her fingers through in a technique she called *shingling*. Her voice changed from the conversational style we'd shared earlier to instruction. As a former teacher, I recognized the instructional tone and knew it was time for me to pay careful attention.

"This will help your curls stay moisturized and defined.

Hydration. Hydration. Hydration. That's what you need." She held up the water bottle. "Whenever your hair feels dry, give it a mist."

"What's that?" I pointed to the Tupperware container.

"This is a special concoction of my own. It's got tons of healthy oils, butters, and vitamins for your hair." She lifted the container and placed it to my nose so I could smell.

"Hmm." There was a light aroma of citrus, which I liked.

After she applied the contents of the container throughout my hair, she squished the ends. Then she moved me to one of the hooded dryer stations, handed me an outdated hair magazine, and sat me down to dry. When the timer dinged and the dryer stopped, she came over and lifted the lid. I could tell by her smile that she was pleased with the results. She grabbed my hands and pulled me to my feet.

"I'm going to need you to trust me one more time."

"Okay." In for a penny. In for a pound. We'd long ago passed the point of no return.

"Close your eyes."

I obeyed and allowed her to lead me to her chair. Once I was seated, she turned me so my back was to the mirror. Then she primped and poked at my hair until she was satisfied.

"Ready?" she asked.

I nodded.

She slowly spun my chair, and I got my first glimpse of my new look.

I gasped and gawked at the woman looking back at me in the mirror. "That's not me."

Behind me, Tabby's face fell. "Oh my God! You hate it."

I turned and looked in her eyes. "Are you joking? I absolutely love it. I just can't believe that's me."

She released a heavy sigh. "Gurl, you scared the crap outta me."

"Holy cow! I can't believe that's me." I stared at my reflection. My dry, brittle mane was full of juicy, spiral curls that bounced. "This is amazing. How on earth did you get all these curls? You didn't use a curling iron?"

"Those curls are all yours. That's your natural hair."

"No way! I don't understand. How is this possible?"

"You've been brushing and pulling your hair and forcing it to do something the good Lord never intended. I just let them be free," Tabby said.

"But, how long will it last?"

Before she could answer, the door opened and a tall, dark, stunningly beautiful Black woman in a navy suit walked in. She walked straight to Tabby, put her arms around her, and hugged her. "Sorry I'm late, but I got trapped in a meeting."

Tabby grinned. "Pris, meet my partner, Carla. Carla, Pris."

Carla extended a hand, and we shook. "Your hair looks fabulous."

"Thanks to Tabby. My hair was a hot mess when I walked in. This woman is a miracle worker." I kept turning my head from side to side to feel the bounce.

"Run your fingers through it." Tabby demonstrated.

I followed her example. "It's so soft."

"Your hot date won't be able to keep his hands out of your hair," she said.

"But, how do I maintain this? What will it look like tomorrow?"

Tabby raised an eyebrow. "Girl, that depends on what you're planning on doing tonight." She laughed and then got serious. "You don't need to shampoo your hair every day. It takes all of the oils out of it. You should probably only shampoo it once per week. If it needs it, then just use conditioner, not shampoo. It's called a cowash. Then, shingle this stuff through your hair like you saw me using and sit under a dryer."

"And it'll look like this?"

Tabby nodded. "Trust me."

"But, how did you know what to do?" I sounded skeptical.

"When I fell in love with a Black woman, I decided to learn as much as I could about Black hair." Tabby smiled at Carla.

I glanced at Carla, whose hair was straight and pulled back into a bun.

"Oh, don't look at this. I'm on the school board and had to do a presentation. As soon as you're done, I'm getting in that chair and letting her work her magic on me." Carla laughed.

"You're on the school board?" I asked.

"Yep." She pulled the ponytail holder off and let her long hair flow.

"Perhaps, we can talk some time?"

"Sure thing. Just give me a call." She reached into her purse and pulled out a business card.

"How much do I owe you?" I turned to Tabby, prepared to shell out whatever sum she said.

Betty had been chatting with her customer and hadn't appeared to pay us any attention until now. She turned and chimed in. "This one is on me, remember?"

I turned to her in shock, but quickly ran over and hugged her. "Thank you."

She laughed and patted my hair. "You look fabulous. No better advertisement than a woman with a beautiful head of hair. You just be sure to tell everyone to come to The Big Tease and we'll fix them up, too."

I pulled out all the cash I found in my wallet and left Tabby a tip that put a huge smile on her face.

"Holy Moly! Dinner's on me, tonight." Tabby stared at the bills.

"You bet it is." Carla grinned.

I don't remember leaving the shop, but I must have because next thing I knew, Bailey and I were in the car. I couldn't stop staring at myself in the rearview mirror and running my hands through my hair. After a few minutes, I put the car in gear and pulled out. This day had been remarkable. Not only did I get a fantastic haircut and get a date with a very sexy policeman, but I'd discovered several new suspects who might have had a motive for killing Whitney Kelley.

Chapter 17

My first stop after leaving the salon was Marcie's apartment. I rang her bell and had my camera ready to snap her expression. She didn't disappoint.

"Wow! You have always looked wonderful, but WOW!" Inside, she examined my hair from all angles. "You look amazing. Please tell me you love it."

"I love it. I just still can't believe this is really me. I mean, I walked in looking like the Scarecrow from *The Wizard of Oz* and I came out looking like . . . the Cowardly Lion after spending a day in the Emerald City beauty salon."

"You look much nicer than the Cowardly Lion. You look like a freakin' supermodel. Your date isn't going to be able to stop staring at you." She winked. "What are you going to wear? You need an outfit that will live up to your new hair."

I hugged my friend. "Thanks for that totally biased opinion. You're so good for my ego."

We talked outfits for several minutes. Just when we had agreed on a dress, I got a text from Pitbull asking how I felt about a new bar that had live music. The bar wasn't a dive, but it reminded me that I was going out with a biker, and perhaps a dress wasn't a good idea.

"You don't suppose he'll pick you up on his bike, do you?" Marcie asked.

"I hope not, but . . . I don't want to ruin my hair with a motorcycle helmet."

After further debate, I decided that I'd pick out jeans and a nice top. I'd deal with the helmet obstacle when I got to it.

"Remarkable that you only went to The Big Tease to get intel on Betty Wilson and—"

"OMG. In all the excitement about my hair, I almost forgot to fill you in on what I found out." I quickly filled Marcie in on what I'd learned about Joe and Betty, as well as the rumor that Whitney was also having an affair.

"Do you believe Betty?" Marcie asked.

I thought about the question for a few moments. "I do . . . at least, I believe *she* believes that Whitney was having an affair."

"What are you going to do?"

"I don't know. I should tell Chief Morgan, but I don't think he'll appreciate me sharing my ideas."

"But you have information that might help him solve

the murder. You have to tell him. It's your civic duty, right?" Marcie asked.

I thought about Marcie's question on the short drive home. Was it my civic duty to tell the police that Joe Kelley was having an affair with Betty Wilson? Or that Betty paid for someone to get dirt on Whitney and that she might also have been having an affair? Wasn't that just gossip that might ruin several reputations? So what if Joe and Betty were having an affair? As long as they hadn't killed Whitney, it wasn't a crime.

At home, I pulled on my best pair of jeans and a figure-flattering black long-sleeved, high-necked top. The yoke and sleeves were sheer, which gave the top a dressier look. Marcie initially suggested I go for a pair of sexy, strappy heels, but on my best day, I wasn't graceful enough for strappy heels. Toss a potential motorcycle ride in the mix and I sensed a trip to the emergency room in my future. Instead, we'd compromised on a pair of ankle boots with a moderate heel. As I zipped the soft leather boots, I couldn't help but think of Whitney's Louboutin pumps. There was nothing moderate about the heels on those shoes.

I changed out my normal stud earrings for a pair of gold hoop earrings and my mind drifted again to Whitney's large diamond earrings with the matching necklace and ring. Even without a jeweler's glass, I knew the pieces were real. A bit large and gaudy for my taste, but then maybe they were family heirlooms that she wore to remember a relative.

Bailey alerted me to Pitbull's arrival long before he rang my doorbell, so I was downstairs and ready to greet him. I opened the door and watched his eyes widen as he took in my new look.

"You look amazing. Wow! I mean . . . wow," he stammered.

"Thank you. Come in." I stepped back for him to enter. He stood gaping.

"Are those for me?" I pointed to the bouquet of flowers he held.

He recalled his manners and extended the bouquet. It was a large bouquet of beautiful flowers that included Asiatic lilies and roses. "These are my favorite flowers. How'd you know?" I sniffed the fragrant bouquet.

"We detectives have our ways of collecting information." He grinned.

I left him in the living room with Bailey while I took the flowers to the kitchen, filled a vase with water, and brought them back to place on my mantel. "They're lovely. Thank you."

He grinned. "Shall we go?"

I shook my head. "No."

He hesitated. "No?"

"I can't go out on a date with someone when I don't know their name . . . their *real* name. I can't just call you Pitbull all evening."

"Everyone else does," he joked.

I folded my arms across my chest, tapped my foot, and waited.

He extended a hand. "Hello. My name is Mark Alexander."

"Pleased to meet you, Mark. I'm Priscilla Cummings." I shook his hand.

He helped me with my jacket, I gave Bailey a treat and told him to be good, and then we left. Outside, he escorted me to a pickup truck. I gave a silent prayer of thanks that I had chosen jeans instead of the black pencil skirt, which, despite the running boards, I knew from experience would have been a challenge. Nevertheless, I was grateful that I wouldn't have to climb on a motorcycle or risk smushing my hair under a helmet.

The restaurant was more like a pub. It had a dining area, a bar, a gaming area with pool tables, and a small stage. It was crowded, but Mark knew the owner and we were quickly shown to a booth with a great view of the stage.

We spent a few minutes perusing the menu before selecting drinks and entrées. We both ordered steaks and when the waitress left, I noticed a look of admiration in the eyes of my date.

"What?"

He chuckled. "I'm just so thankful to see a woman who isn't afraid to order a steak and not some salad that looks like something I'd feed a rabbit or my little sister's pet hamster."

I took a sip of water to hide my relief that I hadn't gone with my original choice of a Caesar salad.

We spent the time before our food arrived getting acquainted. I learned that he was the oldest of seven kids and had moved to Chicago after he got out of the military.

"Chicago? Isn't that where Chief Morgan is from?" I felt my cheeks flush and I was glad the lights were dim in the bar.

"Yeah. We met in the army. We did two tours and then joined the police force. He met Sarah, got married, had Hannah, and climbed the ladder. I went a different route. I went undercover."

"Sounds dangerous."

He shrugged. "I guess so." He frowned and gazed into his beer.

"We don't have to talk about it, if you don't want to."

He took a deep breath. "My youngest brother, Paul, got involved with some dangerous people. The police couldn't do anything about it and . . . well, he died—"

"I'm so sorry."

He shrugged. "I guess that's when I decided I wanted to do something about it. I wanted to be able to help. So, when the opportunity came to infiltrate organizations like that, I jumped at it."

"That's very brave. Is that why they call you Pitbull?"

He shook his head. "Actually, I got that nickname before . . . long before. When I was a kid, my mom used to say when I got something in my head, I was more stubborn than a bull." He chuckled. "When I had to come up with an alias for my undercover work, I chose Pitbull."

"So, what brought you to Crosbyville?" I asked.

"Things in Chicago got a bit hot. I was afraid my cover was blown. I needed a change. I knew Gil was here. A few months after he left Chicago and took the job as the chief of police, I reached out to him. I figured I had an in." He shrugged. "Things were good for a while, but . . ."

After a moment, I prodded. "But?"

He shrugged. "Let's just say we changed. We both changed. He was the chief of police and a stickler for protocol, and I guess he had to make a stand against unconventional cops like me. He thought I was too extreme for small-town Crosbyville. So . . . he suspended me."

"But, you were at . . ."

"You thought because I was at the station today that I was active?"

I nodded.

"I do some private work on the side and still have some friends who help me from time to time."

"That's not fair, that he suspended you. Crosbyville is a small town, but criminals are everywhere." I thought of the irony of the fact that I was relaying the same warnings my aunt Agatha used when insisting that I needed to carry pepper spray in a small town with fewer than thirty thousand people.

"It's okay. I have some money saved up. Plus, I do a little freelance detective and security work on the side. I'm thinking about getting my P.I. license. Seriously, there's a lot more money working in the private sector."

Our steaks arrived, and we continued to make small

talk as we ate. Eventually, our conversation came around to Whitney Kelley, the reason I was at the police station today.

"I want to ask your advice about something."

He leaned back and waited.

He may have been suspended, but technically he was still a policeman, so I told him everything I'd learned about the argument Whitney had with the school board, the fact that Betty Wilson admitted she and Joe Kelley were having an affair, and the rumor that Whitney Kelley was also having an affair. He didn't say anything while I was talking and afterward, he stared at me.

"Well?" I asked.

"Well, what? You said you had a question."

"What should I do? The affair is a fact, but if Whitney was having an affair with someone, then wouldn't bringing this up now just be slinging mud at someone unable to defend herself? Plus, I wonder how she was able to afford shoes that must have set her back at least two grand. That seems weird, doesn't it?"

"Not really. Lots of people buy things they can't afford. But maybe they were a gift. Maybe she bought them at a secondhand store . . . or maybe she saved up her money and bought a pair of expensive shoes."

"Whitney would *never* buy anything secondhand, but . . . I suppose the rest is possible, but what do you think I should do about the other things that I learned?"

"Honestly?"

I nodded.

"Nothing. Don't talk to anyone. Don't ask any questions. Do not get involved."

"Do you think I should tell the police? Should I tell Chief Morgan?"

"In all honesty, I say forget it. Gil's a trained investigator. He'll find out what he needs to know, and he won't appreciate you getting involved. My advice is to stay as far away from this case as you can. Go to work. Write your books, and stay out of it."

I opened my mouth to protest, but Mark held up a hand.

"Look, you've found out a lot of information . . . good information. Information that people should be telling the police. But the bottom line is that investigating a murder is dangerous work." He leaned forward and looked me directly in the eyes. "Whoever killed Whitney Kelley is out there. They haven't been arrested yet. It may be that Gil doesn't even have him or her on his radar yet. They may think they got away with murder. If you come around asking questions, they may think you're causing trouble. They've killed once. What's to stop them from killing a second time?"

I gasped. I hadn't thought of the danger investigating might mean for me.

Mark reached over and lifted my chin. "I'd be very sad if anything happened to you."

We gazed into each other's eyes.

"Uncle Mark."

We glanced up and Hannah Morgan ran to the table and threw herself into the detective's arms.

"Uncle Mark?" I asked.

Pitbull shrugged. "Gil and I were close once. Military brothers." He turned to Hannah. "Hey, munchkin. What're you doing here?"

I turned in time to see Chief Morgan's dark, smoldering eyes boring into mine.

He stepped forward. "Hannah, come on. You're interrupting—"

"No. She's not interrupting anything. We were just having dinner," I stammered. I felt three sets of eyes focused on me. "Would you like to join us?"

"Yes," Hannah squealed.

"No," Chief Morgan said.

Hannah poked out her lower lip and sulked. "Where's Bailey?"

"I left him at home," I said.

"I like your hair. You look so pretty. Doesn't she?" Hannah turned to her dad.

He hesitated a few seconds. "Yes. Your hair looks great." The tips of his ears grew red and the muscle in the side of his jaw pulsed. "Hannah, come on. We need to go. You can talk to Mark some other time."

"Aww." Hannah frowned.

"Actually, I need to talk to you. So, we might as well do it now." I scooted closer to Mark in the U-shaped booth to allow room for the chief to slide in next to me. "Mark, maybe you could take Hannah and show her the games," I suggested.

Mark shrugged and then turned to Hannah. "Hey, munchkin. Did you see that pinball machine near the door?

What do you say I go and wipe the floor with you while your dad and Miss Cummings talk?"

He slid out, took Hannah by the hand, and headed toward the door.

Chief Morgan stood a few moments and then sat down next to me. "Okay, what did you want to talk to me about?"

"Chief Morgan, I—"

"You might as well call me Gilbert."

I took a drink of wine and then turned and shared everything I'd learned.

He listened silently, but the red color that appeared on the tips of his ears deepened and the pulse on the side of his head went from a slow waltz to a quickstep.

When I finished, I waited. Like Mark, he didn't say anything at first. Eventually, his silence grew too much for me. "Say something."

"What are you doing? You could get yourself killed. Stay out of it. Stay out of my investigation or I'll arrest you for interfering in a police investigation."

I blanched. "I'm not interfering in your investigation. I was just doing pet-assisted therapy at the library and getting my hair done. You act as though I did something wrong."

"You're denying that you're acting like some kind of Nancy Drew and investigating this murder?"

"I had no idea the school board met at the library. I go to a lot of libraries and schools." I folded my arms across my chest.

"And you expect me to believe that it's a mere coincidence that you chose the one beauty parlor in town that is owned by the woman who is having an affair with the murder victim's spouse?"

"Yes!" I glared at him for a few moments before my conscience got the better of me. "No."

"I knew it."

"All right, I had heard a rumor that they were having an affair, and since I needed to get my hair done, I did choose The Big Tease because I knew it was Betty Wilson's salon. But I didn't go in there to question her. I just . . . hoped that maybe I'd hear some gossip."

He took a deep breath and then leaned close. "Okay. You got lucky. You got some good leads and now you've told me, and I will follow up. That's my job. But, on no uncertain terms are you to continue asking questions. I don't want you anywhere near anyone that has anything to do with this case. Do I make myself clear?"

Before I could answer, a shadow fell over the table. I glanced up and into a pair of cold, steely eyes.

"Isn't this cozy. Chief Morgan and the prime suspect in my sister's murder out on a date." Chelsea Baxter pulled out a cell phone and snapped a picture of us. "And now I have proof that you're deliberately dragging your feet in making an arrest because you're romantically involved with the murderer."

"Mrs. Davis, I—"

"Baxter," Chelsea corrected him.

"Ms. Baxter, I assure you this isn't what it looks like," Chief Morgan said.

"I assure *you* that the mayor and the town council will

hear about this, and I'm going to make it my personal mission to make sure that this woman will be arrested for murdering my sister and that you will be tossed out of office for misconduct if it's the last thing I do." Chelsea Baxter glared, turned, and marched away.

Chapter 18

Stunned, I looked at the space vacated by Chelsea Baxter. I blinked and shook my head. Surely this was all some horrible nightmare, and I just needed a good shake to wake up and find myself at home, curled up with Bailey. I opened my eyes, but nothing changed.

I was still at the restaurant sitting in a booth. I stole a glance to my side. The red that had initially just been on the tips of the police chief's ears was now covering his entire face and neck. He looked like a volcano about to explode.

I extended a hand, but he wrenched his arm away.

"Gilbert, I'm so sorry. Do you think she will—"

"Yes. Why not? She's been threatening it for two days." He rubbed his head.

"But there's nothing going on between us . . . We

aren't on a date . . . I'm here with Mark. You just happened to come by . . ." As the words left my mouth, I realized how unbelievable it sounded. His face indicated he realized it, too.

"You just happened to be on a date, *and* I just happened to show up at the same time. *And* I just happened to be sitting here talking to you. *And* she just happened to come in while we were talking."

"And she just happened to take a picture of us together."

He nodded. "If I didn't know better, I would believe it, too."

"But, if I go to the city council and I explain . . . surely, they'll—"

He was shaking his head before the words left my mouth. "Just stay out of it. PLEASE. You've done enough."

Mark and Hannah approached the table. I sensed that something was wrong by the inquisitive looks on their faces.

"Come on, Hannah. Let's go." Gilbert took Hannah by the hand and marched out.

"What happened?" Mark asked.

I quickly told him everything. He could see that I was in no shape to continue our date. So he called over the waiter and dropped several bills on the table.

I grabbed my purse and slid out of the booth.

Chief Morgan and Hannah paid for their take-out order and were just getting into their car by the time we made it into the parking lot.

"Gil, wait." Mark rushed to the car. "Pris told me what happened. We can both testify about what happened tonight."

"What *did* happen?" He glared at me.

Mark glanced from Gil to me. "Wait. You can't blame Pris for this. It's not her fault."

"All I know is that there's been nothing but trouble ever since she claimed to have found Whitney Kelley's body."

"Claimed? What's that supposed to mean?" I asked.

"I think you know what I mean." Chief Morgan scowled.

"Now, hold on. You're angry, but there's no reason to take it out on Pris." Mark reached out a hand and grabbed him by the arm.

Gil wrenched his arm away and the two men glowered at each other like two boxers in the middle of a boxing ring. Something told me those angry looks went deeper than me.

Hannah lowered her window. "Daddy, no."

I grabbed Mark's arm.

After a few more seconds, both men came back to their senses. Gilbert pulled open the driver's door and flopped down onto the seat of the car. He turned on the engine and sped away.

We watched the car leave and then Mark took a deep breath and then glanced down at me. "I'm sorry. This is *not* how I imagined this date ending."

"Me, either."

Chapter 19

Mark drove me home and walked me to the door. I thanked him, then reached up and gave him a quick sisterly kiss on the cheek before I hurried inside.

Bailey was there waiting for me, and I flung my arms around his neck and buried my face in his fur. I didn't realize how frayed my nerves were until that moment. "Bailey, tonight was awful. I made a total and complete mess of things with Gilbert . . . Chief Morgan."

Bailey licked my arm and sat still and listened.

"I was only trying to help. I didn't want Chelsea to get him in trouble, but that's exactly what happened." I recapped the situation for Bailey, even though I knew it wouldn't matter. He was always on my side regardless of the circumstances. Tonight was no exception.

He wiggled around in my arms so his face was toward

mine and licked me. He didn't just lick me once. He started by licking away my tears, but then licked my entire face.

"Okay, that's enough," I said.

Bailey didn't listen. He continued to lick. When his tongue went in my ear, I giggled.

"Hey, that tickles."

He continued to lick until I was lying on the floor laughing with one hundred pounds of bloodhound lying on my chest. His muzzle rested on my chin. He gazed into my eyes.

I stared back and a warm glow filled my chest. In that moment, I knew what true love felt like. I squeezed him close and kissed his muzzle. "Thank you."

I lay on the ground and tried to figure out a way out of this situation. Nothing came, and eventually, I must have fallen asleep. I was jolted awake when I felt a vibration in my right butt cheek. It took a few seconds to finagle Bailey off my chest and my cell phone out of my pocket.

"Hello?"

"I've been sending text messages for the past two hours and you didn't respond. You were supposed to text and let me know when your date was over. Is it over? Or am I interrupting something . . . Oh my God, Pris . . . I didn't think. My mind went crazy and I thought Pitbull might be an ax murderer. Even though he's a policeman, he could still be an ax murderer. So, I decided to risk it and call. Just say the code word, Sassafras, and I'll know you're okay and hang up. Otherwise, I'll—"

"It's fine. My date is over. It's okay. You aren't interrupting anything but Bailey and me asleep on the living room floor."

"Oh," she said, sounding disappointed. "I'm relieved you're okay, but why are you on the floor with Bailey?"

I skipped the details of the date and fast-forwarded to Chief Morgan and Chelsea and all the drama that followed. When I finished, Marcie was silent.

"Are you still there? Say something."

"That has to be the worst first date EVER!"

"Say something helpful. Should I ignore Chief Morgan's advice and talk to the city council? Or should I steer clear and let him deal with it himself?"

"My recommendation is to steer clear."

"Really?" I tried to hide the disappointment in my voice.

"Look, the police chief is a grown man. He's capable of fighting his own battles."

"Oh . . . but he doesn't know the Wicked Baxter Sisters like we do. I'm sure he's a highly trained policeman and capable of finding a killer, but Whitney and Chelsea are a different breed. Besides, he doesn't know the people in the community. I mean, look at everything I found out in just one day. People know me, and they are willing to talk to me where they won't talk to the police. I think—"

"Pris. You asked me, and I gave my recommendation. When it comes to the city council, then I say let him do it himself. Plus, Pitbull—Mark was right. This might be dangerous. Whoever killed Whitney Kelley probably thinks they've gotten away with murder. If he or she finds out that you've been asking questions, they might see you as a threat. You could be in danger. I don't want to see anything happen to you, especially not because of Whitney."

"I wouldn't be doing it for Whitney. I'd be doing it . . . Maybe you're right." I sighed. "As long as the police don't think I had anything to do with her death, then there's no real reason for me to get involved, is there?" *Especially, if Chief of Police Gilbert Morgan doesn't want my help.*

I was disappointed, but I knew Marcie's advice came from love and not because she thought I was a meddlesome Nancy Drew. Or because she thought me incapable. We chatted for a few minutes, but it was late, so we called it a night and agreed to meet for breakfast the next morning.

I let Bailey outside to take care of business while I took care of making sure the doors were locked, the curtains pulled, and the lights were turned off inside. According to Aunt Agatha, nothing repelled burglars more than exterior lights. No idea where she heard this, but it was easier to simply turn on the lights than to argue. So, I complied.

Once Bailey and I were tucked in, sleep eluded me. Based on the snoring coming from the next pillow, Bailey wasn't having the same problem.

I tossed and turned and tried every trick I knew to get my brain to turn off, but it refused to shut down. Frustrated, I sat up and checked the time. It was three in the morning, and I was just as wide awake as I'd been two hours earlier. That's when I gave up trying to sleep, sat up, and turned on the lamp.

Bailey lifted his head to see what I was up to. Since there were no treats involved, he put his head back down and was quickly snoring again.

I reached for the notepad and pen that I kept for jotting down book ideas in the middle of the night and pulled them from my nightstand. After a few minutes of gazing at the blank sheet and trying to figure out what to write, I decided to write down what I knew so far.

Whitney threatened to air the members of the school board's dirty laundry.

I scratched out the last part. "No, she said she'd open their closets and expose skeletons." I paused. "Or something like that." *What skeletons? Could one of the board members have a skeleton so bad that they'd kill to keep it concealed?*

I pondered that thought for a few minutes and then wrote:

Who are the members of the school board?

A quick Google search gave me the names and I wrote them in my notepad.

> Whitney Kelley
> Amelia Cooper Lawson
> Carla Taylor
> Lucas Harrison
> Hilda Diaz-Sanchez

Dr. Don Nobles
Dr. Debra Holt

I crossed Whitney's name off the list since she hadn't committed suicide, and thought about what I knew about the others. I also crossed Hilda Diaz-Sanchez's and Dr. Debra Holt's names off the list. Both were wonderful women who had been on the school board for eons, since their children were in school. Now both were older with college-aged grandchildren. Still, they were committed to education and service, as evidenced by their day jobs. Hilda Diaz-Sanchez trained search-and-rescue dogs and volunteered to do searches with law enforcement both locally and nationally, and I knew for a fact that she and her amazing Labrador retriever, Teddy, had been out of the country for the last month working an archaeological dig site in Teotihuacán, Mexico, along with the chief archaeologist, Dr. Debra Holt. A recent article in the newspaper highlighted how search-and-rescue dogs had such amazing olfactory receptors that they were now being used to find buried human remains in archaeological digs.

"If anyone has skeletons in their closet, it's probably these two. Literal skeletons." I chuckled at the idea and glanced at Bailey, who hadn't found my joke funny enough to interrupt his sleep. I sighed. "Of course, both women could have secrets, but they weren't present to hear Whitney's threat." I stuck with my initial decision to cross them off the list and moved on.

Amelia Cooper Lawson had been on the board for over

twenty years. It came as a major surprise when she announced her intention of stepping down from the board and promoted Whitney Kelley as her replacement. She always took pride in her role as a member of Crosbyville's founding family. In fact, a member of her family had been on the school board since its inception. She lived in a large Victorian house set on a hill that overlooked the city. In addition to founding Crosbyville, her family had owned several businesses, including the town newspaper, real estate company, and jeweler. I'd met her several times at various charitable functions, but we didn't run in the same circles. Amelia was a widow. Her late husband, William, had been quite well known. He'd died six months ago from a heart condition.

I moved down the list. Carla Taylor must have been the woman I'd met at the beauty shop, Tabby's partner. From my conversation with Tabby, I knew Carla was an accountant, which is probably why she'd be on the school board. I checked my phone again and Google confirmed that she was the treasurer. She was listed as temporary. She was appointed to fill a vacancy left by the previous treasurer, William Lawson, after his death. I wondered what skeletons Carla could have in her closet. In years past, her sexual orientation might have been a stumbling block to some in the community. Thankfully, many in our small tight-knit community approved and accepted, or disapproved while adopting the adage *Live and let live.*

Did she have other skeletons? Tabby had been so open.

I found it hard to believe that Carla wasn't also. Could Carla have skeletons that Whitney could use to threaten her? I found the idea hard to swallow. Carla struck me as the type of person who would have told Whitney exactly what she could do with her threats, but then I'd met her only briefly. Maybe Carla's skeletons were so secretive that even Tabby didn't know about them? Not likely, but I'm biased. I liked them and I didn't want either of them to be involved. But that's not fair. I couldn't just cross people off the list because I liked them.

I sighed. This was hard. Maybe I should talk to Carla anyway. Not to ask her about her skeletons or to try to find out if she killed Whitney, but maybe I could convince her to go and talk to Chief Morgan about the board meeting, since Charlotte Littlefield refused to do it.

Dr. Don Nobles was an art teacher at Crosbyville College. What did I know about him? I knew he was close to ninety years old but still very active in the art community. He often gave lectures and traveled around the world to various art shows. In fact, he had an art exhibit going on now at the local museum. Once again, I turned to Google to confirm. I was right. His art was on display at the Crosbyville Art Museum. I wrote down the dates and made a mental note to stop by and take a look. *I'm only going to look at the art, not to ask questions about Whitney Kelley's murder.* At least, that's what I told myself.

That just left Lucas Harrison. The Octopus.

I shuddered. He was such a sleazeball. All hands and

teeth—always smiling. I could easily imagine Lucas Harrison with skeletons he wouldn't want exposed. Well, based on what I remembered of Lucas, he probably would want his skeletons exposed. He'd consider them some kind of badge of honor—something to brag about in the locker room at the club. *Ugh!* But he was on the school board. I supposed it wouldn't hurt to talk to him as long as it was in broad daylight and in a public place.

Bailey gave a quick bark in his sleep and a quick shudder. I looked at my goofy boy and couldn't help smiling. "Are you chasing squirrels?" I asked.

He settled down and continued to snore.

During the move, Bailey had discovered a box that was left in the back of the closet under the stairs. Old pictures, a small metal box with a few coins, an old newspaper clipping or two, and a few old books. No signed first editions by William Shakespeare or Leonardo da Vinci— I checked. These were mostly bodice-busting romances and a few P.I. novels by Dick Francis and Erle Stanley Gardner. I could take the box to Lucas's office and strike up a conversation. He didn't strike me as the type who would turn down the opportunity to talk to any woman. I shivered.

The problem with Lucas was that he was too . . . touchy. Had his overly friendly behavior gotten him into trouble—trouble that wouldn't have been something to joke about in the locker room? Of all the school board members that Whitney might threaten, Lucas Harrison seemed the most likely to have skeletons. He'd always had a crush on Whitney since elementary school. To the best of my recollection, she'd never given him the time of day. Whitney was too good for the likes of Lucas Harrison. In high school he'd maintained a competitive rivalry with Joe Kelley, of which he'd consistently managed to take second place. Lucas wanted Whitney. Joe Kelley got Whitney. Both men played football. Joe was the quarterback. What if Lucas was tired of always coming in second in a field of two? Maybe Whitney Kelley's murder was a way for Lucas to get even with Joe in an "If I can't have you, no one will" sort of way? I shivered again.

I didn't want to spend more than five minutes with Lucas Harrison. I should leave this to the police. I flipped my notepad closed, lay down, and studied the ceiling.

Still, sleep eluded me. I couldn't trust that the police would figure this out. Neither Mark nor Gilbert were locals. They weren't from here. They wouldn't know about the high school rivalry between Lucas Harrison and Joe Kelley. Nor would they know about Lucas's longtime crush on Whitney. Love, lust, and jealousy were strong emotions and great motives for murder. If those emotions had been allowed to fester for a decade, then who knows what might have come out of them.

I rolled over and flipped off the lamp. I couldn't leave this to chance. I would return the box to Lucas's office. But I wouldn't question him. I'd just talk to him and if the conversation strayed to Whitney Kelley's murder, then all the better. If not, then I'd walk away and make sure that Mark knew. I'd let him tell Chief Morgan.

I rolled over so I faced Bailey. He opened one eye and looked at me without looking. Then he licked my face, closed his eyes, and started snoring again.

Yep. I was definitely taking Bailey with me.

Chapter 20

*E*verything that made total and complete sense the night before sounded crazy in the light of day. *Why was I going to talk to Lucas "the Octopus" Harrison again?* I had no idea. He certainly wouldn't care about a box full of trash. This was crazy. I had a better idea. I pulled the covers over my head. I could just lie here forever.

Bailey had other ideas. Using his teeth, he pulled the covers back and barked.

"I didn't interrupt you when you were sleeping last night." I grabbed the covers and pulled them back over my head.

I never stood much of a chance of winning the battle of the blankets against Bailey. However, when he climbed onto my chest and used his front paws as though digging to pull the covers back, I was sunk.

"Off," I ordered once I could get my breath.

Bailey bounced back and play-bowed. His tail wagged as drool dripped from his mouth.

How could I be angry when one hundred pounds of pure joy was staring in my face? I smiled and tossed the covers over his head and wrestled with him for several minutes, just as I had when he was a puppy.

After a rousing few minutes of play, I was in a better mood. "Okay, come on. Let's get this day started." I led him outside and left him to sniff and play while I took my shower and got dressed.

I was still tired from lack of sleep, so I spent extra time applying my makeup to hide the under-eye bags. I spritzed and fluffed my hair as Tabby instructed. It still looked great, and I spent more time than usual admiring myself from multiple angles before heading downstairs for coffee.

I loaded the box in the back seat with Bailey and then drove to Harrison Real Estate Properties. It wasn't far, so I found myself parked in the small lot next to the office in no time. I sat in the car staring at the redbrick building for several minutes as I tried to work through a plausible reason why I was here so early with a box of what appeared to be junk. I racked my brain, but I couldn't come up with anything that didn't sound phony and contrived. Eventually, I gave up, and got out. The box was light, but juggling a box and a one hundred–pound bloodhound proved too much. It was daylight and with any luck, the office would be full, so I left Bailey in the car with the windows cracked plenty and a stern warning to be on his best behavior.

I carried the box to the door and after balancing it on my knee, I managed to get the door open enough to squeeze through. Inside, I found Lucas Harrison staring at me through the glass, a lopsided grin on his face. He'd seen me struggling, but instead of coming to my aid, had merely watched in silence.

I swallowed the smart-alecky remark that was floating on the tip of my tongue and forced a smile. "Lucas, I'm so glad you're here to help me. I was afraid I was going to have to manage this by myself."

Based on the twinkle in his eyes, the irony wasn't lost on him.

"What brings you here and bearing gifts on this fine morning?" He walked over and took the box.

"Bailey found that in the closet under the stairs. I thought you could see that the previous owners got it."

"The previous owner was Amelia Cooper Lawson, but she was supposed to remove her stuff before closing. Technically, anything left in the house belongs to you." He glanced inside the box. "This is trash. You should have just pitched it."

"There were some photos in the box, and I thought maybe Mrs. Lawson would have liked to keep them. You know how women are. We can be very sentimental about things like photos." I swallowed hard to keep from gagging on that last statement, but Lucas seemed to be lost in thought.

"Ain't that the truth." He picked up one of the photos and stared hard. I could almost see the gears turning in his head. After a few minutes, a smile spread across his face.

"Lucas?"

"Oh, thanks for bringing these over. I will make sure Amelia gets these." He grinned and mumbled, "You just leave it to me."

"Okay. Sure."

Lucas walked to the door and held it open. Clearly, as far as he was concerned, our conversation was over.

"Great. Well, I'll just head out. If I find anything else, I'll be sure to—"

Lucas closed the door and turned away.

I walked back to the car in a daze. I got in and sat down and tried to figure out what just happened. He didn't make a pass at me. I don't think I've ever been alone with Lucas Harrison when he didn't try something creepy. It wasn't just me—Lucas Harrison flirted with every woman he met. He didn't even make a comment about my hair.

What's wrong with me? "Good grief. What am I thinking? I can't believe I'm upset because he *didn't* make a pass." I glanced in the rearview mirror.

Bailey was lying on the back seat with a small, cross-stitch pillow in his mouth.

"Bailey, Drop it." I reached back and took the now soggy pillow. The cross-stitch pillow said *Home Sweet Home.* I'd seen it in the box. "You took this out of the box."

Bailey avoided eye contact.

"Bad dog."

He slid down and glanced up at me.

"Okay, you're not a bad dog. You're a good dog. But you shouldn't have taken this pillow. It's not ours." I reached back and scratched his ear to let him know all was forgiven.

I got back out of the car and hurried to the door. I flung open the door and barged in. "Lucas, I found one more—"

I was halfway into the office when I realized that I'd just interrupted a couple in the middle of a passionate kiss. They pulled apart. That's when I got a good look and realized who the couple was. Startled, I gasped.

Of all the women in Crosbyville that I could imagine in a relationship with Lucas Harrison, Chelsea Baxter would have been the last person I would have picked. Yet here she was.

Chapter 21

Chelsea adjusted her blouse and then turned to face me. "What do you want?"

It took a few seconds for me to find my voice. "I found this pillow in the back of my car. My dog must have taken it from the box. I was—"

"Well, now you've returned the pillow, so you can just turn around and get out." Her eyes flashed and she fired the words like bullets from a machine gun.

"Fine." I placed the pillow in the box and turned to leave. I made it as far as the door when I was halted.

"Wait."

I turned around. Lucas Harrison was smiling like a Cheshire cat, but Chelsea looked as though she could bite the head off nails. She took several deep breaths. "Look, Lucas and I were just—"

"You don't owe me an explanation. You're both adults. Live and let live. That's my motto."

My attempt to defuse the situation and reduce the tension by indicating that I didn't care what they were doing had the complete opposite effect on Chelsea than the one I intended.

"Don't give me that '*Live and let live*' bullpucky. You know perfectly well that I'm in the middle of a divorce and if my soon-to-be ex-husband found out that I was . . . involved with another man, he'd use that to keep from paying alimony. So, you better keep your mouth shut or I'll make sure your boyfriend never works again."

"Chief Morgan isn't—" I shook my head, trying to make sure I'd heard her properly. "Are you saying you're *not* going to take that picture you took of Chief Morgan and me sitting together at the restaurant last night—having an *innocent* conversation—to the city council to try and get Chief Morgan fired?"

If eye-rolling were an Olympic event, Chelsea Baxter would be the gold medalist. She rolled her eyes and huffed, but eventually she crossed her arms and nodded. "Deal."

I hadn't intended to make a deal, but since one had been placed at my feet, I felt duty bound to accept. After all, I had no intention of telling Chelsea's husband or anyone else about her relationship. Well, no one except my best friend, Marcie.

"Deal." I turned to leave, but my conscience wouldn't let me. "Chelsea, I had no intention of—"

"Just get out already." Chelsea turned and marched away. She pushed open the door to one of the offices, which was probably where she'd been hiding when I'd come in earlier.

Lucas Harrison simply stood, grinning.

I walked out.

Back in the car, I glanced at Bailey in the rearview mirror. "Well, boy, I guess I have you to thank for this. If you hadn't taken that pillow out of the box, I wouldn't have walked in on Chelsea and Lucas, and Chief Morgan would have to go before the city council. Bailey the Bloodhound to the rescue."

Bailey sat up on the seat and basked in his praise.

"How about a walk around the park and then I need to settle down and start writing." I leaned my head on the steering wheel. "Writing. What was I thinking when I agreed to finish my book in a month? I haven't written one word in three days. My editor is going to kill me." I sat up and caught sight of Bailey in the rearview mirror. He looked so happy. "Let's get to the park."

Park was one of the words Bailey recognized. He barked his approval of the plan.

I was just about to back out of the parking spot when I got a text message on my phone. I took a moment to check. It was Tabby. Glad we exchanged numbers before I left.

U need to get over to the salon

Why?

Fur just hit the fan

????

I waited for a few moments, but she never replied. I put the car in gear and headed to The Big Tease.

My first clue that trouble was brewing came at seeing a police car parked outside. I strained my neck, but when I didn't see yellow crime-scene tape, I got out with Bailey in tow.

The salon was crowded. Every dryer was full. I didn't realize so many Crosbyville residents patronized The Big Tease. Amelia Cooper Lawson was sitting in the chair in front of Betty Wilson's station. Charlotte Littlefield was at a shampoo bowl, and Tabby's partner, Carla, was sitting with her feet in a tub of water while her massage chair vibrated and pummeled her backside. Tabby was sitting in her chair, staring at a door that I knew led to the office. When she saw me, she hopped up and beckoned for me to come over.

Bailey curled up on the floor and I sat in the newly vacated chair.

Tabby placed a cape around my neck and leaned down and whispered, "The police came to talk to Betty. She called Joe and he came over. They've been in the office with the police."

"Both of them?"

She nodded. "It's been—"

"WHAT? I'll kill him." Joe Kelley flung open the door and marched out of the office.

Chief Morgan rushed after him and grabbed Joe's arm. "Mr. Kelley, calm down. I don't want to have to arrest you, but I will."

"Arrest me? You're going to arrest me? When that . . .

that . . . gigolo was having an affair with my wife? He's the one you should be arresting. He killed her. You need to do your job and arrest him. That's what you need to do," Joe Kelley screamed. He turned to Betty. "And you knew about this and never told me?"

"I knew you'd be upset. That's why I didn't tell you," Betty said.

Just when I thought things couldn't get any more tense, Chelsea Baxter opened the door and walked in. All conversation stopped; Chelsea's entrance sucked all the oxygen out of the room.

Tabby leaned down and whispered in my ear, "I wish I had some popcorn. It's about to go down."

Chelsea looked at her brother-in-law. "What's going on?"

Chief Morgan tried to keep the situation from spiraling even more out of control. "Nothing. Now, unless you have business here, I think you should—"

"Business *here*? You must be joking. I'd rather let a blind monkey cut my hair before I'd let anyone here near my hair." She looked around the shop.

"Then, why are you here?" Chief Morgan asked.

"I got a text message that I needed to come to this . . ." She waved her arm in a circle. "This harem immediately." Chelsea glanced at Charlotte Littlefield, who immediately pulled up her magazine to avoid making eye contact. Apparently the librarian wouldn't talk to the police, but she had no qualms about stirring up trouble.

Betty Wilson stood behind Chief Morgan with her arms

folded across her chest. "Well, you can just turn around and march right out."

"I gotta hand it to Betty. She's a tough one," Tabby whispered in my ear.

Betty Wilson was certainly putting up a good front, but it's easy to do when you're standing behind an armed policeman.

Chief Morgan glanced around the salon. His gaze landed on me, and his eyebrow went up.

Tabby must have noticed the look because she started fluffing my hair and spritzing it with something I suspected was water.

Betty and Chelsea glared at each other. If looks could kill, both women would have dropped dead on the spot.

Chief Morgan tried to gain control of the situation. "Look, you two, let's continue this conversation down at the precinct."

"I'm not going to any precinct. I have customers waiting and a business to run." Betty walked over to her station and started working on Amelia Cooper Lawson's hair. Some of the air returned to the room and the tension dropped a smidge when it was clear there wouldn't be a catfight in the beauty salon.

Chelsea glared a bit longer but had lost some of her steam. She turned to her brother-in-law. "Joe, what's going on?"

Chelsea may have calmed down, but Joe Kelley was still worked up. He pointed his finger in Morgan's face. "He knows who killed Whitney but refuses to make an arrest."

"We don't know that he killed your wife. But I'll be asking questions, and if he did kill your wife, I'll take care of it."

"You'd better. Because if you don't, then I'm going to kill Lucas Harrison." Joe wrenched his arm free and stormed out of the salon.

Chapter 22

In order to follow Joe, Chief Morgan had to pass Chelsea. But one glance at her face stopped him in his tracks. All of the blood had drained from Chelsea's face, and she was white as a ghost. "Are you okay?"

Chelsea reached out a hand and grabbed his arm. "Lucas? . . . What's he talking about?"

Chief Morgan took a deep breath. "I'd prefer not to have this conversation here. Mrs. Davis—"

"Baxter." Chelsea corrected him. Even in the middle of fainting, she had the strength to correct him.

"Ms. Baxter. I think you should sit down—" He escorted her toward one of the chairs near the window, but before her butt hit the seat, she stopped. Stood up. And turned to face Chief Morgan.

"What did he mean? Lucas Harrison would never have hurt Whitney. Why would he say that? What did he mean?"

"Mrs. Dav . . . Ms. Baxter, please. You don't look well, and I really think you need to—" Chief Morgan tried to gently coax Chelsea into the seat.

Betty Wilson had apparently regrouped and was ready for round two. She marched over to the two and, with one hand on her hip, frowned at Chelsea. "Oh no you don't. You can just escort her right on out the door, Chief. There's no room in the *harem* for people like her."

"Holy cow! This is good. *The Real Housewives of Crosbyville, Indiana.* Who would have thought a small town could have so much drama?" Tabby whispered.

Chief Morgan looked like a lost puppy. I was always a sucker for puppies.

I hopped up and walked over to the group at the front of the shop. "Chelsea, why don't you let me take you to my aunt's diner for a cup of tea."

She looked ready to resist, but what strength she had was gone. I estimated she was about ten seconds from a complete meltdown.

I put one arm around her waist and whispered, "I'll explain everything once we're away from prying eyes."

Chapter 23

The desperate look in Chelsea's eyes combined with her weakened state were probably the only things that gave me the courage to approach her, considering how much she hated me. The shock she'd just received was probably the only thing that allowed her to accept my help.

"Leave Bailey with me. You can swing by to get him later," Tabby volunteered.

"Thanks."

She winked. "Win-win."

I didn't know what she meant by that, but I suspected that Tabby hoped she'd get the inside scoop when I came back for Bailey, but I didn't have time to explain I had no intention of betraying a confidence or the deal I'd made earlier with Chelsea.

Chelsea didn't say anything while I drove to the diner. She looked pale and ready to leap out of the car any minute, so I was glad the ride was short.

When we entered and sat down, Aunt Agatha seemed surprised to see the two of us together, but one look at Chelsea told her this was no time for jokes.

She assessed the situation, brought a steaming-hot cup of tea, and set it in front of Chelsea. "This is strong and hot. It looks like you've had a shock, so I put quite a bit of sugar in it. Now, you drink it."

Chelsea sat and stared as though she didn't understand English, but Aunt Agatha wasn't one to be ignored.

"Hey. You drink that tea. Or do you need me to pour some down your throat?" Aunt Agatha gave Chelsea a stern look, but her lips smiled.

"I'll drink it." Chelsea picked up the cup and took a sip. She winced as the sugary liquid went down her throat, but she forced a smile and took another sip before setting her cup down.

Aunt Agatha gave me a nod and then went back to work, leaving us to talk in peace.

After a few moments, Chelsea leaned across the table. "What did he mean?"

She didn't have to explain who *he* was. I knew she was talking about Joe Kelley. I was probably one of the few people who knew *why* she was taking this so hard.

"You know, don't you?" she asked. "Tell me. Don't sugarcoat it. Just tell me."

I took a deep breath and told Chelsea that Betty Wilson

and Joe were having an affair and that Betty had hired someone to investigate Whitney. When confronted by the police, she must have revealed the name of Whitney's lover. It's the only way that Joe could have found out Whitney was having an affair with Lucas Harrison.

"She's a liar." Chelsea jolted upright as though she'd been struck by lightning and spit the words out with venom. But the burst of energy left as quickly as it came, and she crumpled back against the seat.

I waited. "She hired a detective to investigate."

She looked at me. "No. I don't believe that. I know my sister. We were close. She wouldn't . . ." She shook herself the way Bailey did after a bath. "No. It wasn't Lucas. I know it wasn't. Are you sure that's what that woman said?"

I nodded. Chelsea had been through a lot in a short period of time. Her sister was murdered. She'd learned not only that her brother-in-law was having an affair, but that her lover was most likely also having an affair with her sister. That'd be enough to make anyone's head spin. I wouldn't wish this series of events on my worst enemy, who was probably Chelsea. In a moment of sisterhood and solidarity, I reached out a hand and squeezed hers.

Chelsea snatched her hand away as though she'd been stung by a viper. "Don't touch me."

Okay. Not everyone is into touching. I put my hands under the table. "I'm sorry. I just wanted to say that I'm sorry about . . . everything. If there's anything I can do to help, please—"

"Help? How can you possibly help me? Can you bring

back my sister? Can you roll back time? Can you . . ." Her voice had crescendoed then tapered down to a whisper.

"I'm sorry."

She glared at me. "Well, you can save your sympathy. I don't need it." She grabbed her purse and slid from the bench. "I'm not the person who is going to need sympathy. Save your pity for Lucas Harrison. He's going to need it. I'm going to kill him."

Chapter 24

*C*helsea stormed out of the diner.

I contemplated going after her, but you didn't have to be psychic to know that was the last thing she would want.

Aunt Agatha sat in the seat Chelsea had vacated. "You okay?"

I nodded.

"You wanna talk about it?"

I shook my head. "Actually, I want to go get Bailey and just spend some time with him."

"Then, I think that's exactly what you should do." She patted my hand. "And I love your hair."

So much had happened in the last twenty-four hours, I'd completely forgotten that Aunt Agatha hadn't seen my new hairstyle. We chatted for a few minutes, and then I drove back to the salon.

Chief Morgan was gone, and everything looked pretty much the same as it had yesterday—normal.

Tabby was sitting on the floor while Bailey lay on his back with his paws in the air while she rubbed his belly. His tongue was hanging out and his eyes were rolled back in his head. He looked so goofy, I couldn't help but smile.

"Hey, what's going on here?" I put my hands on my hips.

Bailey glanced in my direction, but otherwise he didn't move.

Tabby laughed and then got up. "We've just been waiting for you to get back. Cruella de Vil came for her car and then sped off like Batman coming out of the Batcave."

I glanced around. "Chief Morgan?"

"He left not long after you did." She narrowed her gaze and tilted her head to the side. "Was he the policeman you had the date with? He's cute."

I felt the heat rise up my neck and quickly shook my head. "No. That's not . . . We're not . . . No."

"Hmm. Methinks the lady doth protest too much," Tabby whispered to Bailey.

"I don't know what you're talking about. We're not even friends. In fact, Chief of Police Gilbert Morgan would probably like nothing better than to arrest me." I slumped in the chair.

"Oh, honey, what's going on?" Tabby asked.

Part of me wanted nothing more than to unburden my soul to Tabby, but another part realized that I didn't know much about her. We'd met only yesterday, and she was so open and honest with me that I couldn't trust that she wouldn't talk. In fact, she'd done nothing but share since I'd met her. I didn't think she was involved in Whitney's murder, but I wasn't sure her partner, Carla, wasn't. Besides, if Chief Morgan found out I'd talked about the investigation, he *would* have me arrested. So, I changed tactics. I deliberately misunderstood her question. "My date was with another policeman. His name is Mark, but they call him 'Pitbull.'"

"I think I'd like a guy named Pitbull . . . Well, if I liked guys." Tabby smiled.

"He's big, covered in tattoos, rides a motorcycle, and looks like he'd fit better behind bars rather than outside of them."

"Now I know I'd like Pitbull."

"He was really nice, and I do like him, but . . ."

"But he's not Chief Gilbert Morgan?"

I took a deep breath. "I like him as a friend, but . . ."

"He doesn't make your liver quiver?"

I gazed at Tabby. "Liver quiver?"

"Yeah, you know, that fluttering feeling inside when he looks at you, like you just swallowed a box of butterflies. Or, when he kisses you, you feel like your toes are going to curl up in your shoes." She closed her eyes and tilted her face to the ceiling.

"No, he doesn't make my liver quiver or my toes curl." I laughed.

"Then he isn't the one."

"Is that how you feel about Carla?" I asked.

A big smile broke out and her face lit up. "Yep. That's how I knew she was *the one*."

"Congratulations. Not everyone finds that special person. You're lucky."

She nodded. "I am lucky. Now, you've got the perfect hair. We just need to help Chief Morgan recognize how special you are."

We talked about dating for a bit, but I told her I needed to go. I glanced around. "Where's Betty?"

"She was so upset, that she left not long after you did. She finished Amelia Cooper Lawson's hair and then canceled the rest of her appointments today." She leaned close to my ear. "I think there's trouble in paradise, if you know what I mean."

"Trouble? What kind of trouble?" I asked.

"That's right, you missed the early fireworks. Well, before you got here, that Chief Morgan came in to talk to Betty, and she called Joe Kelley for moral support, so she said. But, I'll bet you a free perm that if she knew how things would end, she wouldn't have called him."

"Why?"

"Chief Morgan asked her about the private detective she'd hired in front of Joe Kelley. He didn't know she'd done that. So, then he got angry."

"Why would he care?"

She shrugged. "No idea, but he didn't like the idea of 'spying' on his wife. Well, I can tell you Betty didn't take kindly to that. So, they were yelling at each other, and Betty said, 'You never intended to leave your wife. You just wanted to have your cake and eat it, too.' And then Joe got mad and said that Betty was a grown woman, and she knew he was married when she'd started dating him."

"Wow!"

Tabby nodded. "It was ugly and loud. And then when he found out that Whitney was having an affair with Lucas Harrison, well, he just exploded and that's when you got here."

Tabby and I dissected the conversation until we'd removed all the meat from the bone and there was nothing left to discuss. Eventually, Tabby's next client came in, and Bailey and I made our exit.

It was late afternoon, and I still hadn't written one word on my book. But there was still something that I needed to do first. I drove Bailey to the park for his promised walk and considered everything I'd learned today.

At the park, Bailey put his nose to the ground and headed for the maze. I was a little reluctant but realized that the odds of finding another dead body were pretty slim. Besides, it was one of our favorite places to walk. I couldn't allow fear to hold me back.

I pulled back on his leash. "Whoa, boy. Slow down."

Bailey's response was to continue on his path, even if it meant dragging me along.

I adjusted my grip on the leash and was just about to plant my feet and give him a tug when he lurched forward and bolted around a hedge. Zigging and zagging, we flew deeper and deeper into the maze.

"Bailey, stop!"

Months of obedience training meant that despite an occasional stubborn streak, he was usually obedient and obeyed commands. Still, my conscious mind didn't expect him to listen, so when he stopped suddenly after turning a corner, I was shocked. Momentum carried me forward until I collided with a solid wall.

"Oof! You okay?"

I looked up into the face of what I'd initially taken to be a wall but was actually Chief Morgan. I could feel the warmth of his breath on my face as he glanced down into my eyes.

My knees buckled and I stumbled backward. I would have fallen if he hadn't wrapped his arms around me to steady me.

"I'm sorry . . . my dog . . ." I glanced around for Bailey in an attempt to find something else to look at other than Chief Morgan's dark eyes.

Bailey calmly stood by my side as though he had no idea why I was careening through the middle of a maze at top speed without looking.

"That's a lot of dog for a small woman. You might want to consider getting—"

"What? A chihuahua? I'm perfectly capable of handling my dog, thank you very much." I glared. "Just because I'm a woman and shor—vertically challenged, doesn't mean that I'm not capable of handling a big dog."

He raised an eyebrow. "I didn't mean—"

"What? To insult me with sexist comments by implying that because I'm a *small woman* I'm not able to manage my dog. Well, I'll have you know—"

He raised his hands in surrender. "I only meant that a muscular dog like a bloodhound can be a lot, especially when they're on the scent. They can be difficult for *anyone* to handle and that getting a harness might make it easier. That's all."

I felt the blood rush to my head. "Oh . . . I'm sorry. Yes, we have a harness, but I left it in the car."

After a few seconds of awkward silence, he turned his attention to Bailey. "Hello again, Bailey." He reached down and scratched his ear.

Bailey's tail wagged, his butt wiggled, and eventually when he couldn't stand it anymore, he got up on his back legs, wrapped his paws around the sheriff's waist, and placed his head on his chest.

I watched for a few moments and then cleared my throat. "Would you two like a few moments alone?"

Chief Morgan threw back his head and laughed. He gave Bailey a final pat and stood up. "No, ma'am, that won't be necessary. I was just looking for my daughter. Have you seen Hannah?"

"No. Is she missing?"

He glanced around. "She was supposed to come straight home after school, but when I stopped by on my break, she wasn't there. I always call her after school, but she didn't answer. I thought maybe she was still at school."

Bailey nudged my leg.

I shook my head. "I'm sure she's fine. Did you try calling some of her friends?"

"She hasn't made many friends here . . . yet."

I noticed a vein pulsing on the side of his head and his jaw clenched.

"I'm sure she's fine." I forced a smile.

Bailey nudged my leg again. This time, he nearly knocked me over. When I looked down, he barked and whimpered.

Chief Morgan stared at Bailey. "Is he a working scent hound?"

I picked up what he was suggesting. "Of course, but he'd need something with Hannah's scent." That's when I noticed the pink sweater he had in his hand.

He held the sweater up and his eyes asked a question.

I nodded and he placed the sweater to Bailey's nose.

Bailey took a nice long sniff.

"Bailey, *find*," I said.

"Woof." He took one last long sniff and then put his head down and headed deeper into the maze.

Normally, I'm confident in Bailey's ability, but there was the slim possibility that he was on the trail of a stray bacon sandwich or a hot dog that someone dropped in the maze rather than a lost girl. After all, he had been headed into the maze long before he sniffed Hannah's sweater. Nevertheless, I loosened my grip on the leash and decided to trust his instincts as I followed my dog.

Nose to the ground, Bailey followed a trail that I knew led to the center and the fountain.

A few moments later, we entered the center of the

maze. Bailey headed straight for the fountain. On the backside of the large concrete centerpiece, a figure sat on the ground, propped against the base of the fountain. I heard the sigh of relief as Chief Morgan caught sight of Hannah.

Bailey licked her face until she could barely breathe and burst out laughing.

"Hannah, what are you doing? You're supposed to be at home." Chief Morgan marched to his daughter's side.

"I'm sorry, Dad. I just sat down to finish reading this book and I guess I forgot the time. What time is it?"

"It's nearly five o'clock. Didn't you hear your phone?"

She pulled a pair of earbuds out of her ears and hung her head. "I'm sorry, I was listening to music and engrossed in my book." She held up her copy of *The Case of the Missing Maltese* as proof.

Chief Morgan gave his daughter a stern look that didn't bode well. "You know the rules. Now, let's go."

She shoved her book into her backpack, gave Bailey a hug, and then glanced up at her dad. "I'm sorry."

I took a deep breath. "Chief Morgan, I have some new information that—"

His eyes narrowed and he looked like a volcano ready to explode. He opened his mouth, but before he could erupt, his cell phone rang. He glanced at the number and quickly excused himself. He stepped a few feet away and turned away from Hannah and me.

I put an arm around Hannah.

After a few moments, he returned. His face was granite, and he was rigid and intense. "I've got to go." Chief

Morgan glanced at Hannah. "Can I trust you to go straight home this time?"

"Maybe she could come home with me. I can help her with her homework, and then you can pick her up when you're done."

Hannah's face lit up. "Can I, Dad? Can I? Please?"

Chief Morgan didn't look as though he wanted to agree, but he was caught.

"Then, we can talk when you come pick her up. I really do need to talk to you," I said.

He gazed at me. "Why do I think I'm not going to want to hear what you have to tell me?"

I tried to look innocent, but I never was good at acting.

His phone rang again, and he didn't have time to argue with me. "Fine. I may be a little late. So, that would actually work out well for me. If you don't mind."

Hannah cheered.

"Of course I don't mind."

He kissed Hannah on the head. Turned to me. "Thank you." Patted Bailey on the head. "I owe you one, boy." And then he answered his call and hurriedly left the maze.

The last words I heard were "Where was the body found?"

Chapter 25

I drove home while Hannah sat in the back seat of the car with Bailey. She talked nonstop about nothing in particular from the time I left the park until I pulled up to the house. School was boring. Boys were dumb. Dogs were cool, but Bailey was the best. She was obviously excited, and I was thrilled to see it. She was completely different from the quiet, shy girl who barely opened her mouth in the classroom.

Once inside, she sat at the kitchen table and did her homework while Bailey lay at her feet.

I had planned to write, but I certainly couldn't write with company. I decided to cook. Cooking wasn't my love language, like it was for my aunt Agatha. She not only loved cooking, but she loved to feed others. I cooked out of necessity. When I went away to college, I knew how to make a grilled cheese sandwich and how to heat up frozen pizza. After graduation, Aunt Agatha taught me a few simple meals that were great for a single woman on a tight budget. Ground beef was fairly inexpensive and extremely versatile. I could make spaghetti, tacos, meat loaf, chili, shepherd's pie, sloppy joes, or hamburgers—I always had ground beef on hand.

"Hannah, do you like spaghetti?"

"Yep. I love spaghetti. Is that what you're making? Can I help?"

"When you finish your homework, I'll let you make the salad."

"I don't know how to do this," she whined. "It's too hard."

"What are you working on?"

"Conjunctions." She tossed her pencil on the table, folded her arms across her chest and pouted.

"*Conjunction Junction, what's your function?*" I sang.

She sat up. "What are you singing?"

"When I was younger, my aunt Agatha used to sing all these songs that she learned when she was younger. There used to be a program called *Schoolhouse Rock*. It made learning fun."

I pulled out my phone and searched for the *Schoolhouse Rock* song for conjunctions.

Hannah watched in wonder as the 1970s tune played, and then she replayed it. She played the video again and again until she could sing along. After a half hour, she picked up her pencil and tackled her homework again. This time, I heard her singing along as she wrote. After fifteen minutes, she put her pencil down. "Miss Cummings, would you check my homework?"

"Absolutely." I wiped my hands on a dishcloth and walked over to the table. I glanced over the sheet.

Hannah sat anxiously biting her fingernail while I examined her work. When I put down the paper, she said, "Well?"

"It looks perfect."

Her face lit up. "Yay!" She hopped up and danced around the table with Bailey. When they were finished, she flopped back down. "That song is catchy. It made it easy for me to remember. Are there other songs?"

"Oh yes. There's grammar, history, social studies, math, and science."

"I'm going to watch all of them. This was actually fun."

"School can be fun. This is just an aid to help you remember. When I was in school, one of my teachers said he'd pay ten dollars to the student who could recite the preamble to the Constitution. I raised my hand, stood up, and did it right there."

"Did you win the ten dollars?"

"Yep." I nodded. "Now, do you have any more homework?"

She shook her head. "That was the last of it."

"Good. Then, go wash your hands and you can help me with the salad, unless you'd rather go outside with Bailey?"

She waffled for a moment, but eventually decided she wanted to help.

When she joined me, I put one of my aprons on her. I had to wrap the straps around a few times, but eventually, I got the job done.

"What are you doing?" Hannah asked, looking at the stove.

"Browning the meat for the spaghetti sauce."

"My dad just opens a jar."

I chuckled. "My aunt Agatha would never approve of spaghetti sauce from a jar. However, if I'm in a hurry, I sometimes use the jar, too, but I think we have time to make it from scratch."

She watched carefully and asked good questions.

"Can I try?" Hannah Morgan was more of a cooking enthusiast than I was at her age.

I chopped the onions and bell peppers and supervised while she added seasonings, tomato paste, and tomato sauce.

The sauce simmered while we added butter and garlic to some crusty French bread and prepped the greens for the salad. Nothing fancy, but it always tasted great. The great thing about spaghetti is that it's fast, and dinner was done cooking in no time.

The doorbell rang and Bailey barked and ran to the door. Unlike when the mailman rings and my normally calm, tame bloodhound switches into Cujo, he got a good whiff of my visitor and his tail wagged. He pranced in his *I'm so excited to see you, I just want to lick your face* kind of way.

I opened the door. I was half expecting Chief Morgan.

Mark Alexander stood on my porch.

My smile slid off my face, but I caught myself and forced it back up.

Then Mark handed me a large bouquet of flowers and I didn't have to force my lips upward, they moved on their own.

"Hi. I hope I'm not interrupting anything," Mark said. "I just wanted to check on you. You seemed pretty down last night, and I wanted to make sure you were okay."

For an undercover policeman, he was a terrible liar, but I found that rather endearing.

"That's sweet. Please come in." I opened the door wider for him to come in.

One step over the threshold and he was pounced on by a one hundred–pound bloodhound and a fifty-pound eight-year-old.

"Uncle Mark!" Hannah took a flying leap and threw herself into the detective's arms.

"Whoa. Hey, munchkin. What're you doing here?" He glanced around. "Where's your dad?"

Hannah wiggled down and swung Mark's hand as she explained how she ended up spending the evening here with Bailey and me in a way that turned a simple situation into an adventure. "Uncle Mark, I left school but on my way home, I was kidnapped by aliens who wanted me to teach them English so they could take over the planet."

"How terrifying." Mark looked shocked. "How on earth did you manage to get away?"

"Just when they were about to send me into their space-ship, I was saved when Bailey the Fearless Bloodhound found where the aliens had hidden me."

"Wow. You must have been very brave to escape aliens," Mark said.

"No, I wasn't. It was Bailey. He's the brave one. And then Pris . . . I mean Miss Cummings, brought my dad and he locked up all of the aliens in his jail." Hannah sighed. "But, before we could call the president of the United States and tell him to get the military here to pick up the aliens, POOF! They disappeared."

"Hannah, that was a really good story. I need your help writing the next Bailey the Bloodhound book," I said.

Hannah smiled, then turned back to Mark. "Uncle Mark, we made spaghetti. Do you wanna eat dinner with us?"

"It smells delicious, but you can't invite people to dinner at other people's homes." He glanced at me.

"There's plenty if you'd like to stay." I buried my face in my bouquet of flowers.

"Are you sure?"

"Of course."

"Yay! I can tell you all about these cool songs Miss Cummings showed me to help me with conjunctions." Hannah pulled Mark into the kitchen.

I followed behind and found a vase for my flowers and placed them on the table as a centerpiece.

"Wash your hands," I ordered. Hannah ran to the powder room off the kitchen.

"Are you sure this is okay?" Mark asked when we were alone.

"Of course. I just happened to run into Chief Morgan and Hannah in the park when I was walking Bailey. He got called away and I offered to watch Hannah while he got back to work," I explained while I set plates and silverware on the table.

"You don't owe me an explanation. I just wanted to make sure that . . . I wouldn't want to assume anything."

I stopped. "What's to assume? Now, go wash your hands for dinner."

He turned to head toward the bathroom.

"Wait."

He turned to face me.

I walked over, reached up, and kissed him.

When the surprise wore off, he returned the kiss with zeal.

"Ewww," Hannah squealed from the doorway.

Mark and I separated.

"Mark and Pris sitting in a tree. K-I-S-S-I-N-G!" Hannah sang.

Mark rushed toward her and tickled her until she gave up singing and fell onto the floor in a ball of laughter. He picked her up and carried her out of the room toward the powder room.

I thought about the kiss. It was nice, but my liver wasn't quivering, and my toes were completely straight. However, it was a nice kiss. Maybe Tabby was wrong. Maybe everyone's liver didn't quiver. Angels hadn't sung one note. The earth hadn't shaken. Maybe this was as good as it gets. If so, it wasn't bad. It had been quite enjoyable. Mark Alexander was a nice guy, and he brought me flowers.

Their laughter rang through the small carriage house

like bells from a different era. The warmth from the stove mixed with the smell of garlic, butter, and tomatoes, and my carriage house felt like a home.

Mark and Hannah returned and for the next hour, we sat and ate, talked, and laughed. The companionship felt like a cozy blanket.

Hannah was easily distracted and loved to play chase with Bailey. When they were away from the table, Mark reached across the table and clasped my hand. "I was wondering if you'd taken my advice and stayed out of Whitney Kelley's murder investigation."

"If by 'staying out,' you mean have I given up actively investigating? Then the answer is yes."

"Why do I feel like you're holding something back? Go on, spill it." He gazed at me.

I started telling him about the scene at The Big Tease and my chat with Chelsea. Mark asked a few pointed questions. "Did Chelsea really threaten Lucas Harrison?"

"Yeah, she did. But, before you lecture me about staying out of the investigation, I want you to know that I've decided to take your advice. I am going to stay out of it. I'm going to share what I know with Chief Morgan, and then I'm done." I held up both hands.

"I'm glad to hear that. I like you and I'd hate if anything happened to you," he said.

Before I could respond, the doorbell rang, and Bailey ran to the door. I got up to follow and Mark joined me.

"You shouldn't just open the door at night. It could be

an ax murderer. You really should consider getting an alarm system."

"I have an alarm system." I pointed at Bailey, who was wagging his tail like a metronome. "It must be a friend at the door or he would be lunging at it trying to rip the stranger's throat out." I opened the door and stepped back.

Chief Morgan entered. "Hello. I'm sorry I'm late. I got stuck—" He looked up and saw Mark. "Sorry, I didn't mean to interrupt, again."

"You didn't interrupt. Please come in," I said.

Bailey stood on his hind legs and licked Morgan's face.

Hannah heard her dad's voice and ran out of the kitchen and hurled herself at her father. "Dad, Dad. Uncle Mark came and we just had spaghetti and he brought flowers and then he and Pris were kiss—"

"Hannah, your father just got here. Let him catch his breath." I knew by the look on his face that he knew what she was going to say before I interrupted.

"Have you eaten?" I asked.

"No, but I don't want to intrude. I just came by to pick up Hannah. We need to go home."

"Actually, I really need to talk to you, and I think you might take it better on a full stomach. Do you like spaghetti?"

Chief Morgan rubbed the back of his neck and took a deep breath. "Sure. I like spaghetti, but you don't have to—"

"I know I don't, but I want to." I turned and walked into the kitchen. When I got to the door, I turned back and said, "Hannah, show your dad where he can wash his hands."

Mark followed me into the kitchen. "I'm going to take off. I didn't plan to stay this long anyway. I just wanted to check that you were okay."

"Okay, sure, let me see you out." I hoped my relief wasn't obvious. It was going to be hard enough to talk to Chief Morgan without him and Mark glaring at each other. I walked him to the door.

"Thank you for dinner. It was delicious."

"I'm glad you enjoyed it."

He headed for the door but turned at the last minute and grinned. "I enjoyed *everything*."

I swatted his arm and gave him a playful shove out the door.

When he was gone, I took a deep breath and headed toward the kitchen. I braced myself—I didn't think there was enough garlic bread and spaghetti in the world to prevent Chief Morgan from blowing his lid when I told him that Lucas Harrison had been having an affair with both Chelsea and Whitney.

Chapter 26

While Chief Morgan ate dinner, Hannah and I made cookies. When I was a kid, Aunt Agatha and I used to make an easy cookie recipe that had only four ingredients. We whipped up the dough in record time, and by the time Morgan was done eating, the first batch of cookies was coming out of the oven.

Hot peanut butter cookies and a bowl of vanilla ice cream were a fast, easy way to cap off the meal. Aunt Agatha always claimed food could work miracles. I prayed she was right. Based on the "oohs" and "aahs" I got, I knew I'd won over at least one member of the Morgan family.

"Yum! These are the best cookies ever," Hannah said.

"You did a fantastic job," I said, chuckling.

Chief Morgan wasn't as enthusiastic in his praise as his daughter was, but he cleaned his plate and ate at least a half-dozen cookies. When he finished, he turned to his daughter. "Miss Cummings and I need to talk."

I stood up and picked up my iPad from the counter. "Hannah, why don't you and Bailey go in the living room and watch more *Schoolhouse Rock?*"

"Woo-hoo! Let's go, Bailey." Hannah and Bailey raced to the living room.

Alone with Chief Morgan, I was nervous and fidgety. I tried to relieve my anxiety by cleaning.

"Miss Cummings. I want—"

"Call me Pris."

"Pris, I want to thank you for taking care of Hannah this afternoon. She had a wonderful time, and I'm grateful. I also want to thank you for dinner. It was delicious. I don't often get home-cooked meals . . . unless I pick them up from your aunt's diner." He grinned. "Tonight, sitting at the table with my daughter was really nice, and I want you to know that I appreciate it."

"You're welcome. I enjoyed it, too."

"Now, what is it you're avoiding telling me?" He leaned back and yawned.

"Would you like a cup of coffee?" I asked

"Actually, I would love a cup of coffee." He stood and walked over to the single-cup coffeemaker. "This is something I know how to do on my own." He picked up a mug from a rack and pulled a K-Cup from the dispenser and prepared his coffee. When it was done, he asked, "Would you like a cup?"

"Sure."

He handed me his mug and promptly made another and then we sat down.

Sitting at the table together enjoying coffee felt very intimate and comfortable. I didn't want to break the mood, but I knew what I had to do. I put down my mug and took a deep breath. "Chief Morgan, I—"

"Gilbert."

I felt myself blush but hurried on. "Gilbert, first, I need to tell you that I wasn't snooping or investigating Whitney Kelley's murder or . . . anything to do with your career. Not intentionally, anyway. I was just returning a box that Bailey found under the stairs to Lucas Harrison."

He sat up and put down his mug. "Lucas Harrison. You were there today?"

"Yes. He was the Realtor that closed the deal on this house." Gilbert drank his coffee while I told him about my trip to the real estate office and how I'd stumbled upon Lucas Harrison and Chelsea Baxter.

He put down his mug, and coffee sloshed onto the table. "Chelsea Baxter? You saw them?"

I nodded.

He pulled out a notepad. "I'm going to need you to tell me everything you saw and heard. *Everything.*"

I went back over everything, including Chelsea's comments about not filing a complaint against Chief Morgan if I'd promise not to tell anyone about her and Lucas Harrison. I glanced at him and hurriedly explained, "I honestly wasn't trying to get involved. I cross my heart. I had no intention of telling anyone about her and Lucas Harrison anyway. I mean, they're both adults. What they do is their business. So, I didn't feel I was doing anything wrong. Of course, now that I've told you, I'm sure she'll go forward with her complaints and try to make trouble for you, but I felt like telling you was the right thing to do."

He gazed at me so long I was afraid he was really going to blow his top. I was shocked when he said, "I probably shouldn't be telling you this, but you'll find out tomorrow morning."

I glanced at him and waited.

"You know the call I got at the park?"

I nodded.

"That was dispatch. Lucas Harrison was murdered."

Chapter 27

*I*t took several moments for the weight of the words to sink in. When they did, I felt as though I were being crushed. "Murdered? How? Who?"

"I can tell you he was strangled. As to who? I have no idea."

"Do you think his murder is connected to Whitney's?"

"Probably. They were having an affair. They were both strangled. I don't have proof yet, but I'm hopeful the forensic team will find evidence that will tie the two murders together."

I wanted to ask a hundred questions but didn't want to press my luck. He wasn't yelling at me and that was a good thing. Unfortunately, I must not have done a very good job of hiding my thoughts.

"You have questions?"

I nodded.

He sighed. "Go ahead."

"Really?"

He nodded. "Payment for the meal and babysitting." He hid a grin behind his mug as he took a sip of coffee.

"You don't have to pay me for spending time with Hannah. She's a great kid and she's welcome here, anytime. Plus, you don't owe me anything for dinner. It was my pleasure. But, since you're willing to answer questions, do you have any suspects?"

"I can't answer that. This is an open investigation and while I don't believe you killed Whitney Kelley or Lucas Harrison, you are still involved."

"I might not have liked Whitney Kelley, but I certainly didn't have a reason to kill Lucas Harrison. But I know there are at least three people who did."

"Who?"

"Betty Wilson, Joe Kelley, and Chelsea Baxter. All three of them knew about Whitney and Lucas. And Joe and Chelsea both threatened to kill him just earlier today."

"So, why would Betty Wilson want Lucas Harrison dead?"

That took me a bit longer. "No idea. Unless he found out about the private investigator and was afraid that she knew more damaging things about him. Like maybe Betty found out he was involved in some shady real-estate deals or . . . I don't know."

He chuckled. "Damaging things? You've been watching *Perry Mason*?"

"No. Maybe. Okay, yes, but that doesn't mean it's a bad idea. I mean, Perry Mason only lost one or two cases in his entire career."

He laughed. "That's because he wasn't real."

"What does that have to do with anything? Perry Mason would have Paul Drake investigate, and they always uncovered all kinds of skeletons that people were willing to kill to keep hidden. Plus, Whitney Kelley had already threatened to uncover skeletons. Maybe, if the killer heard that and knew that since Whitney was having an affair with Lucas, she might have told him the secrets she knew. You know, pillow talk." I forced myself to ignore the heat I knew was rising up my neck and kept talking. "The killer may have thought their secrets were safe after Whitney was killed, but when he or she found out about Lucas, maybe they thought Lucas knew the secrets, too?"

He shrugged. "Maybe."

"Or, what if Whitney was blackmailing someone?"

"What makes you say that?"

I thought for a few moments. "Remember that jewelry that I told you Whitney had?"

He nodded.

"It looked expensive. I think it was real. If it was, then I can't see how Joe Kelley could have afforded it. Did you ask him about it?"

"He knew she had jewelry, but he claimed he didn't know anything about it."

"Did you ask Chelsea?"

"She knew Whitney had nice jewelry and she confirmed

the pieces you mentioned, but she didn't know when her sister got them," he said.

"If Whitney was blackmailing someone, then she could have bought it with the ill-gotten gains."

He smiled. "Ill-gotten gains?"

"You know. The money. Loot. Payola."

He nearly spit out his coffee. "*Payola?*"

"Well, we don't know what Whitney had on the person, so it could have been payola."

Gilbert finished his coffee and stood up. "You have an active imagination, but now that your curiosity is appeased, I would be remiss in my duties if I did not caution you, yet again. Please, stay out—"

"I know. Stay out of your investigation." I stood up and took the two mugs to the sink. Like a storm that rolls in after a beautiful summer day, the atmospheric pressure shifted. The quiet, peaceful camaraderie that existed moments earlier was gone. A wind of exclusion and separatism blew in, which left me feeling like an outcast.

Gilbert moved behind me and I felt his presence like an electric shock from a light socket. He turned me around to face him.

I kept my eyes averted to shield my emotions but he lifted my chin, so I was forced to look in his eyes. I gazed into his eyes and for a moment, a brief second in time, the veil was lifted. What I saw made me catch my breath.

As quickly as the veil was opened, it was closed. He pushed back a strand of hair that had fallen in front of my face and tucked it behind my ear. His finger lingered a few beats longer than was necessary, but then he quickly dropped his hand. He took a deep breath and stepped back.

We gazed at each other and then he turned and walked out of the room.

I stood at the sink, staring at the small kitchen, which suddenly felt cold and empty. *Yep. My liver was definitely quivering.* I took a deep breath and waited for my toes to uncurl and then followed him out of the room.

Chapter 28

I blamed my lack of sleep on the fact that I don't usually drink coffee late at night. I refused to believe that it had anything to do with Chief Gilbert Morgan. In spite of the fact that I couldn't stop thinking about him, I pushed thoughts of Gilbert Morgan aside, rolled over, and sighed. My tossing and turning must have annoyed Bailey because around three in the morning, he got up, jumped down from the bed, and curled up in his dog bed to sleep.

"Fine," I said, but he ignored me and was snoring in seconds. My sarcasm was wasted on him.

Just as the sun rose, I finally dozed off from exhaustion. It felt like I'd just drifted off when Bailey started barking and I was shocked awake.

Bailey's bark started off short and low. But it intensified

quickly into a deep howl. He ran to the window, got up on his hind legs, and pushed aside the curtains. Looking outside, he howled.

"You have got to be kidding me." I took the pillow and put it over my head and prayed that whatever critter had attracted his attention would make a quick exit.

It didn't.

Bailey continued to bark and when I ignored him, he jumped on the bed and walked on my back.

"Hey, get off. You're heavy." I rolled over and forced him to step off.

Bailey jumped off the bed and ran to the bedroom door.

"Look. I've only had a few minutes of sleep. Can you hold it?"

He howled.

I guess that's a no.

I sat up and tried appealing to his compassionate nature. "I'm exhausted. How about you go inside just this once? I know, we worked hard to make sure you always went outside, but today is an exception. I'll clean it up later." I flopped back down on the bed.

Bailey ran back to the bed and gazed at me.

I could feel drool running onto my arm and knew there was no way he was going to let me go back to sleep. "Fine." I pulled the covers back and got out of bed. It wasn't until we were downstairs in the kitchen that I realized his behavior wasn't his normal *There's a squirrel running in my yard and I need to go out and show it who's boss.* I glanced at Bailey.

"What's wrong, boy?"

He ran to the back door, barking and circling in a way that I'd rarely seen him do before.

That's when I heard a noise outside. "There's someone in the backyard."

For a moment, Bailey stopped barking and gave me a look that I interpreted as *Duh, what do you think I've been trying to tell you?* Then he gave a deep howl, got on his back legs, and started scratching at the door.

I hopped around looking for my cell phone for a few moments before I remembered that I'd left it upstairs. I was alone in my kitchen with no shoes, no cell phone, and no weapon, clad in the sleep shirt Marcie bought me—it had a picture from my Adventures of Bailey the Bloodhound book and read,

I WRITE.
WHAT'S YOUR SUPERPOWER?

I took several deep breaths to settle my nerves, grabbed a marble rolling pin, counted to three, and then opened the back door and released the bloodhound. I stood in the door-way, holding my rolling pin like a Louisville Slugger, ready to clobber anyone that escaped Bailey's assault.

Bailey charged out of the door.

Chapter 29

I expected to hear screams and a raging battle and braced myself against the commotion that would indicate the battle had begun.

A figure stood at the back fence with his back to me.

Right as Bailey approached, the figure turned and faced him.

Bailey skidded to a stop, stood on his back legs, and licked every square inch of Gilbert Morgan's face.

Gilbert walked toward me. He smiled. "I'm sorry. Did I startle you?"

Did you startle me? "No, of course not. What gives you that idea?"

Morgan came inside while Bailey discovered Hannah at the back of the garden, and the two of them hugged and played a game of catch-me-if-you-can.

Standing by the coffeemaker, I took down a mug and quickly made a cup of coffee. When it finished brewing, I handed it to Gilbert and made another for myself.

"We wanted to do something to thank you for dinner last night. Hannah thought it might be good if we worked on cleaning up your garden." He sipped his coffee. "I'm sorry if we woke you, but I have to work and wanted to do this before heading into the station."

"That was . . . really nice. Technically, you didn't wake me. Bailey must have heard you and went crazy. So, he's the one I should be angry with, not you." I sipped my coffee. "Thank you."

He sipped his coffee and glanced at me over the top of his mug, barely able to keep from laughing.

"What?" I asked.

"Nothing. It's just . . ." He picked up the marble rolling pin I'd placed on the counter and held it up. "Do you have a license for this?" he joked.

"That rolling pin is marble, and I'll have you know I broke the record for RBIs and home runs at the Indiana State Softball Championships, and I finished my senior year with a .515 batting average, a .646 on-base percentage, a 1.212 slugging percentage, along with thirty-four home runs and eighty-five RBIs. I used to be a catcher, but I moved to shortstop. Marcie, my best friend, was an excellent pitcher."

"Impressive." He grinned. "Especially when you're barefoot."

It took me a while, but when the realization that I wasn't

wearing anything but a nightshirt with no makeup and my hair pulled up into a weird topknot bun to protect my curls, I screamed, tried to cover myself as I turned, and ran upstairs. When I got to my bedroom, I could hear Gilbert laughing.

It took longer for me to get over the embarrassment than it did to get clothed. For several minutes after I was dressed, I sat on the bed and tried to stop the flush that I could feel in my flaming cheeks. Hunger forced me out of hiding. I took a deep breath and marched back downstairs.

Gilbert, Hannah, and Bailey were outside. Gilbert had pruned all the trees and shrubs and was collecting the limbs into a pile. Hannah and Bailey were raking away years of decomposed leaves, twigs, and dead grass in between bouts of tag. Well, Hannah was raking. Bailey was running around in circles and pouncing on leaves.

I watched for a few moments. A quick glance in my refrigerator confirmed that I had the ingredients for a breakfast casserole. I browned the sausage, chopped onions, and then mixed the spices and eggs. I combined everything and put it in the oven to bake. Then I grabbed garbage bags from the closet and went outside to join the party.

By the time the breakfast casserole was done, my back garden looked neat and tidy. I went inside, washed my hands, and then made a quick fruit salad.

Hannah and Morgan cleaned up in the powder room while I set the table.

"Yum! That smells good and I'm starving," Hannah said.

"Good. I hope you like breakfast casserole."

"I've never had it before." Hannah glanced at her plate.

"Sure you have. It's sausage, eggs, and bread. I just mix it together and bake it. Oh, and cheese."

"I love cheese." Hannah took a bite and smiled. "Mmm. This is good stuff. Could you teach me how to make it?"

"Sure. It's pretty easy."

"Great. Then I can make it for Dad and me sometime. We can have breakfast casserole instead of cereal." She grinned and shoveled food in her mouth.

Morgan's smile didn't reach his eyes. He ate in silence for several minutes.

When we finished breakfast, Morgan went back outside to finish up while Hannah and I cleaned up, and Bailey finished breakfast and curled up for his early-morning nap.

"How did you learn to cook?" Hannah asked. "Did your mom teach you?"

"No. My mom died when I was a baby. That's when I came to live in Crosbyville with my aunt Agatha."

"You didn't grow up with a mom, either."

I shook my head. "No, but my aunt loves me and took great care of me. Just like your dad loves and cares for you. My aunt loves to cook. She taught me how to make a few things for basic survival before I went away to college. It's a lot less expensive and healthier to cook at home than to eat out all of the time."

"Dad doesn't really know how to cook. He knows how to grill. He cooks steaks and hamburgers, but he's really busy and I want to learn to cook."

"Well, if your dad says it's okay, I can teach you how to

make a few things. Or . . ." I grinned. "I can take you to the diner and Aunt Agatha can teach you."

Her face lit up. "Do you think she would teach me how to make carrot cake? I love her carrot cake. And homemade bread."

I laughed. "I'm sure she would. Actually, bread isn't hard. I know how to make a simple bread that only has four ingredients. I'm sure you could do it, too."

She bounced up and down. "Can we do it now?"

"It's easy, but it takes time. The dough has to sit for twelve hours."

Her face drooped. "Ooh."

"I'll tell you what. We'll go ahead and whip up the dough and maybe your dad will bring you over tomorrow to try the finished product."

"Yay!"

I pulled out the ingredients and we quickly mixed up the dough, covered the bowl in plastic, and set it aside to let the yeast do its thing.

"That's it?" Hannah asked.

"It's going to make a crusty bread, not the soft white bread that you buy in the store and use for sandwiches. This is going to be a hearty bread." I gazed in her eyes. "It would go great with a big bowl of soup or chili."

"What are you doing tonight?" Hannah asked.

"I'm going to an art showing with a friend."

"Uncle Mark?" Hannah asked.

"No. My best friend, Marcella . . . Miss Rutherford, your art teacher."

"I like Miss Rutherford. She's so pretty."

"She is pretty," I agreed. Something in Hannah's manner made me ask, "Do you have a best friend?"

"I used to, in Chicago. But I don't have any friends here. Well, only Ben."

"Ben? Who's he?" I asked.

Hannah blushed. "Ben Miller. Sometimes, a lady comes to clean our house. Her name is Ruth. She's Amish. Ben works on the farm. Sometimes, she brings Ben with her, and we play. Sometimes she brings treats, too."

"That's nice. I'm glad Ben is your friend."

"Ben goes to an Amish school. I don't think he's supposed to play with me." She picked at a nonexistent piece of lint on her shirt.

"You know that doesn't have anything to do with you, right? The Amish have their own beliefs and culture."

She sighed. "I know, but I don't see why we can't go to the park and play."

I wasn't equipped to explain to this sad little girl the reason her friend couldn't openly play with her, but I did my best. "Aren't there any other kids at school that you play with?"

"Sometimes Clarice Kelley and I played together, but I don't think her mom liked me very much."

Whitney Kelley didn't like anyone very much, except Whitney Kelley. "I'm sure she liked you just fine. Clarice's mom died, too. I'll bet she might like a little company."

Hannah's face lit up. "Do you think so?"

"I do, and I'll tell you what, we still have about a dozen

of those peanut butter cookies left. When someone has a death in the family, it's common to take food. Maybe your dad would let you go and take her some cookies."

She ran outside to her dad and rushed back in like a tornado, failing to properly close the back door.

"Hannah, close the door," I said.

She scurried back and gave it a hard push. "He said we could. In fact, he said he would take me to the diner, and we could buy a pie." Her face fell. "But I still think she'd like the peanut butter cookies."

I laughed. "Well, I still want you to take them with you. I've got to watch my weight, and having a dozen peanut butter cookies in the house isn't good for helping me stick to a diet."

By midday, Gilbert and Hannah were gone. My back garden looked amazing. I had dough rising in a bowl. And, although I hadn't slept much, I felt a warm glow inside that had nothing to do with the garden or the bread and a lot to do with Crosbyville's chief of police and his adorable daughter.

Chapter 30

*M*arcie came over and helped me finish unpacking, and then we hung wallpaper in the guest bedroom. I'm not a big fan of wallpaper, but I had to admit the blue floral pattern she picked added drama and looked amazing.

I filled her in on Mark, Gilbert, Lucas, Chelsea—everything. Marcie was my oldest and closest friend, and I couldn't hide anything from her even if I wanted to. So, I didn't try.

She picked up on the important silences and gaps quickly. "So, you kissed Mark and felt nothing."

"Nope. In fact, it kind of felt like I was kissing my brother. My liver didn't quiver in the slightest."

Marcie had taken that exact moment to take a drink of lemonade. She spit lemonade down the front of her shirt and nearly choked. When she finished coughing, she turned to me. "And the fact that your liver didn't quiver is a bad thing?"

"According to my hairstylist, Tabby, it is." I laughed and explained.

"I can't wait to meet this Tabby. She sounds hilarious."

"I think you'll like her."

After a few more moments of laughter, Marcie studied me like a specimen in a petri dish. "But Gilbert was . . . different."

"Like an electric shock, and he didn't even kiss me."

"Hmm."

"Don't hmm me. It doesn't matter what I felt. He isn't interested."

"And you're basing that on . . . ?"

"He didn't kiss me. His look said, *I'm not interested, Nancy Drew.*"

"You got all of that from a look?" She stopped squeezing bubbles out of the wallpaper to study me.

"He has expressive eyes," I said. "Besides, you missed the important part. He didn't kiss me."

"No, but he came and spent hours mowing, pruning, raking, hauling away a ton of debris, and basically turning your backyard into a place that you can use instead of a garbage dump all before starting his workday."

I gazed out of the window and smiled. "Yeah, he did."

Marcie stepped back and gave the room a critical appraisal. Satisfied, she put down her seam roller. "What do you think?"

"I love it. You did a fantastic job, and I absolutely LOVE the pattern."

Marcie smiled. "It brightens the room and even though

the room is small, I think the large print works. I'm glad you like it."

"I don't like it. I love it. Now, it's getting late. We better get dressed."

"I love art galleries, but remind me again why we're going to the Crosbyville Art Museum?"

"We're going because the gallery is featuring an exhibit by Dr. Nobles. He's a member of the school board."

"I thought you weren't getting involved in Whitney Kelley's murder," Marcie said.

"I'm not. Dr. Nobles is ninety years old. I doubt if he would have been able to strangle Whitney and certainly not Lucas." I shrugged. "I guess I'm just curious."

*M*arcella had brought her clothes over so changing and getting ready was relatively quick. She was so tall and slender that even in a simple sheath dress, she looked like a runway model.

I wore a formfitting wrap dress that Marcie had convinced me to buy. The neckline plunged deeper than what I was used to, but when I twirled in front of the full-length mirror, I knew she was right, especially with my new curly hair.

Crosbyville Art Museum was in a long brick building near the town square. The building was a converted warehouse, and from one side, you got views of the St. Joseph River.

Dr. Nobles was an internationally recognized artist. His works were featured in modern museum collections throughout the world, and now he was one of Crosbyville's most distinguished residents. The hometown exhibit was well attended. Guests walked around sipping wine and looking at the paintings and sculptures.

Marcie and I slowly toured the exhibition.

Standing in front of a painting that I think was intended to be a sunset, I leaned close and whispered, "What is it?"

"His style is cubist." She then launched into a definition of cubism, Pablo Picasso, and Georges Braque, but I zoned out after a few seconds.

I was shocked to see Tabby and Carla enter the gallery. They grabbed glasses of wine and made their way over to us.

"Marcie, this is Tabby, the Natural Hair Miracle Worker." I hugged Tabby and finished the introductions. Today, Carla's hair was braided into box braids, and Marcie was impressed.

"I love your hair. Who braided it?"

She pointed to Tabby, who bowed. "Just because I'm white, doesn't mean I can't braid hair." She laughed. "Anyone can watch YouTube videos and practice." She wrapped an arm around her partner and examined her handiwork. "I think she looks great in braids. I wish she would wear her hair like this more often."

"Corporate America isn't ready for that yet. Maybe one

day. Right now, I can't afford to aggravate the old boy network too much. I just let her do it because my hair will be flat, and it'll be easy to slap a wig on top of this for one week. We leave tonight for Florida. I worked hard to get on this client's team, so I get a company-sponsored trip to Florida. I'll work at the client site for one week while Tabby lounges around the pool. Then I'm on vacation and we will spend another week enjoying the sunshine on the beach."

"Sounds great," I said.

"Especially for me. I get two weeks at the beach." Tabby shimmied and then did a quick spin.

"And we only have to pay for Tabby's flights, one week at the hotel, and food." Carla and Tabby high-fived and then clinked their wineglasses in a toast.

Tabby sipped her wine. She glanced up and nearly choked. "Who is that?"

We looked in the direction she was pointing.

"That's Mark Alexander," I said.

"Pitbull?" Marcie asked.

I nodded.

"He's cute. If I was into men, I'd be all over him," Tabby joked.

Carla frowned. "Well, it's a good thing you aren't into men."

Mark Alexander strolled slowly into the museum with Amelia Cooper Lawson on his arm. I would have been hard pressed to find two people who were more different—Mark was tall, with muscular arms covered in tattoos carrying a motorcycle helmet and a black patent-leather purse in one hand and Amelia Cooper Lawson on the other. Amelia was in her midseventies, but well preserved. She was thin, prim, and proper, dressed in a classic black-and-white Chanel suit with gold buttons. Her white hair had been curled and teased to hide any thin spots. As a descendant of the founding families, she was one of the most prominent residents of Crosbyville and oozed money with every step.

Marcie leaned close and whispered, "I'll bet she sleeps with a net on her head like my grandmother. Gram used to rip up brown paper bags and use them to curl her hair and then put a net on to hold everything in place."

Mark caught sight of me and smiled. He stopped and bowed to Amelia. However, he lost his balance and dropped both his helmet and her purse. He apologized and quickly squatted down and collected the purse and the few stray items that fell out and rolled across the floor. He replaced the items, bowed again, and handed back the purse.

Amelia patted him on the arm and then turned to greet my former boss, Dr. Freemont, the principal of Crosbyville Elementary School, who never missed an opportunity to suck up to the school board.

Mark walked over. "Hello. Fancy meeting you here."

"What a small world." I introduced Mark to everyone and then turned to look at him. "I didn't peg you as an art lover."

"I'm a man of many talents." He chuckled. "Actually, I'm working, but don't tell anyone." He put a finger to his lips.

I was about to respond when Tabby gasped. She reached across and grabbed Mark's arm and pulled it toward her. "Is that an Arlo DiCristina tattoo?"

Mark chuckled. "Yes. It is."

"I'm so freakin' jealous. That must have cost a fortune." Tabby gaped at his arm.

Carla gave her a jab in the ribs and muttered, "Not cool to talk about money."

Mark laughed again. "It's okay. I'd saved up a long time and decided to treat myself."

"It is the most beautiful thing I've ever seen. Do you mind?" She slid the sleeve of his shirt up so she could get a better look.

Mark and Tabby started talking about tattoos in their own world, oblivious to the rest of us and everything going on around them.

Carla rolled her eyes. "We might as well leave them. She's in tattoo heaven."

We sauntered around the room.

I was getting bored until I felt a tap on my hip. I turned and saw Hannah Morgan smiling up at me.

"You made it." I smiled and tried to hide the fact that my gaze was wandering the room in search of her father. "How'd you get here? Surely, you're not here alone."

"No, my dad's around here somewhere." She glanced around the room and quickly spotted him. "There he is."

Hannah knew Marcie—Miss Rutherford—from school, so I introduced her to Carla Taylor.

"I asked my dad if I could come to the art exhibit tonight. At first, I didn't think he was going to let me, but then all of a sudden, he just said, 'Sure. Let's go.'"

"I think I need another glass of wine." I turned and ran smack into Gilbert Morgan.

"Miss Cummings, we've got to stop running into each other like this . . . literally running into each other," he said.

"Sorry."

"I'm not complaining." He smiled.

Was he flirting with me? I was disconcerted but glanced at Marcie and recovered my composure. "Do you know Marcie Rutherford? And this is Carla Taylor."

Gilbert was carrying a glass of wine and a glass of what looked like Coke. He handed the cola to Hannah and then shook hands with Marcie and Carla. "Did I hear you say you needed a glass of wine? Here, take mine." He handed me his glass.

I put up a slight protest, but suddenly my mouth felt like an arid desert, and I was in desperate need of something to do with my hands. So, I accepted. "Thank you."

Gilbert glanced at Carla and Marcie. "Would anyone else care for a drink?"

When he left to get the beverages, I felt three pairs of eyes staring at me. I decided to ignore Marcie and Carla and focused on Hannah instead. "Do you like art, Hannah?"

"Miss Rutherford says I'm pretty good, but I don't really understand this." She glanced around the room.

"Would you like me to explain it to you?" Marcie asked. Hannah nodded.

"Can you explain it to me, too?" Carla chuckled. "Because

I have no idea what that is." She pointed to one of the paintings that looked like a woman from one angle, a man from another, and a horse from yet another, all in various colored squares, triangles, and shapes.

Gilbert Morgan returned and distributed the glasses of wine to Marcie and Carla. They thanked him and then wandered toward the display with Hannah in tow, leaving Gilbert and me standing in awkward silence.

"Why are you here, Pris?"

"Same reason you are. I'm here to see the art."

He stared. Clearly, he didn't believe me. When I didn't respond, he tried again. "Pris, I thought you agreed to stay out of this."

"I am staying out. I'm at an art exhibit, hanging out with my friends." I took a sip of wine and resisted the urge to check that my nose hadn't started to grow.

"The fact that the artist in question is on the school board had nothing to do with your decision to come here tonight?"

"I didn't say that. I was curious, but I haven't questioned anyone. Although, I think you should."

He sighed.

"At least talk to Carla."

"Why?"

"She's on the board, and I'm ninety-nine percent sure she didn't kill Whitney Kelley. She's only temporary. She's filling in until they pick a replacement since Amelia Cooper Lawson's husband died. She was there when Whitney threatened to expose the board members' skeletons. She could at least tell you if Charlotte Littlefield was exaggerating or not." My voice sounded a bit whiny, but I was also a bit hurt that he hadn't followed up on the clue that I had given him.

He waited several beats, and the silence grew to the point where I was frustrated, disappointed, and more than a bit hurt.

"If this is the way that the police treat people when they give them information, is it any wonder that no one wants to tell you anything? Never mind." I turned to walk away.

He reached out and grabbed my arm. "Okay, I'll talk to her. But, if I do, you've got to promise me that you will stay out of this and stop trying to help."

I raised three fingers in the Girl Scout salute.

"Fine." He sighed. "You wait here and I'll—"

"Oh no you don't. I will just stand by and be completely quiet. I won't say one word. Come on, Nancy Drew would love to see a real cop in action." I grinned. Maybe I remembered how to flirt after all.

He sighed. "You stay quiet and don't say one word."

I pulled my fingers across my lips, indicating my mouth was zipped closed.

He looked skeptical, but he gave in.

We walked over to where Carla, Marcie, and Hannah were looking at a glass ball.

"Actually, I like this," Marcie said. "I love these colors."

Dr. Nobles snuck up behind them. "Then you must have it."

We turned to stare at the artist. Dr. Donald Nobles was a distinguished man. He was tall, thin, with a head full of white hair that looked as though he'd given up trying to tame it years ago. He was wearing jeans, a black shirt, and sandals and looked every bit the beatnik artist.

Marcie protested and offered to pay, but Dr. Nobles would have none of it.

Gilbert tapped Carla on the shoulder and asked if he could talk to her.

We found a quiet corner.

Carla looked from me to Gilbert, confused. "How can I help you?"

"It's come to my attention that you may have information which is pertinent to the investigation into the murder of Whitney Kelley," Gilbert said.

Carla frowned. "I have no idea. What information?"

He took a deep breath and relayed the information I'd learned from Charlotte Littlefield.

"Oh yeah. I was there. I didn't have a clue what she was talking about, so I didn't really pay it any attention."

"Maybe you could come down to the station tomorrow and give us a state—" Gilbert said but Carla was shaking her head before the words were out of his mouth.

"Nope. I'm going on vacation. Tonight. We're leaving after this shindig, going home to get our luggage, and driving to Chicago. Our flight leaves for Florida at five in the morning. I am not going to miss that flight. No way. Nohow."

"Miss Taylor. Surely you realize it's your responsibility as a citizen to assist the police. We—"

"Nope. Not doing it. You might as well save your breath. I didn't like Whitney Kelley when she was alive. She was a spoiled, pampered, privileged shrew who looked down her nose at anyone she deemed beneath her. And a Black lesbian was beneath her. There is no way I'm missing my flight for the likes of Whitney Kelley."

"You realize I could charge you with withholding information."

Carla's gaze narrowed. She put a hand on her hip and lifted her finger. "Well, you could, but I have a really bad memory. It comes and goes, and I promise you that if you ruin my trip, I won't remember one shred of that meeting or conversation." Carla then turned to walk away, but I stopped her.

"Maybe you could just tell him now, off the record?" I suggested.

Gilbert rolled his eyes at me, but Carla's eyes were stone. After a few moments, he nodded his consent.

"What happened?" he asked.

Carla repeated the conversation, and it didn't vary much from what we already knew. "It sounded like she was threatening the other board members, but honestly, I didn't think much about it. I don't have any skeletons she could use against me, but it was weird."

"Weird how?" I asked, and Gilbert shot me a look that said, *You're supposed to be quiet.*

I clamped my lips shut and twisted my finger, indicating

my previously zipped lips were now locked, and then I tossed the invisible key over my shoulder.

Carla thought for a few moments and then shrugged and shook her head. "I don't know. She just had this look on her face like she knew something. All the time, she kept stroking that gawd-awful necklace, like Gollum stroking that ring from *The Lord of the Rings*. I wouldn't have been surprised if she'd hissed, '*My precious*.'" Carla shuddered. "Oh, so weird."

"Were all of the board members present?" Gilbert asked.

"No. Actually, we barely had a majority. Hilda Diaz-Sanchez, Debra Holt, and Dr. Nobles were all out that day. It was just me, Whitney Kelley, Amelia Cooper Lawson, and Lucas Harrison."

Gilbert asked a few more questions, but Carla wasn't able to answer much. Eventually, her attention wandered and Gilbert gave her a break. He reached in his pocket and handed her a business card. "Ms. Taylor, please be careful. If you think of anything that might be helpful, please give me a call."

She took the card and turned to leave, but he stopped her.

"Enjoy your vacation, and I mean it. Be careful," Gilbert said.

She nodded and wandered back over to where Tabby and Mark were huddled together.

Gilbert's silence felt tense, and his mind seemed miles away.

"What's wrong?"

"Nothing."

I stared until he gave in.

"I don't know that there's anything in it, but it struck me that of the four board members who were there that day, two of them have now been murdered, including Whitney Kelley."

Chapter 31

I shuddered and for a few moments, the reality of the situation hit me. I clutched my mouth and hurried to the bathroom.

When I was done retching, I was grateful that Marcie and I had decided to wait until after the exhibition to eat. When I came out of the stall to clean myself up at the sink, Marcie, Tabby, and Carla were there waiting.

I splashed water on my face from the sink and drank from the faucet like a water fountain. When I was as clean as I could get in a public restroom, Marcie handed me a paper towel.

"You okay?" Marcie asked.

"I think the reality of these murders just finally hit home. Two people are dead. Just because I didn't like them doesn't mean they deserved death." I leaned against the sink and faced my friends. "What if it's not over?"

"What do you mean?" Tabby asked.

"You don't suppose there's some serial killer roaming the streets of Crosbyville, trying to take out all of the members of the Crosbyville School Board, do you?" Carla asked.

"Of course not." I shook my head. "At least, I hope not . . . Actually, I have no idea."

"Well, we're leaving tonight. So, if there's a crazy serial killer looking for school board members, they're going to need to look pretty far to find me." Carla folded her arms across her chest.

"I'm sure you're safe. I mean, who kills people just because they're on a school board?" I asked.

"Who kills innocent babies who are just sitting in school minding their own business trying to learn math and science?" Marcie retorted.

I didn't want to terrorize my friends, so it was time to take charge of the situation and de-escalate. "Well, I don't think this is that situation. Those people don't meet you in the park at night, strangle you, and then bury your body in the begonias. This had something to do with Whitney Kelley and Lucas Harrison personally."

"Do you think Joe did it?" Marcie asked.

"On television, it's usually the spouse that did it." Tabby checked her makeup in the mirror and reapplied her lipstick.

"It would make sense if it were Joe. Or Chelsea." Marcie

clasped her hands over her mouth to keep the second lead from falling out, but it was too late. The damage was done.

"Chelsea?" Carla said. "Whitney Kelley's sister?"

"Oh, do tell." Tabby rubbed her hands together and waited.

I thought quickly. "It's just that she was really angry. You saw how she reacted at the salon. She was really close to Whitney. She always put her up on a pedestal. I don't think she can accept that Whitney wasn't the perfect person she held her up to be."

"Especially if she was having an affair with Lucas Harrison, too. Eww." Marcie shivered.

"He doesn't seem like her type, does he?" I asked.

"Absolutely not. I have a pretty active imagination, and I can't imagine the Ice Princess with that sleazeball." Carla shook her head. "She always acted like she couldn't stand him during board meetings."

Other women started coming into the bathroom, so we changed the subject.

"Speaking of off-type relationships, what's with you and Pitbull?" Tabby asked. "He's got some amazing tattoos. Those tats must have cost a small fortune. I mean he has tats from some of *the* most famous tattoo artists. Arlo Di-Cristina, Ryan Ashley, Oliver Peck, Chris Nunez, and OMG, he has two Scott Campbells." She looked at me like I should be impressed.

"Okay."

"Are you freakin' kidding me? The artwork on his body is a masterpiece."

"And how much of his body have you seen?" Carla asked pointedly.

"Not enough. He has some tats in places he wouldn't show me in public, but when he dies, he should be stuffed and hung on a wall like a moose. Ink that beautiful shouldn't be covered up with clothing. He should strip naked and stand on a pedestal in the museum. His skin is a masterpiece. I can't imagine the hours and the money he's spent. I mean, Carla just about busted a blood vessel when she found out how much I paid for my sleeve." She held out her arm to show us the details.

"Five thousand dollars!" Carla said.

"Wow. I had no idea tattoos were so expensive," I said.

"These aren't even that expensive. I mean, I go to the same shop in town, and I get them done a little bit at a time. So, it wasn't just one big hit. But I like the artist, and he cuts me a deal on the tats if I cut his hair." She shrugged. "It works. He's good, not like some jailhouse tattoos that look like they were done by a minor in somebody's basement. He's a real pro, but Pitbull's tats are on a completely different level. Those are masterpieces. He said he travels a lot for his job, and he always schedules work while he's in Colorado or LA or wherever. Still, those had to take a LOT of time, and he probably has close to a half of a million dollars of artwork on his body. That's just insane. I'd kill to have one of those," Tabby said. "And he even has a custom Harley and an airbrushed helmet. Seriously, if I wasn't gay, I'd be so into him . . . Well, maybe. I love his style, but his conversation is a bit . . . limited."

"Glad to hear there's *something* about him you don't like." Carla folded her arms and pouted.

Tabby smiled, but quickly turned back to me. "So, what's going on between you two?"

"Nothing. He asked me out to dinner. We went out once. Then he came by a couple days ago with flowers and I kissed him once. That's it," I said.

"And then he shows up here. Seems like he's smitten," Marcie said.

"How about you?" Tabby looked me in the eyes. "How's your liver?"

"Steady as a rock." I laughed.

"Hmm, shame. Now, I did notice a bit of chemistry between you and the policeman with the smoldering dark eyes," Carla joked.

"Quivers?" Tabby asked.

"On a scale from one to ten, I'd say my liver's quivering around a twelve, and he hasn't even kissed me."

"Yikes!" Carla fanned herself.

"How are your toes?" Tabby asked.

"Curled tightly in a ball."

"Girl, you've got it bad." Tabby pulled me into a hug.

"Too bad he thinks I'm just a pebble in the bottom of his shoes, here simply to annoy him and cause him pain."

"I don't know about that. He and Pitbull exchanged a few looks that might mean there's some friction going on between those two," Carla said.

The bathroom door opened slowly, and Hannah stuck

her head in. "My dad was worried about you. He asked me to come and see if you're okay."

I forced a smile. "I'm fine. Thank you for checking on me."

Hannah nodded and then headed out to pass along the message to her dad.

Carla and Tabby said their good-byes and headed home to finish packing for their trip. They both promised to be extra careful and to text and let me know when they made it safely to Florida.

I splashed water on my face one last time and fixed my makeup. Then I glanced at my best friend. "Let's go home. I'm done. I just want to go home and cuddle with the one male that I know I can trust. He has a serious drool problem, but he's loyal, trustworthy, and I know beyond a shadow of a doubt that he loves me."

Chapter 32

Marcie and I decided we were too tired to go to a restaurant for dinner. Instead of going out, we went back to my house, changed into comfy clothes, and ordered a pizza. When the doorbell rang, I grabbed my wallet while Marcie held on to Bailey to prevent him from pouncing on the delivery driver. Experience had taught us a one hundred–pound bloodhound in full drool could be scary and might lead to a panicked driver who'd toss the pizza on the ground and run screaming to their vehicle. Which might have been Bailey's goal.

When I opened the door, I was surprised to see Chelsea Baxter leaning against the doorframe, and she wasn't carrying a pizza.

"Chelsea, what are you—"

Pale as a sheet, Chelsea Baxter slumped over.

I reached out just in time and caught her before she fell and reached the ground. "Marcie, help!"

Marcie hurried over and between the two of us, we dragged Chelsea over to the sofa. Once she was lying down, the hand that was on her abdomen fell away and that's when I saw the stain. I lifted my hand and saw that it was covered in her blood. I closed my eyes and would have passed out if Bailey hadn't taken that moment to stand up and put his paws on my shoulders. He licked my face to get my attention and then barked.

"Oh my God," Marcie said. "What on earth?"

Chapter 33

My first call was to 911. The dispatcher stayed on the phone until the ambulance arrived while Marcie applied pressure to the wound. My second call was to Gilbert Morgan. As soon as he answered, I blurted out, "Chelsea Baxter's here and she's been shot."

"Where are you?" he asked.

"Home."

"Are you okay? Are you hurt?" I could hear him moving around, opening and closing doors.

"I'm fine."

I heard a sigh of relief. "Thank God. I'll be right there."

The EMTs rushed in, assessed the situation, asked a lot of questions neither Marcie nor I could answer, and then wheeled Chelsea out into an ambulance and sped to the hospital, all while we stood in shock.

By the time the pizza arrived, neither Marcie nor I was in the mood to eat and we were tempted to give it to Bailey, but pepperoni gave him gas, and I wasn't in the mood for that, either.

The doorbell rang and was quickly followed by knuckles rapping on the door.

Bailey's body language told me it was a friend, so I flung the door open.

Gilbert grabbed me by the arms and gazed into my eyes. "Are you okay? What happened?"

"I'm fine. We're both fine." I pointed toward Marcie, who was on her knees trying to scrub Chelsea's blood from my new rug. "And I don't know what happened."

My adrenaline and energy were dissipating and suddenly I felt weak. I would have collapsed had Gilbert not been there to catch me.

He scooped me up in his arms and carried me over to a chair. He lifted up my eyelids and used a pen flashlight to check my pupils, then he eased my head down between my legs.

The blood rushed to my head, and the dizziness I'd felt moments earlier was now replaced by embarrassment. I sat up and waved away his hands as he attempted to look in my eyes. "I'm fine. I just got light-headed."

He stared at me, and I could see the concern on his face and then felt ashamed. "I'm fine, really."

He blinked and his mask was back in place. "Good. Then, maybe you can tell me what Chelsea Baxter was doing here? How did she get shot? Who shot her? And why are you *still* meddling in an active police investigation that I told you to stay out of and that you promised you weren't involved in?"

The rapid-fire questions felt like an assault from a machine gun and a slap in the face. I pushed away and stood up. "I don't know why she was here. I don't know who shot her or why she was shot. I was *not* meddling in your investigation. And I *am* involved. I'm the one who found Whitney Kelley's body. I didn't kill her or Lucas Harrison. And I certainly didn't shoot Chelsea Baxter." I paced from one end of the small living room to the other. I felt my blood pressure rising with each step. "I was just sitting here, minding my own business, waiting for my pizza to arrive, when she showed up on my doorstep and collapsed." I paused to take a breath.

Chief Morgan held up both hands in a sign of surrender. I glared and revved up for round two.

"That put the color back in your cheeks," he said.

"What?" I asked, panting from my rant.

He grinned. "Now, when you calm down, maybe you can give me your statement."

Marcie giggled.

The doorbell rang. Bailey, roused from the nap he was taking on the floor next to Marcie, got up and ran to the door prepared to take a bite out of whoever dared come through the door unless they were carrying another pizza. In which case, he would have relieved them of their burden first, and then attacked.

I moved toward the door, prepared to answer, but was

halted when Gilbert stopped me. He gently shoved me behind him, removed his gun, and glanced out the side window. He returned his weapon to its holster and opened the door.

A uniformed policeman reported that Chelsea Baxter's Lexus was found wrapped around a utility pole about two blocks away from here, and he'd followed a blood trail that led him here. Based on the amount of blood on the upholstery, it appeared that Chelsea already had been shot before she crashed the car.

Vindicated, I folded my arms across my chest and perfected my *I told you so* smirk.

Gilbert ignored me and stepped outside, pulling the door closed behind him.

Note to self, smart-aleck smirks don't work with Chief Gilbert Morgan.

In closing the door, he kept a hold on the knob so it wouldn't lock. That left a slight crack and if I leaned close to the opening and held perfectly still, I heard scraps of the conversation.

He ordered the patrolman to check the perimeter of the house and ordered someone else over the radio to guard Chelsea Baxter at the hospital. "Make sure no one, and I mean no one who doesn't have proof they're a licensed doctor or a nurse, gets within six feet of her."

He opened the door and I barely had time to get away before he swung the door open and stepped back inside.

"Now, I want your statement from the top." He took out his notepad and a pen.

I took a deep breath. "Well, I need a coffee." I turned to Marcie.

"Good idea. Why don't I make it while you two talk? Would you like a coffee, Chief Morgan?" she asked.

"That would be great. Thanks." He ran a hand over his head.

I mouthed, *Coward,* to Marcie, who winked at me and then hurried to the kitchen.

I glared at Chief Morgan, but my anger and energy were gone. I flopped down on the sofa and replayed my actions from the time I left the art museum until Chelsea Baxter arrived on my doorstep.

Gilbert asked a few clarifying questions, but I didn't have answers to most of them. Chelsea hadn't said anything before she collapsed. I had no idea where she'd been or anything that might help him figure out who shot her. I tried to focus on the questions he was asking, but my eyes kept drifting to the wet stain on the rug from Chelsea Baxter's blood.

Gilbert squatted in front of me, took my hands, and forced me to look at him and not the stain. "Pris, there's nothing you could have done."

"What if she . . . dies . . . like Whitney?" A tear rolled down my cheek.

Morgan gently wiped it away.

I gazed into his dark eyes and saw a flame that caused me to catch my breath. He leaned forward, but just then, Marcie came into the room with the coffees. I have never wanted to strangle my best friend more in my entire life.

Gilbert stood up and took the tray away from Marcie and placed it on an ottoman. He picked up a mug and handed it to me.

Marcie must have sensed that she'd interrupted something and when Morgan was occupied with his own coffee and not looking, she mouthed, *Sorry*.

I didn't want coffee, but I needed the warmth that the hot brew provided.

Morgan watched me like a hawk until I took a sip before resuming his questions. "Before she came here tonight, when had you seen her last?"

I shared the conversation that Chelsea and I had yesterday at the diner, after we left the salon.

"She didn't believe Lucas Harrison and Whitney were having an affair?" Morgan asked.

I thought for a moment and then shook my head. "I think Chelsea was surprised Betty Wilson was saying that Whitney and Lucas had been having an affair. She seemed . . . confident that they weren't having an affair," I said.

Morgan surprised me when he asked, "Why do you think that is?"

I shrugged. "Maybe Chelsea was so in love with Lucas Harrison that she didn't want to believe it? I mean, she and Whitney were always really close." I turned to Marcie for confirmation.

"They were close. Chelsea worshipped Whitney. I don't believe Chelsea would have gotten involved with Lucas if she knew that he and Whitney were . . . involved."

"Maybe she didn't know," Morgan said.

I glanced at Marcie. "Chelsea would have told her."

Marcie nodded. "No way she would have kept something like that a secret. Not from Whitney."

"Okay, but what about Whitney? From what you've told me about her, she wouldn't have any scruples about it." Morgan took a sip of his coffee.

I glanced at Marcie and saw the same confusion on her face that I felt inside. "Whitney lacked scruples when it came to hurting others, but I can't see her hurting Chelsea."

Marcie nodded. "Agreed. Whitney wouldn't risk alienating her biggest supporter . . . No . . . I agree with Pris. Whitney Kelley wouldn't have risked losing Chelsea's adoration and support."

Morgan looked from me to Marcie. "Why?"

"What good is a wicked witch without flying monkeys to do her bidding?" She shrugged.

"Ouch." He shook his head. "You two *really* didn't like Whitney Kelley much."

"It's really not that . . . it's just . . . Look, we tried to like Whitney, but she didn't want to be liked by people like us . . . people who weren't rich or important." I shrugged. "Over the course of time, we gave up trying. You heard what Charlotte Littlefield and Carla said she told the school board. It was her way or the highway," I said.

"Pris is right. Maybe it was self-preservation, but there comes a time when you've been hurt one time too many, and you give up and stop trying. You figure out a way to peacefully coexist, and you move on with your life." Marcie shrugged.

"Everyone has some redeeming qualities," Morgan said.

Marcie and I exchanged a glance. Marcie shrugged. "She had great taste in shoes."

We chuckled.

"Look, I'm not saying Whitney Kelley ate children like the evil witch from Hansel and Gretel. She was on the school board, which is a thankless job. She wanted to promote STEM. That's great. Math and science are important. Just not at the expense of music and the arts. There should be a way to offer both, but Whitney was only interested in her agenda," I said.

There wasn't anything else I could add. No matter how many times I went over things and no matter how many different ways Morgan rephrased the same questions, nothing else came to me. Eventually, I was exhausted and could barely keep my eyes open. I'd stifled several yawns, but finally one escaped.

Morgan closed his notebook, set down his mug, and stood. "Okay, you get some rest. I'll place an officer outside to keep an eye on—"

"Why? I don't need security. I wasn't the one shot," I said.

Morgan took a deep breath and turned away. "Let's just say, I like to cover all of my bases."

Before he glanced away, I saw something in his face that made me push. "What's going on? There's more to it. Spill it." I stood and held his gaze until he gave in.

"Maybe I just want to make sure you're safe." His gaze told me he was telling the truth, but only part of it.

"As much as I'd like to believe that, I know you're holding something back. Now, spill it." I pushed.

He hesitated for a few moments, but eventually took another deep breath. "Chelsea Baxter crashed her car about two blocks away and made her way to your door. Maybe the shooter followed her? What if the shooter doesn't know that she didn't tell you who did this to her?"

A shiver went up my spine and I shuddered. "So, you think I'm in danger?"

Morgan reached out an arm, but quickly dropped it. "I'm not saying that, but I prefer to cover all of my bases."

"I can take care of myself. I don't need a babysitter," I said.

"I know." Morgan smiled. "Thirty-four home runs and eighty RBIs."

"Eighty-five RBIs," I corrected him.

"I stand corrected, but listen, slugger. How about you let me and my team do our jobs? You know, *serve and protect* . . . that's what the taxpayers pay me to do," he joked.

Morgan left and one glance out my window showed me a white patrol car parked in front of the house.

Without discussing it, Marcie and I agreed that she would stay over. She moved into the newly wallpapered guest bedroom, and Bailey and I went to our bedroom.

Even though I was tired, I didn't think I'd be able to sleep. Too much had happened for me to drift gently off to sleep. However, maybe it was the comfort of knowing there was an armed policeman sitting outside my house. Or perhaps it was due to the care and concern and . . . something else that I'd seen in Gilbert Morgan's eyes. Whatever the cause, I fell asleep as soon as my head hit the pillow.

My last waking thought was that Chelsea Baxter needed a manicure. Her nails had been in horrible condition.

Chapter 34

I awoke to the glorious smells of bacon and freshly brewed coffee and the weight of a one hundred–pound bloodhound on my arm. I slid my arm from under Bailey's snoring body and shook it until the circulation returned.

I hurried to the bathroom and was showered and dressed in record time. Normally, Bailey would have continued to sleep until I forced him out of bed, but he was up as soon as I was and wandered downstairs, waiting for Marcie to accidentally-on-purpose drop a slice or two of bacon. He was just wolfing down a slice when I joined them.

He glanced over his shoulder at me, and I could see a small piece of bacon stuck to his nose.

"I'll bet that crumb will drive you crazy." I picked the crumb off and held it out for him to finish. Then I opened the back door. "Okay, scoot."

He looked reluctantly from the great outdoors, with not only the normal creature scents luring him out to play but countless prints left from the police last night, to Marcie and the plate of bacon on the counter.

"Out." I pointed.

Accepting that snack time was over, he stood, gave himself a shake, and trotted outside.

When he was gone, I closed the door, went to the sink, washed my hands, and grabbed one of the remaining slices of bacon.

"Hmm. I love bacon." I munched on the crispy bacon, which Marcic had fried just the way I like it.

"I know." She smiled and dropped two pieces of bread into the toaster.

Just as we sat down to eat, the doorbell rang.

I got up and opened the door to find Aunt Agatha standing on my front porch.

"Aunt Agatha, shouldn't you be at the diner?" I glanced at my watch before giving my aunt a kiss.

Aunt Agatha rushed in like a blustery autumn wind. "First thing this morning, Luellen comes in asking if it's true that Chelsea Baxter was shot at Pris's house." She paused for dramatic effect. Just as I started to respond, she continued, "I said of course it's not true. Pris would have told me, her only relative, if something like that had happened." She folded her arms across her chest and waited.

"I'm sorry, I—"

"Then, in comes Macy Thompson. Claims she came for breakfast, but she never comes into the diner on Sunday until *after* church lets out at noon. So, I know, she's just there to get the scoop, but I don't have anything to tell her. Not that I would gossip even if I did have anything to gossip about, but no one saw fit to inform me about anything. So, if a person doesn't care enough about her family to come to the mountain, then the mountain has to come to her."

Marcie had stuck her head out of the kitchen about halfway through Aunt Agatha's tirade, but quickly retreated back. Though she made the mistake of permitting a guffaw to escape.

"And don't think I won't be dealing with you, too, Marcella Denise Rutherford. You have a cell phone, too. And you were raised to know better," Aunt Agatha yelled.

"I'm sorry, Miss Agatha," Marcie yelled back from the kitchen.

"Humph." Aunt Agatha glared at me. "Then, I come over here to see for myself and find a patrol car parked outside! Priscilla Renee Cummings, you tell me what's going on right now, or so help me, I'm going to . . ."

I never learned what she was planning to do to me. At that moment, the steam that had propelled my aunt from her diner to my house went cold. She stopped huffing. Water filled her eyes, and her body began to shake.

"I'm sorry." I pulled my aunt into a hug and held on to her while she sobbed. "I'm so sorry. I didn't mean to worry you. I wasn't thinking, honestly. I've forgotten what it's like in a small town. I should have known that the news about

Chelsea Baxter would travel faster than the speed of sound. I should have called you," I said.

"I'm sorry, too." Marcie joined us in a group hug, and we cried and apologized until we were all out of tears.

Aunt Agatha pushed away and pulled a handkerchief out of her sleeve and wiped her eyes and blew her nose. "I was so worried." Her voice caught and I was afraid she was going to start crying all over again, but Aunt Agatha was tough. "Now, let's go eat some of that bacon I smell in the kitchen while you tell me what's been going on."

I should have known Aunt Agatha couldn't sit and listen quietly. As soon as she entered the kitchen, she put on an apron and started opening and closing cabinets. She took stock of what I had, pulled a bag of blueberries from the freezer, and then went to work while Marcie and I sat and watched.

We told her what we knew about Chelsea Baxter while Aunt Agatha made lemon blueberry bread.

Bailey must have gotten a whiff, because not long after she put the bread in the oven, he came to the back door and howled.

I opened the door, and he bounded over to Aunt Agatha.

She greeted Bailey and then reached into her purse and pulled out a Ziploc bag with a large hambone. "The soup of the day at the diner is ham and bean, so I saved this for you."

Bailey took the bone in between his teeth and went to a corner and went to work.

Aunt Agatha washed her hands, made herself a cup of coffee, and then came over and finally sat down.

"Do the police have any ideas about who did this?" Aunt Agatha asked. "I'm assuming it's somehow related to Whitney's death, but why now?"

"What?" I asked. "What do you mean?"

Aunt Agatha sipped her coffee. "Whitney Kelley's lived in Crosbyville her entire life. She's always been spoiled, pampered, and privileged. Nothing new. I just wondered what changed to make someone want to kill her now."

Aunt Agatha had lived in Crosbyville her entire life, too. She'd known the Baxters long before Whitney was born. When I was in school and complained about Whitney Kelley, Aunt Agatha often compared her to the spoiled Nellie Oleson from *Little House on the Prairie*.

"I don't remember Whitney being rich. Was her family very wealthy?"

"Lawd, no. The Baxters were just regular folks. The only rich person in Crosbyville back then was Amelia Cooper Lawson."

"Whitney had some expensive jewelry. Could she have inherited it?" I asked.

Aunt Agatha shrugged. "I doubt it. Her parents never had anything fancy like that. Then they both died before she or Chelsea finished college. Whitney came home and married Joe Kelley."

"What about his family?" Marcie asked.

"Pshaw. Joe Kelley's family didn't have nothing but big dreams. Joe was going to get a football scholarship and become a millionaire. Then he got hurt his freshman year of college and lost his scholarship. Had to come home and take over his father's insurance business." Aunt Agatha sipped her coffee.

I wondered again how Whitney could have afforded the expensive items she had. The insurance business couldn't be doing that well. Could it? We gabbed about the Baxters and Kelleys until I was tired of talking about them.

The timer on the oven dinged. Aunt Agatha got up to get the bread out of the oven. At the same time, the doorbell rang, and I went to answer it.

Mark Alexander stood on my doorstep. "Hello, beautiful."

He was lying, but I didn't care. It was nice to hear. "Good morning. What brings you here?"

"May I come in?"

"Of course. I'm sorry." I stepped back so he could enter.

"Who's there?" Aunt Agatha came from the kitchen, holding the rolling pin I'd considered a weapon the previous day. Had it been only one day since I'd stood in the kitchen, ready to attack an intruder with that same marble rolling pin?

"Aunt Agatha, this is Pitbull . . . ah, I mean Mark Alexander." She looked skeptical so I quickly added. "He's a friend."

Only then did Aunt Agatha lower her weapon. "Pitbull?"

"Please call me Mark, Mrs. Bell." Mark smiled big and turned up the charm. "You may not know me, but I've enjoyed many meals at the Blue Plate diner. I have to say, I'm particularly partial to your meat loaf and pecan pie. Yum." He rubbed his tummy.

Complimenting my aunt Agatha's cooking was definitely the best way to her heart and Mark laid it on pretty thick. Within moments, my aunt was inviting him into the kitchen for lemon blueberry bread and coffee.

The smell of lemons and sugar filled the kitchen.

Mark went over to pet Bailey, who was lying guard on his hambone and must have felt Mark was after his bone, and he growled.

"Bailey, no!" I yelled.

Bailey snapped his jaw but didn't move.

Mark chuckled. "He must have thought I was going for his bone."

"That's no excuse for bad behavior." I studied my dog, who was rarely aggressive. "Maybe I should take him outside."

"No worries." Mark smiled. "I'm sure he'll be fine. After all, I'm the interloper on his turf." He sat at the kitchen table. "I couldn't help but notice the patrol car outside and just wanted to make sure that you were okay."

Bailey continued to glare, but he made no other moves of aggression, so I let him stay.

Aunt Agatha filled Mark with coffee, lemon blueberry bread, and details of the night's events.

"Wow. That's amazing. You mean, Chelsea Baxter just came here, rang the bell, and then keeled over?" Mark shook his head. "She didn't mention where she'd been or who shot her?"

I shook my head. "She didn't say anything. I think maybe she'd lost a lot of blood." I thought about the stain of blood she'd left on the rug and shuddered.

Mark reached over and squeezed my hand. "You okay?"

I nodded.

"Maybe I should hang around and keep an eye on you," he said.

"I appreciate the offer, but I don't need a bodyguard," I said.

The look in his eyes made my cheeks hot.

"Mercy gracious, look at the time. I'd better get back to the diner." Aunt Agatha took off her apron, hugged me, patted Bailey's head, and then rushed out.

"I'd better be going, too," Marcie said. She hurried up to the guest room, grabbed her stuff, and then followed Aunt Agatha out the door.

That left Mark, Bailey, and me alone in my tiny kitchen.

One look in Mark's eyes and the kitchen felt even smaller and way too intimate. I started clearing away plates.

He must have sensed that I was uncomfortable, because he grabbed his cup of coffee and walked into the living room.

I delayed by cleaning for as long as possible, but eventually, I joined him in the living room.

I found Mark examining the damp rug. He got on his knees and looked under the sofa. After a few moments, he stood up. He was holding a small, shiny object.

"What's that?" I asked.

He held it up. "Looks like a button." He handed it to me. "Must have come off one of your sweaters."

I glanced at the button. "It's not mine. I've never seen this button before."

He shrugged. "Maybe your friend Marcie lost it."

I examined the button—gold and shiny. "Possibly, but . . . I don't think she has anything like this, either."

"Well, maybe the previous owner lost it." He reached out a hand. "Want me to throw it away for you?"

"No. I think I'll hang on to it. I—"

The doorbell rang and Bailey ran from the kitchen to the front door.

His tail wag told me whoever was there was a friend.

Tossing the button onto the table, I opened the door to find Gilbert Morgan and Hannah.

"Hi, Uncle Mark. Hi, Pris—uh, I mean Miss Cummings." Hannah smiled and then hurled her arms around Bailey's neck and then fell to the ground erupting in bouts of laughter as Bailey licked and drooled all over her face.

The smile that started on Gilbert's face froze and then evaporated when he saw my company. He glanced from Mark to me. "Sorry, we didn't mean to interrupt . . . again."

"You're not interrupting. I was just leaving." Mark turned, gave me a quick kiss on the cheek. "My offer is still open. Let me know if you change your mind." He grinned, patted Hannah on the head, and then sidled past Gilbert and closed the door behind him.

Gilbert and I gazed at each other in an awkward silence for a few moments while Bailey and Hannah played. Eventually, my good manners kicked in. "You just missed Marcie and my aunt Agatha."

Gilbert grunted.

"Hannah, do you like lemon blueberry bread? My aunt Agatha made one."

"Yum! Is that what smells so good?" Hannah asked.

"Hannah, you can't be hungry. You ate breakfast before you left home," Morgan said.

Hannah pouted.

"It's okay. No one can resist my aunt Agatha's baking. Why don't you wash your hands and I'll cut you a slice?"

Hannah glanced at her dad. When he gave a reluctant nod, she whooped and raced Bailey to the powder room.

I glanced at Gilbert Morgan and then marched into the kitchen.

After a few moments, he followed me.

I made a cup of coffee and handed it to him and then took two clean plates and put them on the table.

Hannah ran to the table and chatted, completely unaware of the tension that had descended on the room.

I sliced a baby bear–sized portion of bread for Hannah and an extra generous papa bear–sized portion for Gilbert, and an "I have already had more than what's good for my waistline but I need to eat to have something to do" mama bear on a diet–sized portion for myself.

When Hannah had eaten two baby bear–sized slices of bread, she declared herself full and asked permission to play outside with Bailey.

Gilbert agreed, and they ran out the back door. The door didn't catch, and Gilbert got up and pushed it closed.

I stood up, too, and reached for his plate to take to the

sink when he reached out a hand and grabbed my wrist. I almost pulled away at the electric shock that went from my wrist up my arm.

"Pris, I'm sorry."

"For what?"

"I seem to always be interrupting you and Mark."

"You weren't interrupting anything. He just stopped by. I guess he saw the patrol car out front and wanted to make sure I was okay." I shrugged. "If you'd gotten here five minutes earlier, you would have seen Marcie and Aunt Agatha."

He stood up again and paced from one end of my small kitchen to the other. "Look, I don't know what's going on between the two of you, and everything in my head says to stay out of it, but . . ."

"But?"

"But, I care about you—" He took a deep breath.

"Really? I had no idea."

"Having a personal life is not easy. I'm the chief of police investigating a murder."

"And I'm a suspect?"

His silence told me everything I needed to know.

"So your coming here is just part of your service . . . serving and protecting the citizens of Crosbyville? Or is this your way of getting information? Pretend like you care so I'll spill my guts and confess to murder?"

"You know that's not true."

"Do I?" I folded my arms across my chest and glared.

"Look, this just isn't the right timing. You saw how

Chelsea Baxter reacted when she saw us sitting together. I have to be neutral. I can't get involved with a sus—"

I nodded. "I knew it. You think I killed Whitney Kelley and Lucas Harrison and attempted to kill Chelsea Baxter."

"If I thought you had anything to do with those murders, I would have arrested you. Obviously, I don't believe you did, but as the chief of police, I have to be concerned about the perception. That's why I can't . . ."

"I get it. Being seen with a suspected murderer might be bad for your image. Mark was right about you."

"Mark? What does he have to do with this? What has he told you?"

"Told me? About what?"

"About him, about his past. About everything?"

I thought for a few moments and then relayed the information he'd shared from our one-and-only date. When I was done, I realized it wasn't much. I hesitated about sharing his comments about Gilbert, too, but gave it to him straight.

"He thinks I let my position go to my head? That's rich coming from him. Well, there're two sides to every story."

"Why don't you tell me your side?"

He took several deep breaths. He opened his mouth, but then closed it. "I can't."

"Why not?"

"It's complicated."

"Then why did you bring it up?"

He opened his mouth, but the back door flung open, and Hannah and Bailey ran inside.

"Close the door, Hannah," Gilbert said.

She pushed the door shut. Then she held up a large object covered in dirt. "Look, we found a buried treasure."

"What is that?" Gilbert reached out and took the object. He examined it and then hurried to the sink and ran it under the water and used his hand to scrub off the excess dirt.

Hannah chattered a hundred miles per hour while her father cleaned.

When he finished, he held up a diamond necklace with large square rubies.

I gasped. "That's the necklace Whitney Kelley had been wearing the day before she was murdered."

Chapter 35

*A*re you sure?" he asked.

I was positive, but I still walked over and examined the necklace. It was large and gaudy, and definitely real. I was sure. I nodded.

"Can I keep it?" Hannah asked.

"Sorry, squirt, but this is evidence." He turned to me. "Do you have a Ziploc bag?"

I opened the drawer and handed him one of the bags.

He put the necklace in the bag and then turned to his daughter. "Show me where you found it?"

Hannah led her father to the back corner of the yard, where Bailey had apparently buried the necklace.

Two hours later, Gilbert and a small army of policemen with shovels and metal detectors had combed the yard, which now looked like an Egyptian excavation site.

Hannah had long ago gotten bored and moved inside.

I sent a text message to Marcie and Aunt Agatha, updating them on what was going on. Remembering my promise to Hannah, I asked Aunt Agatha if she would teach Hannah how to cook. She was thrilled. She texted that she was going to pick up a few supplies and would be right over.

Aunt Agatha bought a chuck roast and pulled out my favorite cooking equipment, my Crock-Pot. By the time Gilbert came inside, the aroma of freshly baked bread, Mississippi pot roast, and cinnamon and sugar of snickerdoodles filled the house.

"Wow. It smells fantastic in here." Gilbert sniffed.

"You can thank your daughter for that. She made this entire meal," Aunt Agatha said.

Morgan gazed at his daughter with surprise and respect.

Hannah beamed. "I had a lot of help. Miss Agatha is a great teacher."

"Well, I can't wait to try it." Gilbert reached for a spoon, but Hannah smacked his hand away.

"It's not ready yet, Dad." She turned to Aunt Agatha, who nodded. "You have to wait a few more hours."

"I'm not sure I can wait that long." He feigned weakness.

"Then you can have a slice of bread and some jam to tide you over until dinner's ready," Hannah said in a grown-up voice that mirrored a conversation she'd had just moments earlier with Aunt Agatha.

Aunt Agatha sliced the bread and Hannah slathered it with butter. Morgan refused the jam.

He took a bite and moaned his appreciation.

After several minutes, he asked to talk to me privately.

I got up from the kitchen table, where I was supposed to have been writing but was actually watching Aunt Agatha and Hannah work, and I led him into the living room.

The air was tense with static from our earlier conversation, but I was determined to ignore it and behave normally. Or as normal as possible.

When we were alone, he said, "So far, the necklace is the only jewelry we've found."

Something in his tone made me ask, "Did you find anything else?"

He held up several bags containing a hairbrush, several chew toys, my tennis shoe that I thought had disappeared in the move, a gold button, and a page from a scrapbook.

I glanced over at Bailey, who had followed us into the living room. "Bailey, shame on you."

At the sound of his name, he lifted his head, but if he was feeling any shame, he wasn't showing it. Instead, he rolled on his back, paws in the air, and wiggled to scratch his back.

I returned to the bags. I picked up the one with the button and the scrapbook page.

"Assuming these all belong to you, and Bailey is the pilferer, I think we can rule them out as evidence." He watched me as I examined one of the bags more closely. "See something that doesn't belong to you?"

I held up the button and the scrapbook page. "These aren't mine." I explained that Mark found the button earlier under the sofa. A muscle on the side of Morgan's head pulsed at the mention of Mark's name, but I ignored it and continued. "I must have set it down on the table where Bailey could get to it." I shrugged. "But that's not my button."

He examined the button. "What about the scrapbook page?"

"That's not mine, either. It looks like a newspaper article from the *Crosbyville Gazette*, but the bottom of the article's ripped."

Gilbert stood close and glanced over my shoulder at the page.

I could feel his breath on my hair and a current of electricity went through my body with each breath, making it hard to focus. I gave up trying and passed it back to him.

He held the newspaper clipping up to the light. "Looks like it's dated from April last year. Any idea where he might have gotten this?"

I thought for a few moments. "Bailey found a box in the closet under the stairs. It had a lot of pictures and miscellaneous items that had been left by the previous owner. I suppose this could have been in the box, and he grabbed it and buried it in the backyard before I caught him?"

"That's the box you took to Lucas Harrison?"

I nodded. "He was supposed to take it to Amelia Cooper Lawson. Technically, anything left in the house after closing belonged to me, but I didn't want it."

"Do you know if he actually delivered the box?"

I shook my head.

"Do you remember if the button was in the box?"

"It's possible."

"Any idea why Bailey chose these specific items?"

I thought for a few moments and shook my head again. "I have no idea. Bailey's always been a pilferer. He sneaks objects and buries them. His vet says that it's common canine behavior. Animals in the wild typically buried things like food to eat later. They may also bury items they want to protect from others, as a way of keeping them safe. Or they bury items because they're bored." I shook my head. "I don't know why Bailey picks certain things to bury and leaves others." I glanced at Bailey, who didn't seem to know or care that he was being discussed. "I mean, out of everything in the box, why just these items? They seem pretty worthless, but maybe they have some intense smell. It's the only reason I can assume that he would want my smelly old sneaker."

"I don't suppose it's possible that he took the necklace from the box along with the other items?"

I shook my head. "No. Whitney Kelley was wearing that necklace the day before she was murdered."

"Bailey's the one who discovered the body. Could he have found it lying nearby and taken it?"

"I'm sure I would have noticed if he'd grabbed something like that at the park that day."

"So, how did he get it?"

I thought about that, but try as I might, I couldn't come up with a reasonable explanation as to how my dog got that necklace.

"We'll take this stuff back to the precinct, but I'm not holding out much hope that it'll help."

"Including my shoe?" I asked.

"Sorry, but we're going to need everything, but I'll give you a receipt for all of it."

"Never mind. It was time I bought a new pair of tennis shoes anyway."

"Pris, about earlier. I want to explain—"

"No need." I turned to walk away.

Morgan grabbed my arm to stop me. "Pris, please. I just want you to know—"

The radio strapped to his duty belt squawked. Morgan placed the bags on the table, swore, turned away, and then answered the radio.

While his back was turned, I whipped out my phone and snapped a picture of the bag with the button and newspaper clipping and the one with the necklace. I quickly put the bags back on the table.

Between the static, distorted voices, and beeping, I could scarcely make out what was said. However, Morgan didn't have any problems and quickly acknowledged that he understood the message.

He returned the radio to his belt and turned to me. "Chelsea Baxter's out of surgery. I'm going to the hospital to have a talk with the surgeon."

"Is she going to be okay?" I asked.

"They don't know. She's still not out of the woods yet, but with any luck, maybe she'll recover enough to tell us who shot her."

Chapter 36

I knew that Chief Morgan was not having a good day. Still, I was angry and wasn't about to let him off the hook.

When he told Hannah that they had to leave, her response tugged at every one of my heartstrings. Her face dropped, and her disappointment that he would miss her debut meal was palpable. She didn't whine. She didn't plead. Instead, her bottom lip quivered, and one large tear rolled down her cheek. She flung herself in Aunt Agatha's arms and buried her face in my aunt's bosom.

As she comforted Hannah, Aunt Agatha glared down her nose at Morgan in a look that screamed disappointment without uttering one single word.

He looked to me for help. Years of teaching had etched in my brain never to undermine parental decisions, no matter how much I disagreed. However, I wasn't a teacher anymore.

I was a regular woman with an attitude. "She's more than welcome to stay here with Bailey and me until you're done. Or, if you don't want to come back here, then I can drop her at home later this evening."

Hannah pulled her tear-streaked face away and looked up at her dad and quietly whispered, "Please, Dad?"

He caved in like a house of cards. He turned to me. "Are you sure? I don't want to inconvenience you."

"Hannah's certainly not an inconvenience," I said with double emphasis on *Hannah*.

He took a deep breath and then nodded. "It would actually help me out, if you don't mind. My normal babysitter is out of town."

"Thank you, Dad." Hannah flew to her dad and wrapped her arms around his waist.

He gazed down at his daughter with pure love, and it thawed my heart. "All right, squirt. I'll be back in a couple of hours, and I can't wait to eat whatever you've got cooking in that Crock-Pot. It smells wonderful."

Hannah beamed. "I can't wait. When you come back, we can sit down and have dinner together like a real family."

She didn't mean to hurt him. The pain was visible for only a flash before he pushed it deep inside.

"Maybe we can coax Aunt Agatha to make us one of her apple pies for dessert?" I remembered Hannah mentioning how much her dad loved my aunt's apple pies.

Aunt Agatha smiled. "Of course, I'll bring you a pie. Then, maybe later this fall, when the apples are ripe, I can teach you how to make one."

"Really?" Hannah jumped up and down.

"Behave and do everything that Miss Cummings and Miss Bell tell you to do, and I'll be back before you can say Jack Robinson." Morgan laughed.

"Oh, Dad."

He made eye contact with me and inclined his head to indicate he wanted me to follow him out.

When we were in the living room, Morgan turned. "We need to talk."

"Okay, talk."

"I don't believe you had anything to do with Whitney's or Lucas's death. But my job requires that I remain neutral. I can't let my feelings get in the way of my job." He rubbed the back of his neck and paced. "I have to be completely unbiased. You understand, right?"

"I don't see why you're telling me this again."

We gazed at each other, but then he reached out and pulled me close. He gazed into my eyes, and I felt the blood rushing to my head as though I'd just gotten off a merry-go-round.

Then he kissed me.

An electric shock went through my body. Initially, I was too stunned to move, but within seconds, every cell in my body responded. When we came up for air, he gazed into my eyes. "Now do you understand?" he asked.

I nodded.

"Are you sure . . . about Hannah?"

I couldn't get my brain to send words to my mouth, so I nodded again. "Are we going to talk more?" I asked.

"We definitely need to talk more." He grinned. "Later." He walked out and closed the door.

I stood staring at the door with a stupid grin on my face and took stock of myself. My liver was bouncing around like a basketball, and when I tried to walk, I stumbled.

"Pris, are you okay?" Aunt Agatha yelled from the kitchen.

"I'm fine." I shook my leg to uncurl my toes and then limped into the kitchen.

Chapter 37

*T*he rest of the afternoon, I floated. Not long after Morgan left, Aunt Agatha went back to the diner to prepare for the Sunday-afternoon rush, but she promised to bring us an apple pie for dinner.

Hannah and I made mashed potatoes to go with the pot roast, which were both extremely simple to prepare. I thought about adding garlic but remembered that Morgan and I might want to *talk* more after dinner, and I decided to skip the garlic and keep things simple.

Eventually, the army cleared out of the backyard. I refused to look at the devastation, and rather than sending Hannah and Bailey outside to play, we decided to go for a walk in the park instead.

It was a beautiful day for a walk. Bailey put his nose to

the ground and zigged and zagged, following a trail that eventually led to a tree. From the base of the tree, he stood on his hind legs and barked. An insolent squirrel chattered back to him from the safety of a branch high up in the tree.

Hannah ran ahead and sniffed flowers while maintaining a constant chatter. I zoned out most of the one-sided conversation but caught a fragment that halted me in my tracks. "Wait, what was that?"

"I said, I had a good time with Clarice yesterday and she liked my peanut butter cookies. In fact, she said—"

"No, honey. The other part."

"Oh, I said Clarice said she and her dad were probably going to move away from Crosbyville. Her dad doesn't like it here anymore."

"Did she say why?"

"She thinks it has something to do with her mom's death and the other man who died. She wasn't supposed to tell anyone, but she told me." Hannah stopped and turned to stare at me. "Now I've told you. Do you think her father will be upset when he finds out?" Hannah asked.

I dodged the question by asking another one. "Did she say where they were moving to?"

Hannah shook her head. "No, but she did say that her dad was going to take her to get a passport."

A passport? Is Joe Kelley planning to skip out of the country? And why doesn't he want anyone to know? Okay, slow down. Just because he wants to leave Crosbyville doesn't mean he's got anything to hide, like murdering his wife.

"Hannah, let's go pick up our pie from the diner. Maybe

we can take something else by for Clarice and her dad. What do you think?"

"Yay! I'd like that."

Bailey wasn't as enthusiastic as Hannah about leaving all the smells that the park had to offer. However, I eventually persuaded him that it was time to leave.

I drove the short distance to the diner. Inside, I picked up the apple pie that Aunt Agatha had set aside for Morgan's dinner. I glanced at the menu and saw that fried chicken was the Sunday special. No one makes fried chicken like my aunt Agatha, so I ordered an eight-piece meal to go.

Fried chicken was a staple for bereaved neighbors just as much as casseroles. When Marcie's grandmother died, her family received so much fried chicken, they didn't have enough room in their house to store it all. Once the refrigerator and freezer were packed, they ended up taking the rest to the homeless shelter. It's been five years, and Marcie still can't stand the sight or smell of fried chicken.

Crosbyville, like many older towns, had a historic district with some of the town's most elegant homes. Developed between 1840 and 1930, Crosbyville's architecture included a number of buildings that were built in the Italianate and Queen Anne style. The historic district encompassed approximately 751 buildings. In their day, these older buildings and historic homes housed the city's most prominent residents. Over time, many of these buildings had lost much of their regal charm through neglect or unfortunate modern renovations. The houses that still maintained their original period details were often old, drafty, and lacking in modern conveniences. Anyone wanting a house with central heating and air, updated electrical wiring, and modern plumbing built newer homes in the suburbs. Many of the farms, which once held row after row of corn, wheat, and soybeans, were replaced by newer homes that sprouted up as quickly as the vegetables. The farther away from town, the bigger the homes. Whitney and Joe Kelley lived out in one of the newest subdivisions, which catered to Crosbyville's newly moneyed, suburban families.

I pulled through the gates of the subdivision and followed the winding road to a large white house. It was modern and at first glance looked like a ranch. Closer inspection revealed that the house was built on a slope and was even larger than it first seemed.

I pulled up to the three-car garage. The house was new construction and the front yard had been seeded, but the seed had yet to take root and looked like a black moat surrounding the massive structure. Behind the house were green pastures that had yet to be plowed under to make way for more homes.

This didn't look like a house that would welcome a one hundred–pound bloodhound, no matter how well behaved, so I rolled down the windows and left Bailey in the car. He wasn't happy. The nearby fields offered new smells that he was itching to explore, but that would have to come some other time.

Carrying our offering to the front door, I questioned my decision to bring chicken. This was not the type of house where one consumed fried chicken, no matter how finger-licking good it might be. This was the type of home where guests likely brought pâté de foie gras, caviar, and canapés. Nevertheless, I screwed on my courage and pushed the doorbell.

Joe Kelley opened the door. "Pris and . . . you're the chief of police's daughter."

"Hannah," I said as I forced a smile and squeezed Hannah's hand.

"Yeah. You came yesterday with your dad." He got a whiff of the fried chicken, and I heard his stomach growl. "Is that from your aunt's diner?"

"Yes, we wanted—"

He took the chicken from my hands, turned, and walked in the house. He left the door open, so I took that as a sign and entered.

Inside, the McMansion was just as I would have expected Whitney Kelley's house to look. The decor was all white with touches of black—modern and uninviting. The furnishings, art, and decorations all looked as though they belonged in an art gallery. They were items to be admired, not used.

There was a marble entry and white carpet as far as the eye could see. I took one step toward the white carpet, but Hannah tugged on my arm to stop me from making my first faux pas.

Hannah removed her shoes and I quickly followed suit and did the same.

I followed the smell of fried chicken until I found Joe Kelley leaning against the stove, eating what appeared to be his third piece of chicken, if the discarded bones on the counter were any indication.

"Hmm. Your aunt makes the best fried chicken." He sucked the meat off a leg and licked his greasy fingers. "Everyone else brought those fancy foods that I wouldn't feed a dog, if I had one." He glanced at me. "You have a dog. Maybe he'll want it?"

"Thanks, but I suspect it might be too rich for Bailey's stomach," I said.

He shrugged and grabbed his fourth piece of chicken from the box. I wondered if he planned to eat the entire box himself or if Clarice would get any. "Is Clarice around?"

He grunted, waved a piece of chicken to indicate she was in one of the other rooms. "Bedroom."

Hannah stepped forward. "Would it be okay if I went to see her?"

Joe nodded as he ate.

Hannah looked at me, and I nodded approval. Then in search of her friend she went off in the direction he'd waved the chicken.

I spent a few moments watching Joe Kelley eat and then said, "I'm terribly sorry for your loss, especially in light of what's just happened to Chelsea."

"What? Oh yeah. Well, Chelsea wasn't really close to me. Whitney's sister." He shrugged. "Tolerated me while her sister was alive. Now . . ." He shrugged.

"Will her husband . . . um, ex-husband be coming? I know they were in the middle of a divorce, but I would assume he'd come," I said.

"Already here. Came two days ago."

"Oh, I didn't know that."

"Neither did Chelsea." He chuckled. "Found out yesterday when he showed up looking for her."

"Oh wow. I'm sure that had to be stressful. I hope he wasn't upset."

He chuckled. His hunger finally sated, he wiped his greasy mouth and hands on a white dishcloth and then went to the fridge and pulled out a beer. He popped the tab on the can and chugged down the entire can. He then pulled another from the fridge, popped the top, but before he drank, he held it up to me.

I shook my head, declining his offer, and he shrugged and then chugged down most of the can before letting out a belch that would have won him a prize from a college frat contest. "Ah . . . that chicken really hit the spot." He patted his stomach.

"Good. I'm sure my aunt will be glad to know you enjoyed it." I struggled to find a way to approach the subject of his leaving when I heard the garage door go up. After a few moments, Betty Wilson entered the garage, pulling a rolling suitcase and waving her passport.

"I found it! I can't wait to lie on the beach in Mexico and—" Betty entered the kitchen and saw me. "What's she doing here?"

When the shock of her greeting wore off, I opened my mouth to explain but was halted when Joe did it for me.

"Hey, knock it off. Pris brought condolence food . . . fried chicken. Out of all of Whitney's snooty friends, Pris was the only one that brought something I would like instead of all that hoity-toity crap *she* ate," Joe said.

Betty sneered, but Joe waved the box under her nose and the aroma of fried chicken soothed the savage beast of jealousy. "Hmm. That smells good." She reached in the box and grabbed a piece of chicken and took a bite. "Mmm. I spent most of the day looking for my passport, and I missed lunch."

Joe winked at me and then reached over and grabbed Betty's rear.

Betty jumped and gave his arm a playful slap as she ate.

I felt sick to my stomach. Whitney Kelley had been dead only a few days, and Betty Wilson and Joe Kelley were acting as though she never lived. Before I lost my breakfast, I said, "Are you planning a trip?"

"Honeymoon. As soon as the funeral's over tomorrow, we're off to Vegas to get married and then a nice long honeymoon in Mexico," Betty said.

"She finally got me." He grinned. "Besides, I'm going to need someone to take care of all this." He spread his arms wide.

Betty frowned. "No way I'm moving into this ice castle. As soon as we get back, we're slapping a 'For Sale' sign in the yard and finding a nice condo downtown overlooking the river." She frowned as she glanced around the house and finished her chicken. Unlike Joe, she got a paper towel and wiped her mouth. "Someone will buy this mausoleum, it's basically new. Lucas Harrison thought you could make a big profit, even though you've only been here a couple of months."

Joe pounded his hand on the counter. "Don't mention that name in this house."

Betty shrugged. "Well, he's dead now, so we'll need to find another Realtor anyway."

"Do you know if the police know who killed him?" I asked.

"Don't know and don't care," Joe said.

"Beats me. I just know that Joe and I didn't do it, so that's all I care about." Betty folded her arms across her chest.

"I'm sure they never considered you or Joe as suspects," I said as innocently as I could.

"Ha. Don't bet your life on that. That Chief Morgan questioned both Joe and me for hours. Then he went by the Dew Drop Inn and questioned the manager there," Betty said. "As if I'd lie."

You'd have an affair with a married man, but you wouldn't lie?

"Well, I'm glad you two were able to alibi each other. I'm sure that made things easier," I said.

"You're darned right we can alibi each other. Why not? We were together." Betty patted her hair and hooked her arm around Joe Kelley's arm.

Hannah came out from one of the back rooms, arm in arm with Clarice Kelley. Clarice had been crying and her face was streaked with tears and her nose was as red as a beet.

"What's wrong, dear?" I asked.

The waterworks had stopped but Clarice's lip quivered and within seconds, she was crying and howling. Through the garbled tears, I made out that she was upset because she wasn't going to Mexico with Joe and Betty.

Neither Joe nor Betty seemed the least bit concerned by her tears.

"We're going on our honeymoon. You don't take a kid on your honeymoon," Betty said.

"Isn't Clarice going, too? Did something change?" I asked.

"He said I was going. He said WE were all going to Mexico," Clarice screamed. "He promised."

"He never should have promised that you could come, especially without discussing it with me first. However, things are going to be different around here once Joe and I are married. Whitney spoiled you and that's going to stop. We've all got to make adjustments."

Clarice let out a shriek and lunged for Betty, ready to claw her eyes out.

Betty screamed and stepped behind Joe while Hannah and I grabbed Clarice. It took both of us to keep Clarice from attacking her soon-to-be stepmother.

Energy expended, Clarice collapsed on the ground in a puddle of tears.

Betty muttered something about boarding school, and Clarice howled again.

I glanced at Joe. "Perhaps it would be helpful if Clarice came and spent a little time with me and Hannah."

"Great. How about a sleepover?" he suggested.

"Well, I don't know . . . I mean . . ."

"Please?" Hannah pleaded.

"In fact, maybe she can stay with you until we get back from Mexico? Or at least until Chelsea gets out of the hospital. She was going to babysit, but . . . then she went and got herself shot," Joe said as if Chelsea getting shot were solely for the purpose of inconveniencing him.

I wasn't a big fan of Clarice Kelley, but I certainly couldn't abandon her. I sighed. "Okay. Clarice, would you like to come and stay with me for a few days until your dad comes back?"

"Any place is better than this dump," Clarice spat.

"Maybe you should pack a suitcase with your clothes," I said.

Driving away a while later, I glanced in the rearview mirror at Clarice, Hannah, and Bailey. I didn't want to think about what I was going to do with Clarice or how I would explain any of this to Gilbert. Instead, I focused on what I'd learned. Betty and Joe claimed to have been together when Lucas Harrison was murdered. While I didn't have faith that they wouldn't kill Harrison, I had no reason to believe that the manager at the Dew Drop Inn would lie for them.

"I'm hungry," Clarice whined from the back seat.

Chapter 38

*O*ne of my favorite things about using my Crock-Pot is arriving home to the delicious aroma of whatever has been cooking low and slow for hours. It's heavenly. The Mississippi pot roast was no different.

"Wow. It smells delicious," Clarice said.

Hannah's face shone with pride as she proclaimed that she'd made dinner. "It was actually pretty easy."

"When can we eat?" Clarice asked.

I glanced at the time. I had hoped that Gilbert would be back in time for us to eat dinner together. I debated texting him, but just as I picked up my phone, I got an incoming call from him. "Hey, I was just about to text you."

Gilbert was working and wasn't going to make it for several hours. "Hey, I know you've had Hannah there all day, and I can ask Eli to swing by and get her if—"

"That's not necessary." I moved into the living room so that Hannah and Clarice wouldn't hear the conversation. "She's more than welcome to stay here. In fact, I was wondering how you'd feel about her staying overnight?"

He paused. "Is anything wrong?"

"Of course not."

"Pris. Seriously, are you in trouble? Do I need to come over?"

"No, you don't. We're fine. It's just that I picked up a guest. Look, I can't go into a lot of detail right now, but when you're done, swing by your house and pick up some things for Hannah to stay over. I'll explain when you get here."

Morgan was silent for a few seconds and then he said, "How's Bailey?"

"Bailey?" I glanced around, but my bloodhound was enjoying the smells from the kitchen too much to have followed me into the living room. "Bailey's fine. He's in the kitchen begging for food."

"Can you do me a favor?"

"Of course."

"Would you ask Hannah if she has her schoolbooks?"

I glanced down at the phone in confusion but decided to just do it. "Hannah, your dad wants me to ask you if you have all of your schoolbooks?" I yelled.

Hannah stuck her head around the corner. "Yep. I have all of my books and the weather is fair to middling."

I relayed the message and heard a huge sigh of relief from Morgan. "Okay, I'll be a few more hours, but I'll bring an overnight bag for Hannah."

When I'd hung up, I went back into the kitchen. "Okay, girls. Hannah's dad isn't going to make it in time to eat with us, so go wash your hands."

Hannah and Clarice headed for the powder room, and I stopped Hannah. "What's with the weather report?" I asked.

Hannah giggled. "Dad is always concerned about my safety. So, he has all these code words. If I'm in trouble, but I can't say it out loud, then I tell him that I forgot my math book and I need him to pick it up. If I'm okay, I'm supposed to say the weather is fair to middling. He said my mom used to say that phrase all the time. If I'm in danger, like bring-the-Marines danger, then I'm supposed to tell him to bring brussels sprouts or beets home for dinner. He knows I *hate* brussels sprouts and beets. So, if I ever ask for either of those, then I'm in deep doo-doo." She shook her head. "Dads tend to worry a lot, so . . . I humor him," she said in a grown-up fashion, and then hurried to join her friend.

Dinner was delicious and I enjoyed talking with the two girls. Clarice was an intelligent girl. Alone with Hannah, she was vibrant and personable.

After dinner, we cleaned up and I left the girls to play outside with Bailey while I tidied the kitchen.

Something was tugging at the back of my mind, but try as I might, I couldn't figure out what it was. So, I tried to write in the hopes that whatever was lurking around in there would come forward. I was still writing—or attempting to write—when Marcie came by.

I took a few minutes and detailed everything that had happened while we sat and drank tea.

"So, Whitney isn't even buried yet, and Joe and Betty are going off to Vegas to get married?"

"Yup."

"Wow! Just . . . wow!" Marcie shook her head. "How are things going in the investigation? Does Chief Morgan have any idea who shot Chelsea?"

I shrugged. I sipped my tea, but I must not have covered the smile that spread across my face at the mention of Morgan's name fast enough, because Marcie immediately jumped on it.

"What's with the smile? Did something happen between you two that you aren't telling me?"

"I have no idea what you're talking about," I lied.

"Oh yes you do. Spill it."

I should have known better than to try to hide anything from my best friend. So, I told her everything. Her reaction was all I could ask for from a friend. She was enthusiastic and genuinely happy. "Whew! I'm glad he finally made a move. I thought I was going to have to spell it out for him," she joked.

"I need him to solve this case quickly so we can move forward," I said.

"Joe and Betty leaving the country sounds suspicious to me. Maybe he needs to look more carefully at them."

"I agree it doesn't look good, but they swear the manager at the Dew Drop Inn can vouch for them, so they have solid alibis."

"Do you believe them?" she asked.

I thought for a few moments. "Yeah. I don't want to," I

said grudgingly. "Joe is so sleazy that I don't want to believe them, but I do. I mean, if they were guilty, they would act more . . . respectable, wouldn't they?"

Marcie shrugged. "Maybe they're deliberately acting like they're guilty so people will think they aren't guilty, because no one who was guilty would behave like they're doing?"

It took me a minute to process what Marcie was saying, but after a few moments, I gave up trying and shook my head. "Honestly, I don't think Joe and Betty are capable of that level of deception. I mean, they're pretty basic. What you see is what you get. Good, bad, or indifferent."

"You're right. So, who does that leave?"

"I suppose it leaves the other members of the school board—Dr. Don Nobles, Amelia Cooper Lawson, and Carla Taylor."

"I hope it's not Carla. I like her," Marcie said.

"I like her, too. I don't think this is Carla's style."

Marcie joked. "You're right. She's more of the 'I'm going to punch you in the throat, and yeah, I did it' type."

"Both she and Tabby are so nice, plus, they were supposedly on their way to Chicago when Chelsea was shot."

"You think it's the same killer?"

"It has to be, right? I mean, I suppose it's possible that there are multiple killers running around Crosbyville taking out members of the school board, but—" I stopped.

"What?" Marcie asked.

"Maybe we've been looking at this all wrong. I mean, maybe the murders are somehow tied to the school board."

"Well, yeah. That's what you said before, so I don't see the difference." Marcie frowned.

"I don't just mean that the murderer is a member of the school board. I mean, what if the school board is the *reason* for the murders?"

"Whitney and Lucas were both part of the school board, but Chelsea isn't."

"Darn it. You're right." I hesitated. Something didn't feel right.

"Bailey took a necklace and a button. What's with the button?"

I pulled out my phone and swiped until I found the pictures I'd snapped earlier.

"I know that logo on the button." She tapped her fingers on the table and then snapped her fingers. "Chanel."

It took me a couple of extra seconds, but I eventually caught up with her. "You're right."

We studied the picture a few moments longer and then we both looked at each other. This time, the revelation hit us both at the same time. "Amelia Cooper Lawson."

Chapter 39

*A*melia Cooper Lawson was wearing a Chanel suit at the art exhibit," Marcie said. "It had gold buttons just like this. Your picture isn't great, but these look vintage. The interlocking C's are faint, but that's what it looks like to me. Too bad we don't have the actual button."

"Why?" I asked.

"This looks authentic and vintage. Vintage Chanel often featured two interlocking C's for Coco Chanel. Although some of her designs included a four-leaf clover or other motif. However, the older buttons often had her name stamped on the back of the buttons."

"How do you know so much about Chanel buttons?" I asked.

"My head is full of miscellaneous information about a

ton of things." She chuckled. "But I do admire Coco Chanel's clothes. Now, these look genuine to me."

"True, but what does that mean?" I asked. "I mean, how did her button get here?"

"Well, this was Amelia's carriage house. So, it might have been here all along, stuck in between the floorboards or in a corner and Bailey found it," she said.

"Or it could have been in the box that I took to Lucas Harrison. Maybe it fell out and rolled under the sofa," I said. "Or Bailey might have taken it out of the box."

"Your dog is a bit of a kleptomaniac," Marcie joked.

"Or maybe Chelsea realized Amelia Cooper Lawson was responsible for the murders of both Whitney and Lucas. She confronted her and Amelia pulled out a gun. The two women struggled over the gun. During the struggle, Amelia shoots Chelsea. However, Chelsea manages to rip one of the buttons off Amelia's suit and then stumbles out to her car. She drives toward town, but her injuries are too much. Light-headed from blood loss, she crashes her car just a few blocks away," I say in my best Hollywood suspense narrator voice.

Marcie picks up the narrative. "Chelsea claws her way to your door, only moments from death. With her last ounce of strength, she rings the bell."

"Wait."

Marcie pauses. "You've got that *Bailey the Bloodhound, I'm on the trail* look in your eyes. What's up?"

"Something you said triggered a memory. You said, 'Chelsea clawed her way to my door.'"

"Okay, points off for overdramatization, but—"

"No, that's exactly what happened. I mean, not exactly, but the clawing."

Marcie frowned at me. "What are you talking about?"

"When I saw Chelsea the day before at the diner, her nails were perfect. I mean, can you ever remember seeing either Whitney or Chelsea when their hair, nails, and makeup weren't perfect?"

"No."

"Then, why were Chelsea's nails in such bad shape when she was here?"

Marcie shrugged. "I mean, I was more focused on making sure she didn't die on your living room sofa, but now that you mention it, I did notice her hands were in bad shape."

"We noticed because it was out of character for her. We've known them for decades, and I don't recall them ever having ragged nails."

"Okay, so Chelsea's nails were bad. How does that help?" Marcie asked.

"Maybe she damaged her nails in a fight for her life?"

Marcie's lightbulb came on. "Then, whoever killed Whitney and Lucas and tried to kill Chelsea . . ."

"Should have the claw marks to prove it."

Chapter 40

"So, you just need to tell Chief Morgan to look for someone with Chelsea's claw marks on his or her face," Marcie said.

"We don't know it was on their face. I suppose it could have been on their body, but he should be able to get the shooter's DNA from under Chelsea's fingernails either way," I said excitedly. My euphoria didn't last long.

"What's wrong? It sounds logical to me," Marcie said.

"I think the person's DNA would have to be in their computer somewhere to check against. I doubt very seriously if Amelia Cooper Lawson, Carla Taylor, or Dr. Nobles have criminal records." I laughed. "Seriously, can you imagine Dr. Nobles strangling Whitney Kelley?"

"You can't judge a book by its cover; just because he's older doesn't mean he isn't strong. He's in his nineties, but maybe he's strong as an ox. Some of those sculptures are heavy."

"I suppose." The doubt dripped from my words.

Marcie reached inside her purse and pulled out a large glass ball, setting it on the table. "Feel that?"

"What is it?" I lifted the glass ball and nearly dropped it. "That thing weighs a ton."

"I was admiring it at the art exhibit and Dr. Nobles gave it to me."

"Right. But what is it?" I asked.

"No idea. It's art. I'll probably use it as a paperweight. Or maybe I'll just put it on a shelf and admire it."

"It's pretty, but . . ." I glanced at my friend.

"My point is that just because he's older doesn't mean he isn't strong and capable of strangling someone."

"You're right, but I just don't see Don Nobles as a killer. Do you?"

"No." Marcie sighed.

"Heck, as much as I dislike Joe Kelley, I find it hard to believe either he or Betty Wilson killed Whitney and Lucas, either. I doubt they even have police records." I flopped down in my seat.

"Maybe the police don't need to find someone with a police record. Maybe these murders were crimes of passion. I doubt seriously if Whitney and Lucas were murdered by some homicidal maniac who was just passing through Crosbyville looking for someone to murder. It has to be someone local. Someone who knew them. Maybe the police could just find someone who was close to both of them with scratches. I mean, then they could check that person's DNA with the skin under Chelsea's fingernails, right?"

"Maybe . . . I don't know."

We talked about DNA and criminal records for a bit longer, until we'd exhausted our knowledge on the subject.

"Wasn't there something else . . . a newspaper clipping?" Marcie asked.

I swiped my phone and enlarged the picture I'd snapped of the newspaper clipping.

We studied the clipping until we had made out the date, and then went online to the *Crosbyville Gazette* website and looked up the archives.

The article in question was a story about a burglary at Lawson Jewelers a year ago. William Lawson was alone in the shop one night when two thieves broke in. They entered the shop, pulled a gun, and forced him to hand over close to a million dollars' worth of jewelry.

"Was anyone injured?" I asked

"They roughed up Lawson a bit, then tied him up and left him on the floor of the store. One of the staff found him the next morning."

"Holy cow. That sounds violent for Crosbyville," I said.

"It was. I remember when this happened. Everyone went on a safety rampage and the local gun shop had a big surge in gun purchases," Marcie said.

"No town is devoid of crime. But once they had the jewelry, why bother roughing him up?"

Marcie shrugged. "Beats me. He had a bad heart, too."

"But he pulled through, right?" I asked.

"He did, but he was never quite right after that." She tapped the side of her head.

"What about the thieves? Did they ever find them? Or the jewels?"

Marcie shook her head. "I don't think so. The jewelry was insured, so they got the insurance money, but the actual jewels were never recovered. The metals were probably melted down and the stones repurposed."

I glanced over Marcie's shoulder and read the whole article myself. There was a blurry picture of William Lawson from his hospital bed, and a reprinted picture of Amelia Cooper Lawson dedicating a building, adorned in the stolen jewelry. I studied the photo.

"Pris!" Marcie yelled. "Snap out of it."

I glanced at Marcie and tried to fit the puzzle pieces together. "That's the necklace."

"What?" Marcie followed my finger to the picture of Amelia Cooper Lawson.

"That's the necklace that Whitney Kelley was wearing the day before she was murdered," I said.

"It can't be." She stared. "It looks similar, but it can't be the same one. Pris, you can't possibly be sure. The picture quality is horrible."

"This doesn't make any sense." I got up and paced the kitchen.

"Let's say it is the same necklace. Maybe the police recovered the jewels. Or maybe that specific necklace wasn't part of the theft," Marcie reasoned.

"Does it say who the insurance company was?" I asked.

Marcie looked at the article and gasped. "Kelley's Insurance and Casualty."

"Let me think." I walked quicker. "Joe Kelley insures the jewelry store. Then, *someone* breaks in and robs the store. They take the jewels. The insurance company pays Lawson for the jewelry."

"Then, how does Whitney Kelley get the jewels?" Marcie asked.

"No. No. No. Whitney Kelley may have been a mean, self-centered, self-absorbed witch, but there's no way I can imagine her holding up a jewelry store." I shook my head. "There's just no way any of that computes. She might've broken a nail or something."

"What about Joe? Or Lucas?" Marcie asked.

Joe Kelley wasn't the brightest bulb in the pack, but could he be so stupid that he would rob one of his own clients and then turn around and give the stolen jewelry to Whitney? "That would be really dumb."

"Yep. Sounds like something Joe Kelley would do."

She was right. "But would he have given the jewels to Whitney? Or Betty?"

Marcie and I exchanged a glance and simultaneously said, "Whitney."

"Yeah. Betty is more of a beer and pizza kind of girl. Whitney was definitely a filet mignon, champagne, and diamond necklace kind of girl," I said.

We talked through the theory poking for holes, but it was the only scenario that fit the facts.

"Did you notice any scratches on his face?" Marcie asked.

"No, but they don't have to be on his face." I shuddered at the idea of looking at more of Joe Kelley's body. That would be something Gilbert would need to tackle. My stomach couldn't handle seeing much more of Joe Kelley.

I picked up my phone. "I need to tell Gilbert. I—"

The doorbell rang.

"That's probably him now." I put down my phone and ran to the front door.

Chapter 41

I flung the door open wide. It wasn't Gilbert. Instead, Mark stood at the door.

"Oh." I let it slip before I could hide my disappointment.

"Gee. Thanks. Bad time? I can leave and come back later." He turned as if he was leaving, and I reached out a hand to stop him.

"I'm sorry. I just thought . . . never mind. Please, come in," I said more enthusiastically than I would have otherwise, and plastered a smile on my face.

Mark came in. "I just wanted to check on you."

"I'm fine. Thank you for checking. Marcie and I were just having a cup of tea in the kitchen. Would you care for anything?" I escorted Mark into the kitchen. Feelings of guilt kept pushing to the surface, but I shoved them back down as quickly as I could. There was no chemistry between Mark and me. At least, not on my side. I suspected that Mark wouldn't be devastated too badly when I told him about Gilbert and me.

"It smells wonderful in here." He sat at the table.

"Hannah made pot roast." I didn't want to sound rude by not inviting him to dinner, but I wanted to make sure there was plenty left for Morgan. After all, Hannah made it for him. I compensated by offering sweets. "I have pie?"

Morgan declined the pie, but accepted coffee.

I turned to get a mug from the cabinet and walked over to the single-brew coffeepot. When I turned back, he had picked up my phone and was looking at the picture. "What's this?"

My initial reaction was one of irritation, but I swallowed it. "One of the things Gilbert . . . umm . . . it's an article from a robbery last year."

"That would be Lawson Jewelers. I remember that. I had just moved to Crosbyville. It was one of my first cases," he said.

"Really? What happened?" I asked.

"Not much more to say than what's in this article. Some thugs must have noticed the old man in the store alone. They forced their way in the back. Held him at gunpoint and got him to empty some of the jewels into a bag. Then they tied him up. Beat him up. Took off." He sipped the coffee I placed in front of him.

"Do you know if any of the jewelry was ever found?" Marcie asked.

"I seriously doubt it." He shrugged. "If it was, I never heard about it. Why the special interest in a robbery that happened over a year ago?"

"They found the necklace in my backyard." I quickly recapped the events of this morning. Hard to believe it had been only a few hours.

"Wow. That's incredible. What did Gil say?" he asked.

"Not much to me. I'm a civilian, remember?"

"But we saw Whitney wearing that necklace the day before she was murdered," Marcie said.

"Are you sure it was the same necklace?" he asked.

"It's pretty distinctive. Hard to miss," I said.

"How do you think she got it?" he asked.

"Could Joe have been involved in the heist?" I asked.

"Joe Kelley? Newly elected state senator Kelley? Wasn't his company the one that insured the jewelry?"

We nodded.

"So, you think Joe robbed the store and—"

"He could have paid someone else to rob the store," Marcie interjected.

"Okay, let's play this out. Joe either robs the store or pays someone else to rob it. Then he pays out the insurance claim to the Lawsons. He gets rid of all but a few pieces of the jewelry and no one is the wiser." He paused and rubbed his chin. "It could work. It would certainly explain how Whitney came to be wearing the jewelry. Maybe she found it stashed in the house before he had a chance to get rid of it, and either she took some of the pieces or she convinced her husband to give it to her."

"I think she would have convinced Joe to give it to her pretty easily." Marcie glanced at me, and I nodded agreement.

"But why wouldn't he have gotten rid of all of the jewelry as quickly as possible? I mean, it's evidence. He could go to jail if anyone caught him with it, right? I would have gotten as far away from those jewels as possible."

"You're not a thief." Mark smiled.

"What does that mean?"

He took a deep breath. "Sometimes, criminals do things for motives that don't make sense. Murderers sometimes keep some . . . souvenir from the people they've killed."

I shivered.

"Thieves sometimes steal for more than just money. Sometimes, they steal for the thrill of it. It's the adrenaline rush from knowing they've outsmarted the police. Or maybe they want to get back at someone who did them wrong. They murder. Steal. But they hang on to something as a memento."

"Wouldn't that be dangerous?" I asked. "What if someone found them with the item?" I asked.

"That's all part of the game."

"You mean, deep down inside they want to be caught?" Marcie asked.

Mark laughed. "Interesting theory. No. That's psychological mumbo jumbo. I don't think that any criminals have some deep-seated desire to get caught. At least, none that I've run across. I think holding on to some piece of their crime is an ego boost." He leaned close. "They know something no one else knows. They know what they did. Deep down inside, they're laughing. Laughing at the cops. Laughing at the world. They're smarter than everyone else. They did something bad. And they got away with it."

A dark cloud descended on the kitchen, and my feet were rooted to the ground. The mood was broken when the back door flew open and Hannah, Clarice, and Bailey bounded into the kitchen.

"We're hungry. Can we have a cookie?" Hannah got a look at Mark and flew toward him. "Uncle Mark!"

He picked her up and spun her around.

I got up and pushed the door closed. I made a mental note to get the latch fixed.

Clarice skidded to a halt and gawked.

Mark tickled Hannah and then turned to look at Clarice. "And who are you?"

"This is Clarice Kelley. She's Joe and Whit . . . Joe Kelley's daughter." I stood and walked over to the counter and handed each girl a cookie.

"We're playing detective with Bailey the Bloodhound." Hannah patted Bailey with one hand and munched on her cookie with the other. "Come on, Detective Bailey. We have bad guys to catch."

Bailey's gaze never wavered from Mark. He stood unmoved, staring him down and sniffing.

I tugged on his collar and used my body to help propel him toward the door. I held the door open and gave my stubborn bloodhound a shove.

The girls thanked me and hurried back outside with him.

I flopped back down in my seat. I explained that Joe and Betty were leaving for Vegas and then Mexico, and with Chelsea in the hospital, he'd asked me to keep Clarice until Chelsea was out of the hospital.

"Have you heard how she's doing?"

"Only that she was out of surgery. Gilbert went to the hospital to see her, but I haven't heard anything yet. I expect him back with Hannah's stuff soon."

"Then I should probably be on my way." He stood. "Thanks for the coffee."

I followed him to the living room. "Mark, you don't have to leave just because Gilbert is coming . . . I feel like I owe you an explanation."

He held up his hands. "No explanation needed. I sensed there was something between you two from the jump, but . . . you can't blame a guy for trying."

"Look, I don't know what's going on between you and Gilbert, but . . . maybe you should stay and talk things out. Maybe I can help . . . You know, mediate."

"Still waters run deep. Gil and I have too much water under the bridge. We've both chosen our paths. There's no going back now." He smiled and then leaned down and kissed me on the cheek.

Chapter 42

Marcie left not long after Mark.

I sat at the kitchen table and pondered Mark's comments.

Gilbert arrived with a pink duffel with one of the Disney princesses plastered on the front. He came in the front door, pulled me into a warm embrace, and kissed me until I felt as though I were floating. After what felt like an hour, but was more like a few moments, we both needed to catch our breath. "I've wanted to do that all day," he said.

I smiled. "I've wanted you to do that all day."

We went into the kitchen, and I made a plate for him and sat and talked while he ate.

"You can't mean my daughter made this?"

I nodded. "She did with only the slightest bit of help from Aunt Agatha."

He accepted seconds and then leaned back and gazed at me. "Now, what's going on?"

I took a deep breath, grateful that Gilbert was now full and content. I prayed that he wouldn't yell when I explained why I had gone to Joe Kelley's house.

Apart from a clenched jaw and the vein that pulsed on the side of his head when he was angry, he took it surprisingly well. "Pris, you promised me up and down that you wouldn't get involved."

"I know and, honestly, it wasn't like I was investigating. They volunteered the information."

"You shouldn't have been there in the first place." He stood and paced. "And where is Hannah?"

"In the back with Clarice, which . . . is another thing I need to tell you."

He stopped pacing and turned to stare, but I didn't get the chance to explain. At that moment, Hannah, Clarice, and Bailey burst through the back door.

At the sight of her father, Hannah shrieked, "Daddy! You're here. What did you think of the pot roast? I made it all by myself . . . well, mostly by myself."

Gilbert took a deep breath. "The food was delicious." He glanced up at the other girl. "You're Clarice Kelley, aren't you?"

Gilbert glanced from Clarice to me.

"Hannah, why don't you and Clarice go upstairs and watch *Schoolhouse Rock* while your dad and I talk?"

Hannah sensed that all was not right. She glanced from her dad to me, but eventually she and Clarice left.

When the girls were gone, I explained that Joe and Betty were planning a trip to Vegas to get married, and then a honeymoon in Mexico. Chelsea was supposed to babysit, but now that she was in the hospital, Joe asked if she could stay with me until Chelsea could take her.

Gilbert was shocked. "You're joking, right?"

I shook my head.

"He hasn't even had Whitney's funeral yet. Is he even planning to stay and see that his *wife* is buried properly?" He pulled out his phone and made some calls.

If he hadn't wanted me to hear the conversations, he would have gone into another room. Since he didn't, I took it as a sign. Both calls were to the Crosbyville Police Department. One ordered a patrol car to pick up Joe Kelley and Betty Wilson. The second was a request for a warrant.

He hung up and turned toward the door. "I've got to go. I—"

"Gilbert, you might as well hear the rest of it."

He narrowed his gaze but sat back down. The vein on the side of his head looked as though it was pulsing to a quickstep, but he sat still and listened.

I showed him the article from the *Gazette* and explained my theory about the theft and the insurance fraud.

He studied the article and listened carefully. "This explains a lot. This explains a whole lot."

"You're not mad?" I asked.

"Mad? Are you kidding? Apart from giving me a valid reason for a warrant to arrest Joe Kelley for suspicion in a burglary, I can now hold him for more than three days and prevent him from leaving the country while I build a case for murder. You have just helped me more than you know." He jumped up and kissed me hard. "I've got to go." He hurried from the room, but then rushed back and kissed me again. "Are you sure about Hannah? I can get Eli—"

"I'm sure."

"Great. You just gave me the key details that I needed to wrap up a problem that's been worrying me for a long time."

Chapter 43

After Gilbert left, I was antsy. I couldn't settle down. It was getting dark, so I went upstairs and watched *Schoolhouse Rock* and surprised Hannah and Clarice by knowing all the words and singing along. When that was done, the girls took baths and put on pajamas while I made popcorn.

Then we had a great debate over what movie to watch. Clarice voted for horror. Hannah voted for romance. I vetoed both and chose a movie that wouldn't keep me awake all night and also wouldn't get me run out of town by their parents. I chose *Harry Potter and the Sorcerer's Stone*, which was more than fine with them anyway. Both girls fell asleep before the last scene. I crawled out of the guest room bed and left them sound asleep, with Bailey snoring and drooling in between.

The next morning, I woke up to a text from Gilbert asking if I needed anything. I glanced at the time and remembered that it was Monday, a school day, and I had less than one hour to get dressed, get the girls dressed and fed and on their way to school. Let the mad morning rush begin!

Two seconds away from panic mode, the doorbell rang, and Bailey went crazy. Thankfully, it was Aunt Agatha with a breakfast casserole, a bowl of fruit, and a plate of hot cinnamon rolls for the girls' breakfast.

"I love you."

"I know." She smiled as she opened the back door and let Bailey outside to take care of business. "Now go help the girls get dressed while I tend to breakfast."

I grabbed a cinnamon roll and hurried upstairs.

Both girls were dressed, but Clarice was having a wardrobe meltdown, while Hannah's hair looked like a bird had set up a nest. Clarice's wardrobe problems seemed more urgent than Hannah's. Plus, her meltdown was a lot louder than Hannah's, so I tackled her first.

Through her tears, I figured out that she didn't seem to have packed a complete outfit. Nothing matched. Initially, I thought she was exaggerating, but after reviewing everything in her suitcase, I realized she was right. There was a pink summer skirt, an orange winter sweater, striped leggings, and a blue princess dress. Fortunately, Gilbert did a much better job of packing and providing options for Hannah. Thankfully, the girls were close to the same size and Hannah generously offered to share. Once Clarice was calm, she consented to wear black leggings, a T-shirt that read

Keep Calm and Call My Agent, and black ballet flats, so with a quick brush through her hair, she was on her way.

Clothes-wise, Hannah looked great in a denim skirt with a red-and-white cardigan set and red Converse high-tops. Her hair was another matter. Through her tears as I brushed, I learned she'd applied hairspray and teased it in an effort to have her flat hair look fuller and bouncy like Clarice's natural curls. Eventually, I had her lean over the sink while I quickly shampooed out the hairspray, which had hardened to a crunch. Once her hair was movable, I pulled it into a ponytail and sent her downstairs.

Exhausted, I hopped in the shower and quickly dressed myself. By the time I was done, we had fifteen minutes to make it to school. Thankfully, I lived downtown, just blocks from the school.

I came downstairs, and Aunt Agatha handed me a cup of coffee and herded us outside. I pulled up in the drop-off lane, and the girls made a mad dash for the door. They made it just as the bell rang, and I breathed a sigh of relief.

Back at home, Aunt Agatha had cleaned the kitchen and left a note that she had packed lunches while I was getting dressed. Lunches. I hadn't even thought of that. I said a prayer of thanks for Aunt Agatha as I heated up a slice of breakfast casserole and another cinnamon roll. When it was done, I sat at the kitchen table and ate. I savored the peace and quiet as much as I did the sausage, eggs, and Tater Tot casserole.

The peaceful silence was broken when my phone rang. It was Gilbert, and I smiled.

"Hey, just wanted to make sure you were okay? You didn't respond to my text. Everything okay?"

I thanked him for the text and reassured him that the girls were dressed, fed, and delivered to school. "I, on the other hand, have discovered that getting two girls ready for school in the morning must be the reason God created mimosas."

He laughed. "I hope Hannah wasn't too much trouble."

"Hannah is a lovely girl with a vibrant imagination."

"She must get that from her mom." He laughed.

"Gilbert, did you arrest Joe Kelley?" I asked. "I hate to ask, but I don't know what to do about Clarice."

"Yep. I arrested him. It'll be in the papers later, I'm sure. He's lawyered up, so I haven't been able to interview him yet, but I suspect he'll be enjoying the state's hospitality for quite some time."

"Do you know if there's anyone else who might want to keep Clarice? A grandparent? Or some other relative?"

"I think Chelsea is the only close relative Whitney had. I'll try to find out, but I can always call child protective services. They'll need to get involved sooner or later, anyway."

"I hate that. She hasn't been with Whitney and Joe long, and I hate the idea of sending her back into the system."

He hesitated. "Are you saying you want to keep her?"

"No. Yes . . . well, not permanently, no. I was just thinking maybe she could stay until Chelsea's out of the hospital. I'm not family, but she knows me, and it'll be more stable than CPS taking her away."

"I'm sure they'll let her stay with you until Chelsea's out of the hospital," Gilbert said.

"How is she doing?"

"Still unconscious, but the doctors are hopeful. I'll see what I can find out, okay?"

"Thank you."

Gilbert said a few other things that were completely unrelated to Clarice Kelley, but they brought heat to my cheeks and put a smile on my face. He got called away but promised to call back later when he had some news.

I sat at the table and sipped my cold coffee with a huge grin on my face.

Eventually, Bailey reminded me that he, too, needed breakfast, so I scooped his breakfast and topped off his water dish.

I went upstairs and tidied up. One glance at Clarice's suitcase told me that regardless of whether she stayed with me or went to child protective services, she was going to need some clothes.

Once the house was cleaned, I looked for Bailey. After a bit of a search, I found him in the back of the guest room closet.

"Out," I ordered.

His nose was stuck into a box. When he lifted his head, his muzzle, jowls, and ears were covered in dust bunnies. His eyes were sad, but I wasn't sure if that was due to the fact that he'd gotten caught or that he hadn't had time to get his fill of smells before he got caught.

I dusted off the dust bunnies and removed the box. It

was heavier and older than the box I'd taken to Lucas earlier. Inside were pictures and keepsakes. Pictures of bearded men with suits and long-skirted women with high laced collars that dated the timeframe to the late 1800s. I pulled out a gold cameo locket. Inside the locket was a picture of a man with long sideburns and a mustache that might have given Hercule Poirot a run for his money on one side, and a locket of hair on the other. On the back it was engraved with the initials *CCL*—Crosby Cooper Lawson, maybe?—and a date of 1857. I put the locket back into the box and made a mental note to call Amelia Cooper Lawson.

For now, I needed to get going. I packed up Bailey. I dropped the girls' lunches at the school and then we headed for the mall for some power shopping.

Two hours later, the back of my car was full of bags. I'd spent way more than I intended, but there were so many cute clothes for girls that I couldn't decide what to get and what to put back. Plus, I couldn't buy clothes for Clarice without picking up some things for Hannah, too. Hannah didn't need the essentials like underwear, socks, and T-shirts, but cute sweaters and jeans were articles that all eight-year-old girls could use. It wasn't until I was on my way home that I panicked. *What if they didn't like what I picked?* I sent a quick text to Marcie asking her to meet me at home as soon as she was free. Today was a short day for her, so I knew I would have time to return anything she deemed unacceptable.

Instead of cooking, I decided I'd get a family pack of

fried chicken from Aunt Agatha's for dinner. I swung by the diner and placed my order. I ran into Amelia Cooper Lawson sitting at a booth, having a cup of tea. When she saw me, she waved me over.

"Priscilla, I wanted to thank you." I must have looked confused because she quickly added, "For the memorabilia. The box?"

"Oh yes. Well, that was all Bailey." I pointed to my dog, who was lying by her booth gnawing on a liver treat Aunt Agatha made for him. "And actually, he's done it again."

"Really?"

"Before I left, he found a box with more pictures and a beautiful cameo locket. I planned to call you later, but here you are."

"I hate to put you to any trouble. Why don't I just swing by now and pick it up? If that's okay?" Amelia asked.

"Of course it's okay." In fact, it would save time so I didn't have to drive the box over to her later.

I grabbed my box, which contained enough fried chicken to feed a small army, and headed out to my car, Amelia close behind.

One glance in my rearview mirror showed me that Amelia Cooper Lawson was following me at a safe distance. On first glance, you might expect Amelia Cooper Lawson would drive a Cadillac or some other type of conservative and safe sedan, but you'd be mistaken. Amelia was conservative in many ways, but her choice of vehicles wasn't one of them. When the weather was warm, Amelia drove a white Rolls-Royce Dawn convertible with red leather seats. In the winter, she traded the convertible for a white Lexus sedan. Regardless of the season, she drove in style.

Inside, I brought down the box while Amelia admired the updates I'd made to her family's carriage house.

I invited Amelia into the kitchen and made tea and heated up leftover lemon blueberry bread and pastries. Marcie joined us soon after, and we sat in the kitchen and talked while Bailey curled up and slept.

I enjoyed my conversation with Amelia. She was a fount of information, especially when it came to Crosbyville's origins and town facts. She had a wonderful way of speaking that made history come alive. She wasn't just spouting off dates and dull facts. She was sharing stories about real people who lived and loved right here in my hometown. I was enchanted by her stories and was reluctant for her to leave.

"I've always enjoyed young people, which is why I always wanted to serve on the school board," she said. "My husband, William, and I never had children of our own."

The same question must have been floating around both Marcie's and my head. She beat me to it.

"Mrs. Lawson, why did you plan to retire from the school board?"

She hesitated so long that I didn't think she was going to answer. She took a deep breath. "I hear they've arrested Joe Kelley for robbing the jewelry store. It'll all come out now, so . . ."

"I'm sorry. If it's too painful, you don't—"

She waved away my protest.

"Actually, I think it will be good to get the truth out in the open." She took a sip of her tea. "My husband, William, was a very handsome man." She gazed into space for a few moments, remembering the man. "I fell head over heels in love from the first moment I saw him." She smiled.

"Love at first sight. How romantic," Marcie said.

"Oh no, dear. It was love on my part, sure, but I don't know if William ever loved anyone but himself . . . except money. He did love money."

I tried to hide the shock that revelation caused, but I must not have done a very good job. Amelia Cooper Lawson took one look at my face and burst out laughing.

"Oh dear. I didn't mean to shock you."

"I'm sorry. I didn't mean—" I stammered.

"It's quite all right. I've had more than forty years to get accustomed to the fact that my husband didn't love me. I do think he liked me. I think he appreciated and respected me, but I don't think he was capable of anything like love. My father knew it. He made his will so that William would only be able to have access to my money as long as I lived and as long as we were married. If he divorced me, or heaven forbid, if I died first, then he would be out on the streets without a bean."

"Wow. That's . . . just wow!" Marcie said.

Amelia nodded. "Yes, dear. Well, William had a choice. He knew the conditions before we walked down the aisle. He chose a life of comfort and prominence in Crosbyville without love, but again, I don't think he was capable of love, so I guess it wasn't such a great sacrifice for him." She paused. "Anyway, he rode through my family's money faster than a Ferrari taking a turn at a Formula One race. Then he started selling off anything of value. Paintings, furniture, and finally my jewelry."

I reached out a hand and squeezed her hand. "I'm so sorry."

"I managed to hide a few of the better pieces."

I smacked my forehead. "Is that why Bailey keeps finding your mementos?"

She nodded. "Yes, I stashed some things here in the old carriage house, but after all these years, I'd forgotten about it. Anyway, William found a necklace, earrings, and ring that belonged to my great-grandmother. I'd forgotten about the pieces, or else I would have hidden them years before. But now he owed a lot of money to some dangerous men . . . gambling debts. Well, he needed more than he could get by pawning my great-grandmother's jewels. By now, he had gotten himself mixed up with some unsavory characters, like that Joe Kelley and some other person in town."

"You don't know who?" I asked.

She shook her head. "Sadly, I don't. Anyway, they cooked up this scheme which would get far more money than he'd get simply by selling the jewels. They would insure the jewels, fake a robbery, and then they'd get both—the jewels and the insurance money."

"Could the third person have been Whitney?" Marcie asked.

"No. I'm sure Whitney wasn't involved in the original theft," Amelia said.

"How can you be sure?" I asked.

"Because she found out the jewelry hadn't been stolen. I made the mistake of wearing the earrings to an event in Europe sometime later. Somehow, I'd gotten my picture taken and it made its way into the *Crosbyville Gazette*. The picture was blurry, and no one noticed the jewelry, except . . ."

"Whitney." Marcie finished.

Amelia nodded. "She always noticed my jewels, even as a child. She used to spend hours in the jewelry store pointing out pieces that she would have one day. She was probably one of the only people who would have recognized those earrings, but she'd spent enough time looking at them that she spotted it at once. She knew that they couldn't have been stolen since I was wearing them. She confronted her husband, who spilled everything, from our silent financial ruin to co-planning William's scheme for insurance money. Then William died. He was never quite the same after the robbery. I think they hit him too hard." She smiled. "They must have knocked some sense into him at last, but by then it was too late. He was much more attentive and . . . loving during that last year than he'd ever been before." She shrugged. "Anyway, that's when it started."

"The blackmail?" I asked.

"Yes. She wanted her family to be the next dynasty of Crosbyville, and she wouldn't believe that I wasn't rich. I sold the businesses, stocks, bonds, real estate to pay off William's debts and Whitney Kelley's demands for money."

"That's why you sold the carriage house?" I asked.

"Yes, but I'm glad you bought it. I know you'll take good care of it. It deserves to be lived in and loved." She patted my hand. "But Whitney wanted the town's admiration. She wanted the jewels—my great-grandmother's jewels. She wanted to be on the school board. She wanted everything. When she'd bled me dry, then she wanted me to use my influence to help her get what she wanted." She wrung her napkin. "If someone else hadn't beat me to it, I would have wrung that woman's neck."

We were so focused on our conversation, we didn't notice that we weren't alone until it was too late.

"Too bad. I guess I should have waited and let you do all the dirty work."

Chapter 44

I turned and stared into the unrecognizably cold, dark eyes of Mark Alexander.

"Mark? How did you get in? What are you doing here?"

"I'm tying up a few loose ends before I leave town." He pulled a gun from his pocket and pointed it at us.

Bailey growled. Drool dripped from his lips, and he tensed like a coiled spring.

Mark pointed his gun at Bailey. "Do I need to kill him first?"

"No! He won't hurt you," I yelled. "Bailey, come."

His fur stood on end and for a few seconds, I thought he would disobey. Instead, he inched closer to my leg. When he was close, I reached out and grabbed his collar.

Mark grinned and for the first time, I noticed that something wasn't quite right with him. "I may still need to take care of him, but I'll leave that for later. The Pitbull takes on the bloodhound . . . sounds like a good match." He laughed. "Now, isn't this convenient. I was heading up the hill to take care of you, Old Lady, when I saw your car parked outside."

"Why do you want to hurt Amelia?" I asked.

"Somebody has to take the fall for killing Whitney and Lucas. It might as well be her."

"No one will believe that. Gilbert has already arrested Joe. He'll talk," I said.

Mark shook his head and gave me a *you poor, pitiful fool* look. "Joe's weak, and he probably would have talked, but thankfully I got to him first."

"How?" Marcie asked.

"Let's just say a man in my line of work gets to know some lawyers who don't mind getting their hands dirty. I got word to Joe to keep his mouth shut or I'd shut it permanently."

The lightbulb went on in my head and suddenly everything made sense. "You were the third man involved in the robbery."

"Good job, Sherlock! You're smart. I learned that during our first date. I knew you'd come in handy."

"That's why you went out with me," I said.

"Well, you are pretty cute." He grinned.

My hand itched to smack the smile off his face.

"Actually, I knew Gilbert had the hots for you. I thought if I could stay close to you, then I could stay one step ahead of my ole friend."

"He's smarter than you. He knew you were dirty. That's why he suspended you," I said.

Mark glared. "He suspected that I had my hand in the till, sure, but he couldn't prove it. I hoped he'd let it go, but I should have known he wouldn't give up. He's like a dog with a bone."

Amelia stood up and faced Mark. "Okay, young man. Why don't you shoot me and get it over with, and let these two young ladies go."

Mark laughed. "Oh no, I can't let them go. Not now. They know too much."

"Just how do you plan to get rid of us?" Marcie stood and faced him.

"Amelia Cooper Lawson is going to shoot both of you. You were getting too close to her secret. Then, overcome with grief, she shoots herself. Yeah, murder and suicide."

I was holding Bailey and was the farthest away from Mark. If I hadn't been standing behind Marcie, I wouldn't have noticed that she was inching her hand closer to the glass paperweight. I glanced over and saw the marble rolling pin on the counter near the sink and started to slowly wind closer to it. I was just about close enough to reach it when the doorbell rang.

"Who's that?" Mark asked.

One glance at my watch and I knew it was Hannah and Clarice home from school. Whatever happened, I couldn't let them come into this.

"No one. It's no one," I said.

Bailey barked and started to lunge.

"Do something about that dog, or he's going to be the first one I take out." Mark pointed his gun at Bailey.

"No. If you shoot, someone will hear. Let me put him outside."

Marcie gave me a look that said, *Are you crazy?*

I reached back, opened the door, flung Bailey outside, and let the door shut behind me.

The doorbell stopped.

Mark waited a few seconds, then grinned. "Great. Now, that's better. I can hear myself think."

I closed the door, but I forgot about the latch. It didn't close completely. That's when the back door reopened, and Hannah and Clarice rushed inside.

"What's going on? Didn't you hear us ringing—" Hannah saw the gun and stopped. "Uncle Mark? What are you doing?"

Chapter 45

*H*annah, come here," Mark said. "That lady is bad and she's trying to hurt Pris and Marcie." Mark glared at Marcie and me, daring us to speak. He turned his gaze toward Clarice. "You're Whitney Kelley's daughter, Clarice?"

"You're the man my mom was dating," Clarice whispered.

Mark nodded. "I wondered if you saw me with her."

"It was you? *You* were having an affair with Whitney?" I asked.

"Don't sound so surprised. Good girls like you and Whitney like bad boys." He laughed.

Clarice stared at the gun, frozen.

Hannah took a step forward.

Mark smiled and reached out a hand toward her.

Clarice hadn't closed the door tightly, either, and Bailey

pushed his way through. Teeth bared, Bailey jumped in front of Hannah and Clarice. He stood between the girls and Mark.

"Get that dog out of here," Mark yelled. "He's dangerous. See, he's foaming at the mouth. If you don't stop him, I'll shoot."

"No," Hannah yelled. "Don't hurt him." She moved to grab Bailey's collar, but that's when Bailey turned and growled at her.

Hannah stopped and Bailey turned his attention back to Mark. If Hannah moved toward Mark or he moved toward Hannah, Bailey growled. He nudged Hannah with his muzzle, but he refused to allow Mark near her.

"Hannah, please stay where you are. I—" My phone rang. I glanced down. "It's Gilbert."

"Dad!"

"Don't answer that," Mark yelled.

"He always calls after school to make sure I made it home okay."

"If I don't answer he's going to know something's wrong," I said.

The phone stopped, but after a few seconds it rang again.

"He's not going to stop," Hannah said.

"Okay, but put it on speaker," Mark said.

I put the phone on speaker.

"Hey, what's going on? I've been trying to reach Hannah, but she's not picking up her phone." Mark pointed the gun at Hannah, who was silent and pale as a sheet.

"She's here with me. She's fine," I said.

"Mind if I talk to her?" Morgan asked.

Mark shook his head, no.

"She's outside playing with Clarice," I said.

"Okay, well if you're sure everything's fine. I should be wrapping up soon. It looks like Chelsea Baxter's going to be fine. I talked to her, and she had some big revelations. Turns out Mark was the one having an affair with Whitney, not Lucas. He tried to keep it quiet, but Whitney told her sister. After I suspended him, he took on some private investigation work, and he's the one who spread the false word to Betty that Whitney was with Lucas. I've got a warrant out for his arrest, but I should be back to your place soon. What's for dinner?"

"Fried chicken." I was about to hang up when I had a thought. "Gilbert, Hannah forgot her math book. Can you swing by the house and bring it before you come?"

He hesitated. "Okay. Is that all you need me to bring?"

Mark motioned for me to speed things up.

"Dinner will be ready, but we could use some brussels sprouts and beets." I prayed he knew what I was saying and didn't actually want him to bring root vegetables.

"Got it."

I was about to hang up when Gilbert said, "Pris, I love you."

He hung up before I could respond.

Chapter 46

Mark chuckled. "Dinner? Do you seriously think any of you are going to live long enough to eat sprouts for dinner?"

Marcie's fingers were inches from the paperweight.

I took a step backward so my back was against the counter and my hand was inches from the rolling pin.

My heart raced so fast that I could feel the blood pounding in my ears loud enough that I could barely hear.

Mark's lips were moving, but I couldn't understand him. He stopped and listened.

That's when I heard the sirens blaring.

Mark swore.

Marcie glanced at me and nodded. It was time. I recognized that gaze from the pitcher's mound in high school. One glance at her hand showed me she had her index and middle finger over the top and her thumb underneath. It was going to be a two-seam fastball pitch.

I looked at Hannah and nodded toward the back door.

She gave a slight nod.

I prayed Amelia Cooper Lawson wouldn't get hurt, but the sirens were getting louder, and I couldn't focus on anything other than the girls' safety.

"Now," Marcie yelled.

"Get down," I screamed.

Hannah and Clarice hit the floor.

Marcie leaned back, wound up, and delivered an incredible fast pitch with the glass paperweight right as I grabbed the marble rolling pin and swung hard at Mark's ribs.

Not to be left out, Bailey leapt into the air and bit the hand holding the gun.

The back door flew open just as Gilbert burst through from the living room with his gun drawn.

Chapter 47

Within seconds, my small kitchen was teeming with police. Weapons drawn, yelling orders.

Mark lay on the ground, writhing in pain. Blood dripped from the wound on the front of his head. He clutched at his ribs with a limp arm and screamed until he passed out.

Amelia Cooper Lawson picked up the gun he'd dropped and pointed it at the now-limp man on the floor.

"Hannah?"

"I'm fine, Dad." Hannah ran and threw her arms around her dad's waist.

Gilbert's face went from rage to relief. He glanced at me. "You okay?"

I nodded and held up my marble rolling pin.

A police officer was trying to get Amelia Cooper Lawson to hand over the weapon. "Ma'am, it's over. Please hand over the weapon."

"He's an evil, evil man. He's killed two people and tried to kill all of us. He assaulted my husband. I—"

"Amelia, please. Not in front of the children," Marcie said.

That snapped her out of her daze. She turned and glanced at Clarice and handed the gun to the policeman.

Clarice ran and flung herself into Amelia's arms.

Between the police and EMTs, it was hours before the house was quiet, and everyone had cleared out. As the paramedics were working on Mark's broken ribs, that's when I saw the scratches on his chest.

Amelia Cooper Lawson refused to go to the hospital, but eventually allowed Marcie and Aunt Agatha to take her home. Clarice curled up on the floor with Bailey, and they were both snoring in a corner.

I sat on the couch next to Gilbert. Hannah refused to leave her dad's side and had fallen asleep with her head in his lap.

Gilbert clasped my hand. "I was so afraid . . ."

"So was I." I laid my head on his shoulder.

"I knew Mark was dirty. I just had no idea . . . murder . . . In the army, we were like brothers." He gazed down at his sleeping daughter. The vein on the side of his head pulsed and he clenched his jaw. "I can't believe he would almost hurt—"

"She's fine." I reached up and stroked the vein until the pulsing slowed down.

He kissed her forehead and then turned and kissed me. "Mark . . . will he . . ."

"He's going to be fine," Gilbert said. "Eventually. He's got a concussion, at least three cracked ribs, and a dog bite, but he's going to live."

"I suppose that's good," I said.

"I don't suppose he mentioned why he planted the button and the necklace here?" Gilbert asked.

"He didn't, but I think it was all part of his plan to frame Amelia Cooper Lawson for the murders. I think Whitney got too greedy and too careless. Once Joe spilled his guts and told Whitney about the theft, insurance fraud, and William's role in the scheme, Whitney must have realized that she had Amelia Cooper Lawson over a barrel. Amelia may not have been involved in the crimes, but she loved William and wouldn't have wanted him humiliated. Besides, she had her pride and wouldn't have wanted her family's good name dragged through the mud. Whitney saw her chance and she took it.

"She forced Amelia to give her the jewelry as part of her blackmail scheme. She wore the jewelry as a measure of control. Every time Amelia saw her, she knew that Whitney could destroy her with one word. Whitney could find some way to explain away money, but the jewelry was an entirely different matter. As long as Whitney had that jewelry, she had the upper hand. She had the power to force Amelia to do whatever she wanted, not thinking . . . or caring about the fact that she was endangering Joe and his accomplice by wearing the jewelry in public. So Mark killed Whitney."

"According to Chelsea, Lucas picked up on it from a picture in that box you brought. He must have tried to blackmail Mark. That's when Mark killed him." Gilbert shook his head. "He didn't use to be that way. After his brother died, he changed. I think he snapped. I'd hoped that getting away from Chicago might help him remember who he used to be, back in the military."

I could hear the guilt in his voice. "This isn't your fault. Mark chose his path. You tried to help him."

He gazed down at his daughter, but then shook himself. "I still don't quite get how you and Marcie took down a trained policeman with a gun."

"Remember when I told you about being high school state softball champions? Well, did I mention that Marcie holds the record as the only person in state history to strike out all twenty-seven batters in one nine-inning game?"

He chuckled. "No, you didn't mention that."

"Plus, we had Bailey the Bloodhound, Pet Detective, on our side. He refused to allow Mark to get close to Hannah and Clarice." I gazed down at my brave bloodhound. "He was amazing."

"He wasn't the only one."

"How is Chelsea? Is she going to be okay?" I asked.

"She's going to be just fine." He turned to me. "And you? Are you okay?"

I snuggled into his chest. "I am now."

The Adventures of Bailey the Bloodhound, Pet Detective:

....

The Case of the Barking Beagle

After a long, exhaustive search, Bailey the Bloodhound picked up the scent.

His faithful companion, Anna, followed.

To the back of the fence, Bailey led the way.

He pulled the missing necklace out from under the rock where it lay.

"You're wonderful," Mrs. Smith exclaimed. "Name your price, we'll be glad to pay."

Bailey shook himself. Anna waved her hand. "We can't take your money. Finding things is what he does. He's Bailey the Bloodhound, Pet Detective!"

THE END

Acknowledgments

I have been blessed to know people who possess a vast amount of information with unique skill sets who are willing to share their knowledge and expertise with me. Thanks to Derrick Hembree, Jordan Beqiri, and Dakia Taylor for sharing their love and appreciation for tattoos. Thanks to Abby Vandiver for legal help. Thanks to Debra Goldstein for legal help and for brainstorming, supporting, and listening. Thanks to Larissa Ackerman for sharing your stories, pictures, and love for your bloodhound, Bocephus.

Thanks to my family: Benjamin Burns, Jacquelyn, Christopher, Carson, Crosby, and Cameron Rucker. Thanks to Jillian, Drew, and Marcella Merkel. I also want to thank my friends Shelitha Mckee and Sophia Muckerson for supporting my dream.

Special thanks to my amazing agent, Jessica Faust at BookEnds Literary, and editors Liz Sellers and Michelle Vega at Berkley for bringing this dream to reality.

Author photo © Lifetouch Inc., 2023

Valerie Burns, writing as **Kallie E. Benjamin**, is the author of three mystery series. She is a mentor in the Master of Fine Arts program for writing popular fiction at Seton Hill University in Greensburg, PA, where she earned her own MFA degree. Valerie currently lives in North Georgia with her two poodles, Kensington and Chloe.

VISIT VALERIE BURNS ONLINE

VMBurns.com
🅕 VMBurnsBooks
🅞 VMBurnsBooks

Ready to find
your next great read?

Let us help.

Visit prh.com/nextread

Penguin
Random
House